# When the Lantern Swings

## Allen T. Grimes

NewLink Publishing

2024

Copy Editor: Janelle Evans
Interior Design: Jo A. Wilkins
Cover Design: Janelle Evans
E-pub design: Richard R. Draude

1. Fiction/Mystery & Detective/Police Procedural
2. Fiction/Fantasy/Paranormal
3. Fiction/Ghost

ISBN   978-1-957374-10-9- Hard Back
ISBN:   978-1-957374-05-5- Trade Paper
ISBN:   978-1-957374-09-3- E-Book

www.newlinkpublishing.com
Henderson, NV

Published and Printed in the United States of America

1 2 3 4 5 6 7 8 9 10

For
Deltrina and Aelacia

# When the Lantern

# Swings

# Chapter 1

**Ed Freemen looked down** at the mangled body of a young woman on the old Moonville Rail Trail. The way her remains were spread in two evenly spaced lines made it evident she had been run over by a train. The problem was that there were no tracks — and hadn't been for a very long time. So how in the nine circles of hell had she been run over by a train?

A senior ranger at Lake Hope State Park was a cushy retirement job for a burned-out cop according to Ed's former supervisor, Sergeant Harry Dean. The sergeant hadn't added the part about a burned-out cop, but Ed knew that was the gist. Ed didn't have much to worry about beyond taking a few kids on a nature walk to show them how beavers build their lodges, talk to families about conservation, warn them to cover their fires with dirt, and occasionally break up a domestic fight when too much alcohol flowed.

The body lay in a clearing near Little Sandy Run, a tributary of Racoon Creek. An early morning mist crept down from the lake, pulling a thin blanket over the girl's body — sadly, too late for comfort. The victim had pulled her car off the road near Park Road 9 and State Route 278. Ranger Peace Officer Nancy Sullivan crouched near the corpse, digital camera in hand. Her long ginger hair had slipped from its bun into an unintentional ponytail. She side-lunged and snapped a photo, stretching the green polyester uniform to its limit. When Ed approached, she looked up.

"Morning, chief."

"Good morning, Nancy."

Ed always wanted to laugh when someone called him chief. With only three rangers under him, he was more like a squad sergeant than a chief, but that was what they called his predecessor, Jeff Waddell. So who was Ed to buck tradition? He took a sip of Nature Boost. Although they were stimulants for most people, energy drinks calmed Ed. He needed calm that day. When he left Akron a few months ago, he thought he had seen his last dead girl.

Ed's other ranger, Andy Tabachnik, moved around the scene carrying small yellow flags. He occasionally stooped to mark where evidence had been found. He walked hunched over, rocking back and forth as though bipedal locomotion were a foreign concept. Nancy followed behind with the camera, snapping photos as Andy went.

Unlike television, there were no CSI units in Tyvek suits combing through the grass for microscopic clues. In sleepy southern Ohio, investigators had to bag, tag, and in many cases, analyze their own evidence.

The girl wore a white blouse and teal skirt. Lying perpendicular to the trail, she looked like the heroine of one of those cheesy 1930s serials. Only there was no last-minute rescue revealed in the next installment.

Her head and legs were gone, mixed up in the bits of bone, flesh, and brain matter. A train—Ed kept coming back to that. It was like the old rail line was still operating, still transporting coal from Marietta to Cincinnati, but it wasn't. Her clothing was amazingly, disturbingly pristine, with just a few drops of crimson on her blouse.

In Akron, Ed had responded to a suicide. A man had sat in a chair and placed the barrel of a shotgun under his chin. The resulting blast splattered the wall behind him. It looked like someone had poured ketchup into a bowl of oatmeal and thrown it against the wall. If someone had seen the man from the chest down, it would've looked like he had just leaned back to take a nap, save for the teardrop of blood soaked into the thigh of his blue jeans. That was the thing that bothered Ed. How could there be just one drop?

Ed looked around. There appeared to be no evidence of a rope or chain, nothing to indicate that the young woman's assailant had tied her down. So, what kept her on the tracks? Ed closed his eyes. There were no freaking tracks.

Something in the forest caught his attention—a deer nosing its way through the trees. Ed watched its delicate steps for a few moments before doe eyes turned his direction and it melted back into the woods.

Ed rubbed his bald head. He had shaved it a few years ago after his bald spot had grown from dime to quarter size. His girlfriend at the time hadn't liked the new look, telling him that bald, muscular black men looked dangerous.

"Andy, when was the last time a train came through here?"

"About forty years ago, chief."

"And what would you say killed this young lady?"

"I'd say a train."

"Yeah, me too."

Nancy rose quickly, only shooting up to about five feet. "Wait a minute, how could it be a train?"

"Well, that, as the bard would say, is the rub." Ed knelt close to the body. From the low vantage point, he could see the laces on Nancy's boots were not completely secure. He started to mention it, then wrestled his focus back to the matter at hand.

"I don't like Shakespeare." Nancy frowned, and Ed couldn't help but crack a smile.

"Seriously, though, chief," Andy said. "How did this happen?"

"I don't know." Ed stood, his eyes tracing the length of the trail once more.

"Well, could it have been one of those things you see in the old movies? You know, with the two guys pumping the lever up and down?" Nancy gestured, her small hands vigorously pumping an imaginary handle. She snapped her fingers. "Hand cars. Isn't that what they call them?"

"They haven't used those things in years. They got motorized maintenance vehicles now," Andy said.

"What about that, motorized whatever?"

"They're heavy as hell, and they got the same problem as a train engine—no tracks."

Nancy looked down the trail. "Maybe they killed her somewhere else and brought the body here?"

"And spread her blood and brain matter all over the ground? That's a lot to go through. Naw, she was killed here, Nancy. What about a truck, chief? A big one."

"Possibility," Ed said. "But I've seen people run over

4

by trucks and they had tire tracks across the body. They didn't look like this."

"That kinda takes care of what it wasn't." Andy wiped sweat from his forehead.

Ed's rangers turned to him again and it annoyed him a little. What did they expect, rapid-fire deductions à la Sherlock Holmes? *Elementary, my good fellow, obviously a thousand strong men from a nearby circus dragged a train engine down here.* He forced himself to calm down. Of course they looked to him for answers. He was the big city (well, medium city) detective who worked hundreds of crime scenes. For them, this case was their first experience with crime, unless you counted writing citations for fishermen sans permits.

"Speculation without sufficient evidence is counterproductive," Ed said. "Tie your shoe, Nancy. For now, let's stick with what we know. All indications say that this young lady was run over by a train—a fact for which we have no explanation. The probability that this was some kind of accident is at best remote, so we treat this as a homicide. We must accept that there are aspects of this case that we do not understand at this time and instead focus on the circumstances that brought the victim to this place."

Ed noticed Nancy and Andy staring at him, thin grins on their faces. Perhaps he had channeled a little Holmes after all. Ed smiled back, then turned and started up the hill where the girl's gray Nissan Sentra sat in the middle of a trail. Tucked among the cedar and pine, it was barely visible from 278, but Nancy had spotted it on her last patrol run of the night. Ed made a mental note to place a commendation into her file.

A woman's purse lay on the ground near the vehicle.

Its spilled contents formed a rough trail in the direction of the body.

"Andy, what do we have on the car?"

Andy withdrew a small plastic bag from a paper evidence sack and followed. From the side, Andy looked like a bent stick. His Sam Browne belt kept slipping off what should have been his behind. He absent-mindedly adjusted it with long, thin fingers. He caught up to Ed and held the bag up to the light to read the driver's license inside. "Meghan Haynes from Zaleski, sixteen. Pretty girl."

*She's not pretty now.*

"We found her cell phone here." Andy pointed to one of the yellow flags on the ground. "It's busted up pretty good, but I'll see what I can get from it."

Walking to the car, Ed dropped to a knee in front of the open door. He caught a faint whiff of wild cherry from one of those cheap air fresheners in the plastic envelope. "Her assailant dragged her out of the back seat and along the ground. See how the grass is matted down?" Ed's hand hovered over the flattened grass. "She must have grabbed her cell phone on the way out, tried to record or dial nine-one-one. Check with county dispatch."

"Dragged her out and then what?" Andy looked at the ground in front of him.

Ed lifted a finger. "Let's focus on the *why*. Who was with her and who wanted her dead."

Andy pursed his lips. "Who was with her?"

"Young girls don't drive out into the woods alone." Ed gestured but noticed a squirrel. He hesitated as the rodent scurried up the hill, an acorn in its mouth.

Ed turned back to see Andy and Nancy exchange smirks.

"Go," Ed said.

"Yes, sir."

A Vinton County Coroner's van arrived as Andy drove off, and two men in jumpsuits got out. They waited for a nod from Ed before moving toward the body.

Ed turned to Nancy. "Get some rest after you log in the evidence. You have to go on again tonight. I'm going to follow these guys to the coroner's office."

"I'm good, chief."

"Go get some rest. That is not a request."

"Yes, sir."

Ed stood and stared at the trail. The wind changed direction, whipping sideways across his face and sweeping the familiar smell of the lake over his nostrils. He imagined a train chugging along tracks no longer in existence. Though he would not admit it to his rangers, in his mind, he was 100 percent sure that a train had run over that young woman. The question was how. So much for the stress-free retirement job.

**The powerful** surgical light reflected a glint off of the titanium tray of bloody scalpels, scissors, and retractors. The coroner had already closed and begun to sew the Y-incision shut. Neither man seemed bothered by the smell, a combination of burned tires, methane, and rotted fruit. Despite the cliché, Ed had become accustomed to the stench long ago. Charlie Cook's hands shook as he worked. He could never have been a surgeon.

The examination table had been lowered to accommodate Cook's diminutive frame. Leaning over the remains, his garish green-and-red Mickey Mouse tie hung dangerously near the gore. Holding a curved needle in one hand, Charlie looked over his shoulder.

"Well?"

Ed frowned. "Well, what?"

"I know what you're going to ask me." Charlie shakily pulled a suture through Meghan's skin. It snapped back unnaturally as if made of some polymer instead of the delicate flesh of a young woman.

Ed scratched his scalp. "The cause of death would be nice."

"You talk to Waddell?" Charlie looked up from the body and back at Ed.

"About what?"

"Your transition meeting. You ever make it happen?"

Ed wondered why Charlie was acting so strange. They had hit it off during Ed's first joint law enforcement meeting. He had been impressed with Charlie's credentials. Most coroners were mere administrators, but Charlie was a bona fide forensic pathologist. He and Ed had talked about cases in the news. It was unlike him to be so reticent.

"No. He blew me off," Ed said. "Wouldn't take my calls when I tried to follow up. You know this. We talked about it."

"Yeah, well, you're going to need to talk to him about this."

Naked on the table, Meghan looked more like a pile of scraps at a butcher shop than a human being. Lacerations on her torso meant that she had been dragged across the gravel, maybe rolled over a few times. Ed wondered why Charlie even bothered to close the incision. It wasn't like they were going to have an open casket.

"You going to give me the cause of death, or do I have to talk to Waddell about that too?"

Charlie looked up from the body and quickly turned

back. "I can't give you what you want. I'm sorry."

"What do I want?"

"You're not thick, Ed, so stop pretending. You want me to say she was killed by a train. I can't do that."

"Wasn't she?"

Charlie finished the stitches and pulled a paper blanket over Meghan's remains. He rolled the table over to a row of mortuary cabinets and pulled one open. There were only eight, a fraction of the cabinets Ed had seen in Summit County. It was well known that drawer number seven contained a bottle of whiskey.

"You're not listening. You need to talk to Waddell."

Ed came over to the other side of the body and prepared to lift it.

"I got it," Charlie said. "She's not very heavy."

"I'll help."

The two men slid the corpse over. Charlie was right. In her current condition, Meghan weighed next to nothing.

Ed looked at his friend. "You have to rule it a homicide, Charlie."

Charlie peeled off his surgical gloves and tossed them into the red bio-waste container. "Don't try to bluff me. That's bullshit TV logic. You know as well as I do that the county coroner has the final say on the manner of death. I can rule any damned way I please. I can call an inquest or not call one. I can say the cause was unknown. I could rule it death by misadventure. Hell, I could say she committed suicide!"

"I don't know what's going on with you. But you need to tell me something."

Charlie waved his arms. In his oversized lab coat, he looked like a child who had appropriated his parent's clothing. Ed had only seen him this animated after a few

9

too many drinks.

"That would serve you right. I should call an inquest," Charlie said. "Make you testify in front of the whole county that Meghan Haynes was killed by a ghost train."

"I didn't say anything about a ghost. Why are we talking about ghosts? I just—I need something I can work with."

"Are you listening to yourself?" Charlie put his hands on his hips, smudging gore onto his lab coat. "You have any idea what we're dealing with?"

"No. That's why I'm asking my friend, the coroner, for help."

"I'm sorry, Ed." Charlie took off his glasses. "But you're going to have to talk to Waddell."

Ed looked at the ceiling. "Why can't I just talk to you?"

"There are things about this you don't understand, okay? And Waddell has the answers." Charlie went to a drawer, pulled out an autopsy face sheet, and handed it to Ed.

Ed perused it. "Object of immense weight, moving at considerable speed. What's this crap?"

"Preliminary report, and the only reason you got that is because I *am* your friend."

"Charlie, talk to me." Ed held the report out.

"Waddell," was Charlie's only reply.

**On Second** Avenue in Zaleski, the sight of a tractor was as common as an automobile. Most homes boasted large red barns and sprawling fields. The setting harkened back to a time when all the neighbors were friendly, and all knew the names of everyone's kids and pets. Perhaps it was a time that never existed but only looked as if it did in home movies and faded photographs.

The Haynes family's roof seemed much newer than their two-story colonial. The bright orange-and-brown shingles clashed with the soft gray exterior. Andy's cruiser and a Vinton County sheriff's vehicle sat deep in the driveway. Ed climbed the stairs and knocked before gently pushing the door open and going inside. Mrs. Haynes sat on a couch with her entire upper body slumped over a Saint Bernard. She caressed the animal, her frumpy housedress hiding its face in her sleeve. A ceramic bull crouched on the coffee table as if preparing to charge. At the opposite end, a cigarette lighter in the shape of a revolver aimed at a pewter Conestoga wagon.

"Mrs. Haynes, I'm Ed Freemen. I'm so sorry for your loss."

She looked up at Ed and motioned toward the stairs.

During his time in the Akron Police Department, Ed had made several death notifications and realized that each was different. A sister who had been notified of the death of her estranged sibling shouted "no" over and over again for a full minute. In another case, a mother who found out her son had died in a single-car collision mused, "Well, that was bound to happen sooner or later. That bastard was born with a whiskey bottle in his mouth and a tag on his big toe."

Ed quickened his pace when he heard shouting.

"I want to see it! It's my house, goddamnit! I have a right!"

Henry Haynes stood at the entrance to his daughter's bedroom. Ed's swing-shift ranger, Doug Weems, did his best to hold the enraged father back. Weems had been a skinny wide receiver for Athens High School and retained that build, adding a receding hairline over the years and a two pack a day smoking habit. He struggled with the rotund Haynes who looked at Ed with wild-eyed desperation.

"Are you in charge here? Make 'em let me see!" Haynes pushed against Doug, dragging both of them toward Ed.

Ed looked into the room. Andy, along with Vinton County Sheriff's Deputy Carl Bergan, were crowded around an iPad. Andy looked up and gave a slight shake of his head. Ed pulled the door closed.

"That's probably not a good idea."

Haynes moved so quickly that Weems was unable to stop him. He launched forward, grabbing Ed's uniform with both hands. "You get out of my way! This is my house. *My* house!"

Ed took the man's hands off his shirt and pushed him firmly. "Your wife's downstairs. She needs you."

Haynes's hands dropped to his side, and his voice dropped to a whisper. "I'm sorry, but I have a right to know what she was doing."

"You're right, sir. This is your house. You have every right to look at that iPad before we take it into evidence. But if what you *think* is on there is really there, you have to ask yourself whether you want to see that with your own eyes. If the answer is yes, we won't stop you." Ed stepped out of the way and gestured for Doug to do the same.

Haynes stared at the unblocked door, then turned slowly and walked down the stairs. Ed tried to imagine what it would be like to be Haynes at that moment and came up short.

Ed went into the bedroom. A five-foot poster of a tattooed Justin Bieber stared down at him from the wall above Meghan's bed. The caption below the pointing pop star asked, "Are you a Belieber?"

An assortment of carnival-prize stuffed animals struck various poses from a pressboard shelf. A collection of actual paperback books sat on a lower shelf. Ed picked one up. It appeared to be set in a dystopian world where oppressive government agents pursued a group of nonconformist youths. Not at all original, but Ed had to give Meghan points for being an avid reader in the age of shorthand information. Out of the corner of his eye, Ed saw a brown piece of paper poking out between the mattress and box spring—just a bit—but Ed spotted it.

"Andy, did you look under here?"

Andy looked away from the iPad. "No, chief. Didn't seem to be a reason."

Ed grabbed the side of the mattress and flipped it off the bed. There was a thin paper bag wedged between the mattress and box spring. Ed pulled on latex gloves and looked inside. Lingerie.

Andy stared at Ed with his mouth open. "Forgive me, chief, but how the hell did you know something was under there?"

Ed waved him off. "A corner of the bag was sticking out."

Andy glanced at Bergan, and both men shook their heads.

Andy turned back to the iPad and said, "You got to see this. She has some pretty—" He leaned over to make sure Henry Haynes was out of earshot. "—nasty pictures on her iPad, Fifty Shades stuff. You were right. She was involved with someone."

"Can you tell if she sent the photos to anyone?"

Andy stared back at the screen. He looked out of place sitting at Meghan's desk, where she kept up with her friends and completed school assignments.

"She had to be sharing them, but I'm gonna need time to get into her social media accounts."

They went downstairs to find Meghan's parents hugging on the couch. Ed sat across from them until they looked up.

"I'm sorry to ask you this, but we need to know who Meghan was seeing."

"Seeing?" Henry Haynes said. His neck turned red. "She was sixteen!"

Ed glanced at Andy. "We're not here to judge anyone, but evidence shows that she was — parked with someone when she was killed."

"Parked? *Parked?*" Haynes said, beginning to rise from the couch. "My daughter is dead, and you come in here accusing her of being a—"

"They're just trying to help, Hank." Mrs. Haynes spoke up for the first time. She grabbed his wrist and pulled him back down. "They didn't know our Meghan. Mr. Freemen, our daughter wasn't allowed to date."

"Perhaps you can give me a list of her friends." Ed smiled warmly. "People she would confide in. As much information as you can give us. Addresses and phone numbers."

"And maybe you can give us access to Meghan's social media accounts," Andy added.

"Oh, Meghan wasn't on social media," Mrs. Haynes said. She left to get a pad and paper. Henry Haynes continued to assault the two law enforcement officers with his gaze.

Mrs. Haynes returned with a list in neat cursive. Ed thanked her and walked out with Andy.

"How can the parents be so strict and clueless at the

same time? Kinda hard to blame Meghan for going a little wild."

"It's an old story," Ed said. "I'm sure they mean well, but in my experience, the tighter parents hold on to the child, the further the kid strays."

Andy shifted the evidence bag from his right hand to his left. "How could they not even know she's on social media? What'd they think the iPad was for?"

At the edge of the driveway, they stopped.

"The father probably grew up in a house where the parents told the kids what to do, and they did it," Ed said. "Besides, do you think either of them even knows what a URL is?"

"Nope."

"We have to do this the hard way. Contact all the friends on that list and go to Meghan's school. Until we find who she was with, we're spinning our wheels. And do your thing with her accounts."

"Yes, chief."

# Chapter 2

**For the third time**, Nancy's head hit the printer behind her. She kept the lights dimmed in the office when she was alone. To her, bright lights ruined the mood of the night shift, but it was not conducive to staying awake when she wasn't on patrol. Her desk sat near a line of printers and file cabinets, and leaning her chair back on two legs provided a visceral alarm. When she dozed, her head would impact the printer. It was one of the few useful things she learned from Doug Weems when she took over the night shift.

Nancy got up and staggered to the break room. Pulling the coffee pot from the machine, she tilted it to look inside. Empty. Still holding the pot, she went to the sink, filled it with water, then went to the cupboard to retrieve a can of Maxwell House. Nancy dumped two scoops into the filter and filled the water reservoir. She leaned against the counter, closed her eyes, and listened to the bubbling of the coffee maker.

Nancy looked at her watch. *Five past three. Three hours to go.* Technically, her shift didn't end until seven, but the chief always got in at six and usually let her go early. The chief was an interesting character — well-read, philosophical, and hot for an older man.

She wondered why a man of such obvious talents had given up big-city police work for the boonies. There must have been a good reason, but she didn't know him well enough to ask. She knew from the internet he had been involved in a shooting of a teenager but had been cleared of any wrongdoing. As far as she could tell, he had an impeccable record. Nancy decided to let it go for now. If the chief had wanted her to know, he would have told her. Maybe he would, one day.

The office phone rang. Nancy jolted, speeding to her desk. She pushed the speaker button and opened her computer. She rarely got calls on the night shift.

"Rangers' office. Sullivan," Nancy said.

"Nancy, this is Bea."

"Yeah, Bea, what's up?"

"A lady called the office pretty upset. Said someone chased her kids. She's threatening to check out."

"Okay. What's her name, and where is she?"

There was a pause on the other end before Bea's voice came back.

"Her name is Cheryl Tate. She's in cabin seven."

*Lucky seven*, Nancy thought.

Nancy arrived at cabin seven, one of the rustic sleeping cabins for families who wanted the camping experience without sleeping in the elements. The woman who answered was one of the most striking human beings Nancy had ever seen. Jet-black waist-length hair and thick eyebrows contrasted perfectly with her olive skin. Her eyes were the color of a Cabernet Franc, and Nancy found that she could not look away from them.

"Thank goodness," Cheryl said. She backed away

from the door to allow Nancy in. "Some man chased my boys through the woods."

The park brochures didn't lie. The cabin consisted of a small room and a fireplace. Bathroom facilities were down the street. Four sleeping bags, two full and two medium-sized, were arranged on the floor. Fishing rods, lures, and hiking boots formed a pile in the northeast corner. Four cloth folding chairs were lined up against the west wall. A tall, thin man with wavy brown hair sat three chairs from the right, his arms folded.

"Well, 'chased' is a strong word," Mr. Tate said.

Cheryl stared daggers at her husband.

Nancy looked at the two boys, who appeared to be twins. Possibly eleven or twelve. They knelt on their sleeping bags in an identical pose. The twins possessed the same striking features as their mother and the rail thinness of their father. Nancy turned to Cheryl. "May I talk to them?"

Cheryl nodded. Nancy dropped to one knee in front of them. They looked at each other and giggled in the way little boys do when they begin to discover girls are actually kind of nice.

"What are your names?" Nancy smiled.

"Mike," the twin on the left said. He looked to his right. "This is my brother, Mark."

For seemingly no reason at all, this drew more giggles, which stopped abruptly after a stern look from the twins' mother. Nancy thought they were adorable.

"Nice to meet you. My name is Nancy."

The boys looked at one another again. Big grins spread across their faces, but they did not laugh again.

"Can you tell me what happened that scared you?" Nancy asked.

"We were camped by the lake, fishing," Mark said.

"They were supposed to be out back where I could see them," Cheryl said, eyeing the twins. Mr. Tate rolled his eyes.

Both boys avoided their mother's gaze.

"We wanted to get some catfish. So we went down by the lake and set our poles."

"Okay," Nancy said. "Then what happened?"

"This big man chased us," Mark said. "We ran home — left all our stuff."

"Do you know which trail you took?"

"Copperhead!" the boys shouted together, then playfully nudged one another.

"Okay," Nancy said. She took out her notebook. "When you say he 'chased' you, what do you mean, exactly?"

"Well, he came up the trail after us," Mark said.

"Was he running, trying to catch up to you?"

"No."

"What are you trying to say?" Cheryl interrupted. "Some maniac stalked my boys."

Nancy turned around. Cheryl Tate stood with her arms folded, her left hand clutching a gold necklace with twin hearts. Her fingers worked as she fondled the necklace as well as the suprasternal notch at the base of her neck. The chief had taught Nancy that this gesture meant she was nervous or afraid. "I know you're worried. I would be, too, if I had these little fellas to protect. But in order to help, I need to get the full picture." She turned back to the boys. "Can you describe him?"

"Uh," Mike said. "We didn't see him that well, but he was big, and he had a lamp."

"Did you see what he was wearing?"

20

"No, just the light swinging back and forth."

Nancy stood and shoved her notebook into her back pocket. "Did you put out your fire before you ran?"

"We didn't have a fire," Mark said. "Just our lamp."

"Is it possible the man had your lamp? Maybe he tried to return it?" Nancy felt Cheryl shift behind her. Nancy understood. Whether Cheryl's fears were rational or not, something had scared her babies, and she was in protection mode. Nancy hoped to have children one day. At thirty-four, her biological clock wasn't sounding the alarm yet, but the yellow light was blinking.

"No, ma'am," Mike said. "It was different."

"How was it different?"

Mike squinted. "I don't know. Ours is electric. New. His was, I don't know...different."

"Okay," Nancy said. "You guys are doing great. How do I get to your campsite?"

"Just follow Copperhead to the lake."

"Did you see the man come out of the woods at the end of the trail?"

"No, ma'am," Mike said. "We didn't exactly look back."

Nancy was about to leave, but the boys were staring at her, their eyes wide. She looked down at them. "Is there something else?"

"You're pretty," Mike said and immediately covered his mouth. Mark punched him in the arm, and they giggled uncontrollably.

"Boys," Mr. Tate said but he was grinning.

"I think your mother is pretty, but thank you," Nancy said. She turned to Cheryl. "I'll make a report on this and check out their campsite. In the meantime, you might want to keep them close."

"Is that all?" Cheryl said. "You're not going to arrest him?"

"Arrest who, Mrs. Tate?" Nancy kept her voice even. "The boys couldn't give a description, and there is no way of knowing if the man was just walking the trails or stalking them. In any case, at this point, no crime has been committed."

Mr. Tate got up from his chair, went to Nancy, shook her hand, and mouthed, *I'm sorry*. Out loud, he said, "Thank you for coming out at this late hour, officer. You have a good rest of your night."

Mr. Tate hooked his wife's arm and led her to the cabin's interior. She continued to glare at Nancy until she went out the door.

**In the** Vinton County High School counselor's office, Andy Tabachnik sat with McArthur Police Officer Greg Encanto as a string of girls were called out of class to be interviewed. School had only been open for a week or so. The building still had that clean, polished wood smell that brought back memories, mostly unpleasant, of Andy as a gawky teenager trying to fit in.

Things weren't going well. Most kids didn't want to talk about Meghan at all, and those who did gave one-word answers. Not all of the girls on Mrs. Haynes's list were friends of Meghan's. Perhaps they had been at one time but had fallen out as high school girls do. The fifth girl to walk in was Darlene Chambers. She was tall and chubby with blonde hair and tight jeans. She plopped down and folded her arms. Her mouth moved in circles as she aggressively attacked a wad of gum. Andy prepared for another flat refusal.

"Yeah, I knew Meghan. She wasn't the little angel that

her parents made her out to be," Darlene said.

"How do you mean?" Andy said. Darlene was absolutely murdering the gum, making wet clicking sounds. Andy wanted to jab his pen into both his ears.

"You know what I mean." Darlene glared at him.

"If you know something, you need to tell us," Encanto said.

"She didn't see any of the boys around here if that's what you mean." Darlene rolled her eyes as if Andy and Greg were the dumbest people on the planet.

Andy turned to Greg then looked back at Darlene. She was trying to tell them something without telling them, and he felt like the dumbest person in the world. "You wanna explain that young lady?"

"Ughhh!" Darlene jumped out of her chair and stomped out.

"Miss Chambers!" Andy called, but she continued down the hall.

"That went well," Greg said.

"She's trying to tell us something."

"And trying very hard not to tell us at the same time," Greg added.

"Meghan was boning someone, but not a student." Andy stood and walked around the room.

"A teacher?" Greg suggested.

"Teacher, coach, staff, somebody," Andy said. He stopped pacing. "She sounded almost pissed about it. Like she was jealous."

Greg cocked his head. "Why talk to us at all?"

Andy snapped his fingers. "She's playing us like a fiddle. Wants to trash Meghan's reputation and torpedo him while staying out of the line of fire. It's a damned good strategy if you think about it."

"Or her," Greg said.

"What?"

"The adult might be a woman," Greg said.

Andy shrugged. "Or her."

"We got to get one of these girls to talk," Greg said. "How many are left on the list?"

"Seven." Andy came back to the desk and sat.

They were about to call the next girl when the door opened, and a tall, balding man with a gray beard walked in. The corners of his mouth pulled down, and he directed his gaze at Andy.

"Mr. Greeves," Greg said.

"I have a student in my office crying her eyes out. She says you're traumatizing her."

What the hell was going on? The principal knew why they were there. "Sir, we're investigating a murder," Andy said.

"I'm not talking to you!" Greeves snapped. "You have no jurisdiction here. Officer Encanto, do you need me to get your chief on the phone?"

"No, sir, that won't be necessary," Greg said. "Andy, we have to go."

"No, wait," Andy said. "Darlene has information we need for the case—may even involve a staff member."

"You're done here. Or do you need me to call your chief as well?" Greeves opened the door.

Andy started to open his mouth, but Greg grabbed his arm.

"Let's go, Andy. We lost this one."

When they entered the hall, Andy turned to Greg. "What the hell?"

Greg frowned. "He and my chief are golf buds. We're never going to win that one."

"Well, he doesn't golf with mine," Andy said. "He would've backed us up."

"It doesn't matter. He's right about the jurisdiction, and you know it."

They passed the principal's office and saw Darlene staring at them, a Cheshire grin on her face. She lifted her right hand as they walked by and wiggled her fingers. Andy raised his hand, intending to flip her off. Greg pushed it back down. They moved farther down the hall and students began to poke their heads out of classrooms. Teachers yelled for them to return to their seats.

Darlene Chambers was a manipulative little witch, but Andy had to admit a grudging respect for the teen. In the space of a few minutes, she had seized control of the entire situation, fed them just enough information to put them on the scent, then sabotaged their ability to get more information from other students—perhaps about her own involvement. Even her little tantrum was probably contrived. They had come in with a checkerboard, and Darlene was playing three-dimensional chess. Andy wouldn't make that mistake again.

"You know any girls like that in high school?" Andy asked Greg.

Greg thought about it. "Yep."

According to the public-school review website, Vinton County High School had a diversity score of 0.04, so Andy was surprised to see a Black girl lingering in the hallway. She was about five-eight with curly hair, light brown complexion, and a beauty mark under her left eye. The girl stood erect, with the confident bearing of a top athlete. She caught his eye and lifted her chin slightly. Andy didn't know if Principal Greeves was watching and didn't want to look back. He reached into his pocket, grabbed a business card, and trapped it between his first and second fingers. When he and Greg passed the girl, he flicked the card in her direction. It hit the wall behind her and slid to the ground. She gave no indication that she saw it.

*Good girl.*

**Andy finished** briefing Ed on the day's events and was typing his report when his phone rang. He snatched it on the second ring.

"Mr. Tabachnik, please." The girl's voice was barely a whisper.

"This is Andy Tabachnik," Andy said.

There was a long silence, and Andy was afraid that she had hung up. Finally, she came back. "This is the girl you passed in the hallway earlier."

Andy caught Ed's attention and pointed vigorously to the phone. Ed nodded, went into his office, and pushed a button.

"What's your name?" Andy asked.

"Can't tell you that," she whispered. "I don't want to get into trouble."

"You know I could find out," Andy said. He saw movement out of the corner of his eye and looked up to see the chief shaking his head.

Her voice became louder. "Please don't do that."

"Okay," Andy said. "What do you have to tell me?"

The girl's whisper softened. "There's a teacher."

"A teacher?"

"He likes girls," she said.

Andy pressed the phone closer to his ear. He had to consider the teen mastermind, Darlene, had put this girl up to calling him, but his instincts told him no. "He's having sex with some of the high school girls?"

"Yes." Her breathing quickened.

"And what is this teacher's name?"

The voice on the other end caught and went silent long enough for Andy to think she had hung up.

"Hello?"

"I—I have to know my name won't be out there. My parents—they can't know."

"I don't even know who you are," Andy said.

The girl blew a puff of air into the phone. "Please, there's only a few Black girls in the whole school."

"Okay, I promise you won't be involved." Andy looked at Ed, who gave him the thumbs up from his office.

"Mr. Malone," the caller said.

"Was Meghan one of the girls Mr. Malone was—seeing?"

"I don't know that. He—he has a few girls."

"Can you tell me who the girls are?" Andy asked.

Heavy breathing. "No, I don't want to do that."

Andy lowered his voice. "We can take him down. You won't have to testify."

"No, I can't."

"He won't hurt any other girls. You did the right thing by calling, young lady. Please give us what we need to get him."

"No, I've told you too much."

"Wait," Andy said. "He do anything to you?"

The line went quiet.

"Sorry, chief," Andy said as Ed walked into the room.

"No, that's fine. That's all you were going to get out of her anyway," Ed said.

"Should I look her up, chief?" Andy asked.

"No, let her go for now. We'll have her parents screaming that we're harassing her. She might call back. Just see what you can get on this Mr. Malone."

**The following** morning, Ed stood with Andy near the scene of the murder. They hiked the Moonville Rail Trail from the Zaleski terminus, looking for signs of a large vehicle. Ed kept looking at the spot where Meghan's body was found. He didn't know what he expected to find, a rail line hidden just under the gravel or maybe a note from the Riddler. Though it seemed impossible—what didn't in this case—Ed felt he had to explore the theory that some kind of vehicle had been placed on the trail to run over Meghan, perhaps a large truck. Of course, a truck, even a semi, would not cause the wounds found on Meghan.

So far, they had found nothing. There were no ruts in the grass where a vehicle had been driven from the road, no grooves on the gravel and dirt trail. Ed asked around and was informed that people hiked, ran, rode horses, and even dirt biked on the trail, but they had never seen a car or truck.

Ed stopped, pulled off his backpack, and grabbed a water bottle. Andy followed suit, and the two men stood staring at the crime scene. The technicians had done an admirable job of collecting the remains, but sticky black blood still clung to the gravel.

"I wonder if she saw it comin'," Andy said.

"Better not to think about it." Ed put his water bottle away, pulled out a can of Nature Boost, and drank. He heard the sound of Andy's shoes on the gravel path, birds in the trees, insects buzzing, and a mild breeze. His visual senses were jacked up as well. Whenever an animal, leaf, or blade of grass moved, it drew his attention. When the Nature Boost kicked in, the world around him would slow down, or more accurately, his brain would catch up to his thoughts. Ed would get a pleasant tingling at the edges of his brain and sense, rather than hear, a low buzz. The buzz signaled that everything was in sync again, and he could use his powers of observation without distraction.

Andy cocked his head. "Chief, can I ask you a question?"

"Sure."

"Why do you drink that stuff?"

Ed chuckled. "Helps me concentrate."

Andy squinted at the can. "You don't seem to have trouble concentrating."

"Exactly." Ed smiled, downed the rest of the can, crushed it, and put it in his backpack. His mother would be proud to hear that. She had worked with him daily on how to control his symptoms so he wouldn't have to stay on Ritalin. She had a practical reason in addition to her aversion to medicating kids. As a single mother working minimum wage, she couldn't afford even the modest co-pay or the loss in wages when she had to take off work to pick up an unruly child. Ed learned it was his responsibility to keep the family going by controlling his behavior. Only Ed's best friend knew his secret. When Ed turned fifteen, his mother contracted cancer. He studied at home to care for her until her death. His sense of responsibility for others played a major role in his decision to become a police officer.

They shrugged on their backpacks and continued down the trail.

"We going all the way to Mineral, chief?" Andy asked.

Ed looked down the trail. A sprawling field straddled either side, but a wooded area lay ahead of them.

"No, just to the Moonville Tunnel. We've had rain off and on the past couple of weeks, and the ground is soft enough to show any marks. If there are none by the time we get to the tunnel—"

"Then that theory is busted," Andy finished.

They continued, entering a wooded area.

"What did you find out about Malone?" Ed turned to Andy.

Andy pulled out his cell phone and flipped through images until he found a picture.

"David P. Malone. English teacher and soccer coach. Well respected by faculty and staff."

"You think he's diddling the students?"

"Oh, yeah," Andy said. "English teacher. You know he's got a line of bullshit six miles long. He starts throwing Shakespeare at those high school fillies, it's all over."

Ed looked up at a bird scrambling up the branch of a tree, feasting off insects. He pulled his attention back. "How are we going to prove it?"

"I don't know." Andy wagged his head. "I'm working on Meghan's computer. She was sending images to a 'Spartan two-four-seven.' Dollars to donuts that's Malone, but all the traffic is on the dark web and hard as hell to trace. Message board administrators claim they don't even know who's posting content, but that's a load of crap."

"What do you need?" Ed asked.

"Got to get a search warrant for Malone's computer. If he downloaded any of those images, his ass is mine."

"So he can't see us coming?"

"Right," Andy said. "If he ditches his computer, he'll

be pretty hard to catch, but if he just tries to delete the images, that won't work."

"We're lucky to have you here." Ed patted Andy on the shoulder. "Otherwise, we'd have to send everything to the crime lab in Columbus."

Andy's face lit up. "Thanks, chief."

"So when did you become interested in computers?" Ed asked.

Andy looked up. "Oh, since I was a kid."

"You grew up on a farm, right?"

"Yeah," Andy said. "Near Athens, but we had internet and all that stuff. Built my first computer from parts I found at the thrift shop, and I was off to the races. Worked my way through college selling refurbished computers, fixing crashed hard drives, and setting up networks. What about you, chief?"

Ed frowned.

Andy took his hat off and ran a hand through his sweat-soaked hair. "What's a big-city cop doing in the ass-end of Ohio?"

Ed looked away. "This is my retirement job."

"You ain't that old, chief. Did something happen? I know there was a shooting—"

"That's a conversation for another day, okay?"

"Copy that, chief."

Ed knew Andy and Nancy must have googled his name when they learned he would be the new chief, so they had some knowledge of the Anthony Deavers shooting. They may even suspect that it had something to do with his retirement. Still, the memory was a painful one, and Ed wasn't quite ready to share.

They arrived at the tunnel. Vines crawled up the sides of the entrance, caressing the name "Moonville" carved into the ledge. Workers regularly cleared foliage from either end of the tunnel, making passage by a large vehicle possible, but it would only travel a short distance before the forest closed in again.

"Should we go farther?" Andy asked.

"No. Any vehicle that came to the trail between here and Mineral would have to pass through here, and it just didn't happen."

Ed and Andy stood there for a moment before turning back and hiking to the park, no closer to finding out what happened to Meghan Haynes.

# Chapter 3

**Gareth "Big Wheel" Cauthorne** drove south on Ohio Route 356, passing Scott Street and Biddyville Road. He pulled his 1987 Blazer over to a clearing.

As a kid, his family could never afford a new bicycle. Whenever a part fell into disrepair, Gareth stole what he needed from the more affluent families in Albany, Ohio. Once, his rim was bent beyond repair. The only replacement wheel he could steal was two inches smaller than the standard twenty-six. As he rode his bike through the neighborhood sporting a front wheel considerably larger than the back, the kids began to call him "Big Wheel." However, as his front wheel was of average size, perhaps "Little Wheel" would have been the more appropriate nickname.

In any case, the name followed him into adulthood, though it had been shortened to "Wheel." The other thing that followed him into adulthood was his penchant for methamphetamine, cultivated at an early age by his older brother, Kenny.

*Thanks, Bro.*

Wheel stopped the truck and got out. No cars came

in either direction. He went to the passenger side where Julie was scooting to the edge of her seat. The truck had oversized tires, raising the cab about four feet. Julie stuck out her arms like a small child at a swimming pool and dropped into Wheel's arms. It wasn't that he was a gentleman. Last year, Julie tried to negotiate the drop while high on meth and broke her nose. The broken nose didn't detract from her looks, however. Meth had done that job much better than gravity ever could.

Once the fantasy of every boy at Alexander High School, Julie could now pass for an extra on *The Walking Dead*. Meth had ground her top teeth down to black stubs, and her lips looked as if they had been scorched by a butane torch.

He started to lower her to the ground, but she wrapped her impossibly skinny legs around his waist. He turned toward the woods where an abandoned camper trailer served as their home. She tried to kiss him, and he turned his head in disgust. They'd come up short that week, and the scent of alternate payment still clung to her breath.

"None of that now."

"Come on, Wheel." Julie leaned over and moved her face in front of his.

"You kiss me, I swear I'll drop you on your head."

Julie was not Wheel's girlfriend. They had more of a symbiotic relationship based solely on the acquisition of meth. Wheel worked odd jobs or sold stolen goods, and if that wasn't enough, Julie made up the difference.

Wheel knew her shelf life as a prostitute was coming to an end. She was long past the point where even the most desperate man would have intercourse with her, and only the cover of darkness allowed her mouth to be an adequate orifice for a transaction. Not that Wheel was a prize catch. With long, greasy hair and a dirty American flag bandana, Wheel looked like the last attendee at a long-forgotten Grateful Dead concert.

Like most meth users, Wheel's gums were black, and every tooth from the premolars forward had been pulled. His skin was a blotchy patchwork of black circles and pale white. The difference between them was that Wheel had always been strung out, and Julie wouldn't have given him the time of day if it had not been for her spectacular fall from grace.

"Hurry up, Wheel, I'm gettin' the itch." Julie wiggled in his arms.

"Hang on!"

Despite his emaciated frame, Wheel carried her easily. He ducked through trees, occasionally whipping her with branches. She made no sound of protest because it didn't matter. Nothing mattered but the temporary euphoria of the drug, a feeling that was just a little less with each hit.

They arrived at the trailer just off the old Moonville Rail Trail and went inside. They were impervious to the salty, dank stench of sweat and mold steeped in the candied chemical twang of meth haze. With no light inside, they stumbled through the twelve-foot compartment like blind rats in a maze. Wheel went to a cabinet above the sink to get a glass vial while Julie skittered about the trailer, lighting candles with a butane torch. Carefully pouring the crystals inside the vial's small opening, they held it over a candle and took turns inhaling the white vapor that wafted out.

They never spoke while getting high. What was there to say? Their relationship was based on mutual self-destruction, and to discuss it would be pointless. After the contents were empty, they sat on the bed, drinking warm cherry soda and watching the candlelight flicker on the ceiling.

"Gotta take a leak," Wheel said.

He pushed off the bed and started toward the door, his lanky arms dropping to his sides.

"You said you were going to fix the toilet." Julie's head lolled to the side as she looked at the broken folding door. Behind the door was a toilet stained brown with age and fecal matter.

"Yeah, I just need to get a septic tank," Wheel said.

He paused at the door and looked back at her. In the shimmering candlelight, she didn't look quite as hideous. For a moment he wanted her, then dismissed it. The last time they had sex was a year ago when they were so wasted they barely knew what was happening. He chuckled to himself and continued outside. He wasn't *that* damned high.

"Use the stick."

The "stick" was an old broom handle that they wedged through the aluminum door handle and against the wall. It would prevent someone of moderate strength from pulling the door open. Wheel didn't know why they used it. What would a possible intruder take, some moldy cheese crackers? The case of cherry soda a guy had handed them off the back of his truck? Julie? This last thought made him laugh aloud.

"What the hell you laughing at out there?" Julie called from inside.

"That somebody out here would want to get you." Wheel looked up to see a middle finger shoved through the sliding window.

He laughed again and walked toward the trees. Wheel found a tall oak and unzipped his pants. A light

36

flashed over his right shoulder. He turned and saw a man holding an old lantern, the red light illuminating half his face like a fun-house ghoul.

Before Wheel could say anything, the man punched him in the throat. Wheel's hands flew to his neck. He staggered in a circle, spraying piss in all directions. The man paused until Wheel's bladder emptied and stepped forward.

"What's up, man!" Wheel shouted.

The man hit Wheel hard in the solar plexus. Wheel groaned and bent over. His head dropped. The stranger popped his head back up with an uppercut. Wheel's head hit the tree behind him with a loud *clunk.* Pinned against the tree, the attacker fired a series of right leads into Wheel's face, bouncing his head repeatedly off the bark in a sickening rhythm.

Dazed, Wheel slid down the tree fully expecting the beating to be over. He was wrong. The man grabbed him by the hair and dragged him into the clearing.

"Please take — what — want." Wheel hyperventilated.

The big man made no indication that he even heard. They stopped near the trail with Wheel sitting on his butt and the man holding his hair.

"Man, why you kicking my ass?" Blood ran from Wheel's nose into his mouth. He coughed.

The man turned to look down at him, then up at the moon, high and bright in the sky. With his mouth closed, the man began a rhythmic chant. Wheel's eyes widened. The guy was as loopy as a cross-eyed cowboy.

Wheel clawed at the man's arm and kicked his side. Strung out and skinny, Wheel wasn't a match for the big man, but if he could get loose, he'd make a run for it.

The man dropped his lantern and looked down at

Wheel.

*Oh, shit.*

With his left hand free, the man punched Wheel in the nose. Wheel rolled over and tried to crawl away, but a hand clamped around his left foot and dragged him back.

"Please, man, just tell me what you want!"

His assailant twisted the foot, rolling Wheel over on his back. He straddled Wheel and pounded him with heavy blows.

The sky spun. Wheel's arms slipped to his sides. The big man stood again and resumed his chant. Wheel looked up and saw—*holy shit*—like a hole—a hole in reality. Inside the hole was a mirror image of the night sky, except the moon was in a different position. Wheel's mouth dropped open. In the distance, he saw a point of light and heard a familiar sound. *Chug-a-lug, chug-a-lug.*

Wheel wondered what the hell was going on. Maybe Streamer had cut his meth with LSD. Maybe the whole thing was a bad trip, but Wheel's pain belied that conclusion. The big man grabbed Wheel by the scruff of the neck, his large hands closing around his throat.

As the light approached, Wheel saw that it *was* a train. The roar grew louder like an approaching tornado. Wheel punched and kicked his attacker's shin. The man threw Wheel into the path of the train. Wheel only had time to lift his head before it hit.

**Wheel had** been gone a long time when Julie thought she heard a train in the distance. Maybe he had gone to get more dope from Streamer. She paced back and forth in the trailer, one hand on her hip, the other holding a Marlboro to her desiccated lips. *He'd better not smoke it himself, or —*

*or what?* What would she do if he did hold out on her, kick his ass? She laughed, then heard the train again. Her drug-addled mind finally made the connection. There couldn't be a train. There were no tracks.

She threw the lit cigarette down, pulled the broom handle from the door, and ran outside. In the growing darkness, something glowed behind the trees. Julie ran to the rail trail and looked to her left. A man ambled down the path carrying what looked like a lantern.

"Hey!" Julie called, but the man continued to walk down the trail. She followed him, wondering where Wheel was. Her foot stepped into something gooey. She looked down but couldn't see anything, since the moon had temporarily retreated behind cloud cover. Julie knelt close to the mushy substance, still unable to see anything. She tentatively stuck her hand in it and felt a viscous fluid between her fingers. She held it to her nose. The metallic smell was unmistakable. *Blood.*

Julie popped up so fast that her foot slipped, and she fell sidelong into the gore. She scrambled to her feet, chipped bone and flesh dripping from her body. Julie stumbled toward the road, following the trail. If someone had been watching her, strung out and emaciated with blood and flesh coating the side of her body, they would surely believe zombies were real. Julie made it to Route 356 and dropped to her knees. The last thing she remembered was the sight of taillights receding in the distance.

# Chapter 4

Jeff Waddell lived in a one-story farmhouse just outside of Logan, Ohio. A large field of freshly mowed grass spread majestically over the east side of the property where there were once rows of crops. As Ed approached the front door, he heard creaking floorboards. Someone was coming. There were only two stairs leading up to a small porch, adorned with a swing and a hanging flowerpot devoid of flora. Up close, Ed noticed that the white paint had peeled, and a slight separation stood between the bright green faux shutters and the wall. Ed had only placed one foot on the first step when the door opened, and the muzzle of a shotgun slid out.

"Whoa." Ed raised his hands instinctively before lowering them, realizing how ridiculous he looked. "I'm Ed Freemen."

"I know who you are." The muzzle shoved forward in a quick jerk. "Now, see how fast you can get back to your car."

Ed's eyebrows pressed together. "First of all, you can get that shotgun out of my face!"

"First of all, I ain't got nothing to say to you. I warned

you once to get off my property. Now I'm within my right to shoot."

Ed heard Waddell chamber a round. Seeing little available cover, he slid his hand down to the thumb break of his Glock 40 holster. Ed hoped Waddell was bluffing. "Your shotgun is loaded with buckshot, right? At this distance, you can't incapacitate me with a single shot. You won't get a second."

There was a long pause where Waddell held his ground, his face obscured by darkness like a troll under a bridge. Ed didn't think he would have the right answer to the riddle.

"You got guts, I'll give you that. But I still ain't got nothing to say to you. Now get!" Waddell lifted the barrel of the shotgun toward the road.

Ed backed down off the porch. He couldn't think of a good outcome. Waddell couldn't be serious about shooting him, but if the encounter did end in gunfire, Waddell's actions could be construed as a man protecting his property. Ed had no more jurisdiction at Waddell's home than the paperboy, and in an increasingly red state like Ohio, the right to defend one's home was sacrosanct.

"I just wanted to talk, you crazy old coot. You didn't have to pull a gun on me. I should report you."

"Report it to who?" Waddell poked his head out the door. Ed saw a grizzled, mostly white beard. "I don't work for the state no more."

"Whom," Ed said. He turned, walking the long path toward his car.

"What?" Waddell said, coming onto the porch.

"'Report it to whom,' you ignoramus!" Ed knew his response was childish and stooping to Waddell's level, but he didn't like backing down to the gun-toting idiot. Behind him, he heard Waddell's dry, gravelly laugh.

**That night**, Ed called Charlie. "You're going to have to tell me what's going on, Charlie."

There was a sigh on the other end of the line. "I told you to talk to Waddell."

"He didn't seem in the talking mood. Met me at the door with a shotgun."

"Oh, that stupid old bastard," Charlie said. "I'm not the one who's supposed to tell you."

"You keep saying that."

"All right, all right. Don't get mad. Meet me at the Corner Pub in half an hour."

"Why the Corner Pub?" Ed said.

"This is not a story you tell sober." Charlie hung up.

**There were** only three other customers at The Corner Pub in Jackson. Lambent lights blended perfectly with the soft country music wafting down from tiny speakers overhead. The narrow pub had room for one row of tables that ran along the front window. There was just enough room to walk between the tables and the mismatched wooden stools that lined the bar. On karaoke night, patrons would squeeze onto a small makeshift stage near the far wall and belt out country tunes with all the fervor they could muster.

Ed and Charlie sat at the end, under a television suspended from the ceiling. The air was thick with the smell of onion rings, French fries, and beer.

Near the bar, a large blonde woman wearing a tight denim skirt and cowboy boots did a sultry dance to Blake Shelton's "Do You Remember." Her friends giggled as Charlie stared, mesmerized by her hips and ample bosom. Ed, with the side of his head leaning on one hand, patiently dumped one catfish nugget after another into his mouth. Charlie turned away from the dancing woman, took a long drink from his beer, and leaned forward. He had gotten a head start before Ed arrived, and the pitcher between them was only half full.

"I don't know the whole story," Charlie said. "They play it pretty close to the vest."

"Okay."

"When I took over as coroner, the outgoing coroner, Alice Camden, told me that I might get a case like this."

"Involving a train?"

"Not really." Charlie looked around, but there was no one in earshot. He took another drink. "I mean, she didn't go into specifics, but she said I might get a case that I couldn't explain. If I did, I was to play it vanilla. You know, leave anything crazy out of the report."

"You mean lie." Ed sipped his ginger ale.

"Not lie. Just don't volunteer anything, just like the report I gave you."

Ed looked at three women engaged in animated conversation. Another Blake Shelton tune played, "Who Are You When I'm Not Looking." He fixed his gaze back on Charlie. "Why?"

He drained his glass and reached for the pitcher again. Unlike at the autopsy, his hands didn't shake. That might seem to be a good sign, but Ed knew it meant Charlie's tremor was a symptom of withdrawal. They had only been friends a little over a month, and Ed didn't know how to broach the subject with him.

"Alice didn't say." Charlie put down his glass. "She

only told me one day I might get a case where the circumstances seemed impossible. She said I should water down the report and talk to Waddell. That's why I keep telling you to talk to him. He's the gatekeeper."

Ed knew that some medical examiners tailored their reports at the request of the investigators, in most cases altering the time of death to defeat a suspect's alibi. As elected officials, coroners enjoyed much more leeway.

He lowered his head in disappointment. "Charlie, you're not just a paper pusher or political hack. You're a licensed pathologist and medical board member."

"I know, I know," Charlie said. "I hoped I would never see anything like this. Maybe Alice was losing it. She was pretty sick at the time. But then you come in with this girl, and I think, this is it. Has to be."

The waitress came to check on them. Ed waved her off, but Charlie pointed to the pitcher.

"Charlie, why don't you take it easy?" Ed felt he had to say something, though he had dealt with enough alcoholics to doubt it would do any good.

He looked at Ed over his empty glass. "There ain't a Cook alive who can't hold his drink."

"How many are still around?"

"That's not funny, Ed."

Ed interlaced his fingers. "It's not meant to be. Didn't you say your dad's death was alcohol related?"

"I'm a big boy."

"Fair enough." Ed picked up his drink.

They sat in silence for a while. Ed didn't care if he had overstepped or hurt their friendship. He had to say something and probably hadn't said enough.

Finally, Charlie spoke. "Your dad still around?"

"He's out there somewhere." Ed fondled his glass.

"Womanizing, cheating, stealing."

"Reconnect with him before it's too late. None of that stuff is going to matter once he's gone."

Ed shifted uncomfortably. He didn't like talking about his deadbeat father. "There's still something you're not telling me."

Charlie impatiently tapped the counter while waiting for the waitress. Ed looked over at the three women. Periodically, they glanced at Charlie then returned to their conversation. At least one seemed interested, no doubt encouraged by Charlie's earlier attention. In his mid-fifties with salt-and-pepper hair, Charlie wasn't a bad-looking guy, and women responded to his quirky taste in clothing.

"Everyone's predecessor is supposed to brief them. Waddell was in the thick of it, so he has the whole story. That's why you have to get him to talk."

"That's not happening," Ed said. "I don't know how crazy he is, but I really thought bullets were going to fly."

The waitress came back with a new pitcher. Charlie waited until she left before reaching under the table and pulling a spiral-bound notebook from his bag.

"I did some research after I took over. Every ten years, there's a spike in deaths in the area. They're listed as accidents. Whenever the remains are extensively damaged, it's attributed to animal predation."

"Maybe lead with that next time," Ed said.

"I had to see how you were going to react first." Charlie handed the notebook to Ed.

Ed waved a hand. "Anything could account for these numbers. An increase in traffic in those years, more visitors to the area."

"Okay." Charlie pulled out a map from the back of the notebook. The map showed dots in various colors clustered along a single line. "Tell me what that line is, Ed."

"The Moonville Rail Trail."

Charlie thumped the map with his finger. "Exactly. I could only go back to nineteen-fifty. Before that, the records get fuzzy. But guess what?"

Ed stared, intrigued.

"The deaths all begin in August, and this is the ten-year anniversary."

Ed scratched his head. He had been a cop most of his adult life and had seen some strange things on the job, but everything could be explained by a thorough analysis of the evidence. Still, despite his drinking problem, Charlie was a scientist, not given to flights of fancy. Ed had to admit that the deaths along the Moonville Rail Trail were hard to explain, especially after the tracks were removed. "I don't know what I'm supposed to do with this. I'm a cop. I deal in evidence and eyewitness accounts, not ghosts and goblins. Besides, we have a flesh-and-blood suspect."

"You're supposed to talk to Waddell."

"You're just going to keep saying that. What about Alice Camden? Why can't we talk to her?"

Charlie turned away. "We would find the conversation a bit one-sided."

"No," Ed said.

"Yep. Cancer. That's why she quit."

Ed looked down and stirred the crumbs of his catfish with his fork. "Okay, the first thing that's going to happen is you're going to get me a real autopsy report."

"Ed."

47

"I mean it, Charlie. No more of this Waddell crap."

"I really hope you know what you're doing," Charlie said.

Ed signaled for the waitress and ordered another plate of catfish. The sweet honeyed voice of Trace Adkins came on, but Ed didn't know the tune.

# Chapter 5

"**Chief, can I talk** to you?" Andy Tabachnik stood outside Ed's office, with a wrinkled uniform and his hair matted to his face.

"You've been up all night." Ed motioned for Andy to sit. He took a chair across from Ed's desk and scooted it closer.

"Still working on that Spartan two-four-seven," Andy said.

Ed pulled a can of Nature Boost from the little refrigerator behind his desk and offered one to Andy. "Any luck?"

"Nope. That site has him covered pretty well. Chief, I want to go after the girl."

"What girl?" Ed said.

"Mariela Campbell." Andy held up his phone. On the screen was a smiling girl in a VCHS track uniform.

"Andy—"

"I know, chief. But if I can get her to talk, we can get a search warrant on Malone's place." Andy put the phone away.

"We have no jurisdiction there. If you talk to this girl

49

and she tells her parents or the school, it's going to open a can of worms. You can't even take Encanto with you because he's already been warned off."

Andy looked down, playing with his fingernails. "Chief, for the past six years, I've been citing litterers and people fishing without a license. I've got a chance to help take down a child molester and possible murderer. You got to let me take the shot."

Ed rubbed his chin. He liked Andy's enthusiasm, but making waves with the locals could make him a pariah at headquarters. Ed had to face it — he was way out over his skis on this one. He didn't care that much about the job or the money. People in his jurisdiction were in danger, and it was his responsibility to protect them. Getting involved in a homicide investigation was the last thing he had wanted when he "retired" to Lake Hope. But he had no intention of leaving it for someone else to clean up.

Ed remembered his first few years on the force when he was full of piss and vinegar. He couldn't help but smile at the eager young face looking up at him. "Okay. You go in plain clothes. She sounded like she was feeling guilty on the phone. Play on that but don't push. If she insists that she wants no part of it, let it go."

Andy beamed. "I got this, chief."

**On West** Main Street in McArthur, Andy sat outside the Main Eatery. Most students were attending Vinton County's home game against Athens, and only a few walked by the shop.

Andy wore blue jeans, a Polo shirt, and a dirty John Deere baseball cap. No one seemed to take notice as he sat outside, sipping a mocha Frappuccino. After about forty minutes, a light-skinned girl wearing tan shorts and a red-and-white VCHS T-shirt walked down Main Street. Her arms were folded over her chest, and she looked down like a Buddhist trying to avoid insects on the ground. She turned left toward the eatery, not even glancing at Andy.

"Hey," Andy said.

Mariela let out a short, high-pitched squeal, her hands shooting up to her mouth.

"*Shh!*" Andy said. He took her arm and guided her inside, ushering her to a table.

"You can't be here, Mr. Tabachnik," Mariela whispered. A tall man in a white cap stared from behind the counter. She waved to him. "Hey, Mr. Johnson. I'll have a latte."

"Of course." Mr. Johnson eyed Andy suspiciously.

"I'm sorry. I had to talk to you," Andy said, sliding into the chair across from her.

"If somebody recognizes you, I can get into so much trouble," Mariela said. She turned to look out the window. "You're lucky there's a game tonight."

He didn't want to freak her out, but he wanted her to know he had done his homework. "It's not luck."

The girl inhaled. "You've been stalking me?"

"I'm not stalking. I just needed to follow up on our conversation about Malone."

Mariela went to the counter to retrieve her drink. When she came back, she was frowning. "You said you wouldn't do this. You gave me your word."

"I know. I'm sorry," Andy said. "I tried to keep you out of it, but things aren't going well. He might get away with it."

Mariela sipped her latte and looked out the window

51

again. "I was going to call you back anyway. Darlene is in the hospital. She tried to — hurt herself."

"Malone?" Andy said.

"Yeah. He stopped seeing her after Meghan. Darlene was obsessed with him. I told her he was just a perv, but she wouldn't listen. I think she did it to get back at him."

"There were other girls?" Andy said.

"Yes." Mariela put her drink down. "He knew just what to say. Told them they were special and the high school boys were too immature to notice."

"He ever try that with you?"

Mariela's eyes became dark balls of ferocity. "No. He knew who to pick on. The girls with self-esteem issues or whose parents didn't pay them enough attention and shit. Sorry."

"That's okay." Andy wanted to ask her why she hadn't told anyone sooner but was afraid she would clam up. "How is she? Darlene?"

"She's doing better now. I was headed to the hospital after stopping here." Her eyes dropped, and she looked at her drink.

"How many girls does Malone have?" Andy asked.

"I don't know." Mariela continued to look down. "I only know about Meghan because Darlene hated her so much. Sorry I lied to you."

Andy thought Mariela knew more but if he pushed, he might lose her. It was better to get enough to nail Malone and expand the investigation later.

"That's fine. You're a good friend, but I think you know now that these girls are in danger."

Mariela looked up at him. "I know, but I don't think Mr. Malone killed Meghan."

"Why?"

"Mr. Malone's kind of a wimp. I think Meghan could have kicked his ass. I know I could." Mariela glanced at her watch.

Andy pressed his lips together to stifle a laugh.

"I'm sorry, Mr. Tabachnik, but I have to go." Mariela stood.

"Wait," Andy said. "Do you think Darlene would talk to us?"

She sat again. "You can't talk to her. I'm the only one she confides in. If you talk to her, she'll know it was me."

Andy leaned forward. "I know this is a lot to ask, but could you ask her? Malone can't be her favorite person now. It might be the right time."

"I'm not sure. I'll let you know." Mariela stood again.

Andy shook her hand. "That's all I can ask."

**The following** morning, Andy and Greg entered the psych ward where Darlene was under mandatory observation. Mariela stood next to the bed, and the girls joined hands when the two officers came in. Andy introduced himself to Darlene's parents, who opted to stay in the room during the interview. Though he knew they had already been told, Andy was worried Darlene would be less than candid in front of them. Andy and Greg pulled up chairs to the side of the bed. On the opposite side, Mariela tightened her grip on Darlene's hand.

"How are you feeling?" Andy said. Darlene's eyes were bloodshot.

"I'm doing okay, thanks," she said.

"Sorry to have to do this, but I need to ask you about your relationship with Mr. Malone." Andy couldn't see the parents from his angle but heard someone shift positions behind him.

"I understand," Darlene said.

Andy flipped open his notebook. "When did you first begin to see Mr. Malone?"

Darlene looked at Mariela, who smiled reassuringly. She turned back to Andy and said, "It was my sophomore year—"

She stopped at the audible gasp from behind Andy. The parents must not have been told everything.

Mrs. Chambers took charge. She tapped Andy on the shoulder. "We'll be in the hospital cafeteria." She grabbed her husband's arm. He stiffened, but she tightened her grip.

"Please go on," Andy said after the Chambers left.

"Well, all the girls were talking about how cute Mr. Malone was, and that he liked young girls. I guess I was just curious at first, so I stayed after class one day and talked to him."

'Talking,' Andy assumed, was code for flirting. A brief image of Malone ogling the young girl gave Andy a sudden urge to punch something. "Okay."

"He invited me to a study group at his house. I guess I knew what he had in mind. When I got there, he was alone."

"Were you guys intimate there at his house?" Andy asked.

Darlene crinkled her nose. "No, never at his house. We would take a drive to the lake or in the woods."

Andy flipped his notebook to a new page. "Was he involved with other girls then?"

Darlene's face heated up. Red blotches appeared on her pale cheeks. "He started asking me to bring other girls. He would pay me or buy me nice things. I didn't want to do it. I thought he—" She buried her face into Mariela's side. Mariela stroked her hair.

The chief had warned Andy to keep his emotions in check, to not show judgment or surprise. He relaxed his facial muscles. "Wasn't your fault. He's a predator."

Darlene turned back toward him, dabbing her eyes with the edge of her gown.

"Meghan?" Andy asked.

The corners of Darlene's mouth turned down. The embarrassment and guilt drained from her face. "She was the last one I took to see him. After that, she was the only one he wanted to see."

Andy chose his words carefully to avoid dropping too much of the burden on Darlene. "Why didn't any of the girls tell on him?"

She looked at the ceiling. "He had us send nasty pictures of ourselves to him. If we talked, he would put them on social media."

Andy now understood why Darlene staged her delicate dance with him at VCHS.

"He told you that?"

"He didn't have to," Darlene said. "So stupid."

"You're not stupid." Andy put down his notebook. "These guys have all the time in the world to study you, tell you just what you want to hear. Besides, you had Greg and me running around like blind dogs in a meat house."

Darlene met Andy's gaze. Tears ran down her cheeks, but laughter escaped her mouth. She wiped her face with the backs of her hands. "Do the pictures have to come out at trial?"

"These guys never go to trial," Greg said. "They don't want what they did on public display. Even if he does, only the jury will see them."

"Will she have to testify?" Mariela asked. Darlene sobbed again. Mariela cradled her head.

"As I said, most of these guys plea out, but it is a possibility," Greg said. "Would you be willing to do that?"

Darlene hugged Mariela tighter and uttered a muffled, "Yes."

"I'm going to need a list of the other girls," Andy said.

"I'll get that to you, sir," Mariela said.

Greg and Andy left the room and met down the hall.

Greg pounded his fist into his hand. "We have to get this guy. He's going through these girls like a rooster in a hen house."

"Agreed," Andy said. "I'll start on the search warrant. Can you talk to the parents, make sure they keep this under wraps? I don't want Malone to see this coming."

"Count on it," Greg said. The two men shook hands.

# Chapter 6

**David Malone lived in** a one-story brick home on West Mill Street in McArthur. Downtown, as it was, sat one block to the north, putting Subway and Giovanni's Pizza within easy walking distance. Maple and hackberry trees lined the homes on Mill Street, and the residents maintained their lawns with the utmost care. Next door, Ed could hear children playing in a pool. A woman opened the door and called to the children that it was time to come in. The sun sat low enough for residents to begin turning their lights on in the shadiest parts of the house.

Ed could see Malone at his dining table with a laptop. Ed and Andy dropped back, allowing Vinton County Sheriff's Deputy Arthur Robinson and Greg Encanto to take the lead. Ed lacked jurisdiction to execute a search warrant within city limits. Andy had attempted to obtain a "no-knock" warrant, arguing that Malone could easily destroy evidence contained in computer files, but the tech-savvy judge denied the request on the basis that data retrieval technology was sufficiently advanced to render such an intrusive measure unnecessary.

Because statutory rape charges in Ohio required the victim to be under sixteen, and all of Malone's victims were sixteen and over, the officers only had a search warrant. The investigators agreed that they would secure Malone until the search turned up probable cause for his arrest on child pornography charges. After, they would transport and question him about the murder of Meghan Haynes.

The officers moved so they would remain out of Malone's field of vision before knocking. Malone opened the door with a smile. His whole body tensed when he realized his mistake. Malone's eyes, wild as an animal stalked by a predator, darted from the officers to the laptop on the small dining room table and back again. Ed preferred the encounter to be peaceful, as it was more likely that Malone would cooperate.

"Police. We have a search warrant," Greg said. He handed the paper to Malone. Malone looked at the warrant, then turned to look at the computer again.

"Don't make this hard," Ed said. Despite their jurisdictional issue, he and Andy nudged their way to the front. "It's just a search warrant. No one's going to jail today."

Malone remained silent, looking over the officers one by one. Ed knew he was estimating his ability to get to the laptop before they grabbed him. Ed didn't think he had a chance. Malone wore a salmon polo shirt and gray slacks. His arms didn't fill in the sleeves. He had probably never seen a dumbbell, let alone lifted one.

When he continued to hold his silence, Ed said, "We're coming in. Are we going to do this the easy way?"

Malone stepped away from the door with his left foot partially pivoting toward the dining room. Ed blocked the door with his foot. "Don't."

Malone paused, and Ed saw him bend his knees.

"Don't," Ed warned again.

Malone turned and dashed across the room with an ungainly stride, waddling back and forth like a toddler. Ed sprinted after him. Andy tried to cut him off at an angle but was blocked by a chair.

The room was small, and despite his lack of athletic ability, Malone was close to the table. He turned to look over his shoulder. His eyebrows rose above his glasses, and his mouth dropped open. Ed was closer than he anticipated.

Malone stretched out his arms to dive but Ed hit him in the hip, wrapping his arms around Malone's legs and driving him up into the air. Ed tried to angle Malone away from the table, but the teacher clipped the edge. Like a seesaw, the table flipped, catapulting a cup, saucer, and the computer into the air and over the heads of the tumbling men. They were all sprayed with warm liquid. The laptop crashed into the wall with enough force to break the keyboard, sending black tiles into the air like a demonic Scrabble board. Ed rolled Malone onto his stomach, straddled him, and cranked his hands behind his back. Greg Encanto dropped down next to him and handcuffed the teacher's wrists.

"That was stupid!" Andy said. "Now, you picked up assault and resisting on top of everything else!"

Malone twisted his head to look over his shoulder at Andy. "What else?"

"You know. We found your girlfriend," Andy said.

"Andy," Ed said, shaking his head. He stood and pulled Malone to his knees. "Get up."

"Look, I swear to you I didn't kill her. It was someone

else. A man attacked us! Took her!" Malone scrambled up. With his glasses askew, he looked like a battered Mr. Rogers after waking up in the wrong neighborhood.

"You have the right to remain silent," Ed said, pulling Malone to a standing position and continuing the Miranda warnings.

"I want a lawyer," Malone said after Ed finished.

"Son, you're gonna need one," Andy said.

**"You think** he's gonna talk, chief?" Andy asked.

"Well, based on the photos you found on his hard drive, we've got him bagged and tagged on kiddie porn. His career is gone, and he's going to jail no matter what. His only incentive to talk to us is if he's innocent of murder," Ed said. He stood in front of the large orange star of the Vinton County Sheriff's office.

"You think he could be?" Andy squinted at the sun and tugged at his collar.

"I don't know," Ed said. "Does he look like someone who could do that?"

"Jeffery Dahmer's neighbors said he was a nice guy, chief," Andy said. "What if Meghan threatened to expose him?"

The right side of Ed's lips curled up as he pondered the question. "To be honest, I'm not sure anyone could have done it like that, let alone a high school English teacher."

"Maybe he had some help," Andy said. "Some of his pedo friends."

"Hmm." Ed frowned. He hadn't thought of accomplices. It was a possibility, but then there was the matter of the train.

"I can't believe he didn't ditch his laptop after Meghan

got killed. He deleted his photos on the hard drive, but I was able to retrieve them."

"You did a great job with that." Ed reached out and gently punched Andy's shoulder. The younger ranger beamed. "I'm surprised he deleted the photos."

"What? You worked these cases before, chief?"

"My partner, Al Sherman did. We were both assigned to the crimes against persons unit. I specialized in homicide, and he worked child porn. We backed each other up. These guys don't give up their candy box unless they have to."

"Candy box?" Andy said.

"That's what Al called it. You see, these guys like to relive the experience, share photos, and discuss in detail what they do to the kids. It's a compulsion, no different than an alcoholic or drug addict."

"That's sick." Andy looked away.

An electric-blue Mustang convertible pulled up. A petite brunette emerged from the driver's seat carrying a small briefcase. She had dark features and wore bright red lipstick. Long bangs covered most of her hazel eyes, and she wore a tight gray pantsuit. She walked into the building without looking at the officers.

"Must be his attorney," Andy said.

Ed and Andy went inside and waited in the lobby. A man with white hair and thick rectangular glasses stood in the reception booth, casually flipping through reports. He had the carefree demeanor of someone who was on KMA or "kiss my ass" time. It was the same in Akron. Officers on desk duty consisted of those recovering from injuries, pregnancies, burnouts, drunks, those under investigation, and short timers. A door to the right of the space led to offices, and the door to the left led to the jail and interview rooms. Ed and Andy sat on a black leather sofa built for the leaders of the Lollipop Guild. An elderly couple sat in front of them, their legs extended under the equally low coffee table.

After a nod from the desk officer, they went inside. Malone sat with his lawyer, who introduced herself as Sandra Kay-Smith. Neither Ed nor Andy had heard of her. She snapped open a small briefcase and pulled out her tablet with the demeanor of a person who brooked no fools. Malone squatted on a barstool made of the same stainless steel as the table. His face wore the mask of sleepless nights on a metal cot. Kay-Smith sat next to him on a folding chair that had been brought in for her.

Andy and Ed sat across on a bench seat. The table had an eye hook on top, but Malone was not cuffed to it. Ed wished the table was wider. He felt uncomfortably close to the pedophile.

"What are we looking at, officer?" Kay-Smith spoke in a detached, businesslike voice.

"Possession and distribution of child pornography. Maybe statutory rape as well," Ed said.

At the word "distribution," Kay-Smith shot a glance at Malone, then returned her gaze to Ed. Defense attorneys never wanted to let the police know that their clients kept information from them. Malone looked down and away.

"Distribution?" she said. "That's not on the sheet."

"County's filing it today, ma'am." Andy kept his eyes on Malone. "Found out he's been on the dark web, sharing images on the pedo network."

She turned the reproving stare on Andy. Ed shot him a look that said, *tone down the lingo.*

She said, "I assume you have evidence of this?"

"Yes, ma'am," Andy said.

"How do we know it's my client who sent them?" Kay-Smith asked.

Ed thought it was perfunctory. She must have known the answer.

"He backed up the images to his laptop, and the IP address comes back to him." Andy hesitated, looking at Ed.

Kay-Smith looked down at her notes. "My client is prepared to talk about the day Meghan Haynes was killed. He will make no statements about the images on his computer at this time."

"That's fine," Ed said. "The county is handling the other charges."

Andy leaned forward. "They got him seven ways to sundown and halfway over the hill on the kiddie porn."

Ed caught Andy's eye and shook his head almost imperceptibly. From the time he was a patrol officer, Ed made it a point to be polite and professional, no matter what crime he was investigating. His training officer told him that they see people often at the lowest point in their lives, and it never did any good to kick someone when they were down. As a result, he often got tips from those he had arrested. Some of them became sources when he moved to the detective bureau.

"Why did you go to the lake with Meghan?" Ed asked.

"He's not going to answer that," Kay-Smith said.

"What time did you get there?"

Malone squirmed on his stool. He looked at Andy, then at his lawyer. "About eight thirty."

"So just after dark?"

"Yes." Malone kneaded his hands. He looked at the door, the ceiling, his lawyer—anywhere to avoid Ed and Andy. The interview room lacked ambient light and was illuminated only by four fluorescent bulbs. The poor lighting washed Malone out, enhancing the look of exhaustion on his face. He was in a world of hurt, and he knew it.

"Who was driving?"

"Meghan."

"And at some point, you got into the back seat?"

"He's not going to—" Kay-Smith started.

Ed cut her off. "I'm not going to ask him what they did, but their position in the car is relevant to the homicide."

The attorney nodded to her client.

"Yes," Malone said.

"How long were you there before the incident occurred?" Ed looked at Kay-Smith to see if she would object to this. Hearing nothing, he looked at Malone.

"Hard to say. About an hour, I guess. We fell asleep—" he trailed off, and Ed knew why.

"What happened then?"

"It happened pretty fast," Malone said, his eyes moving back and forth, seeking the memory. "We didn't know anything was wrong until he ripped the door open."

"Who ripped the door open?"

"This big, hulking man. He grabbed Meghan by the hair and dragged her out of the car. She tried to fight, but he was strong. She kept punching and kicking, but it did no good."

"Did she try to use her phone?" Andy said.

"She took it out. I think she was trying to record him, but he smacked it out of her hand."

"What happened next?" Ed asked.

"I told him to leave her alone," Malone said.

Ed could feel Andy squirming. They all knew this was

a horribly inadequate response, but there was no need to say so.

"I started to get out. He kicked the door into my head. I got a contusion right here." Malone leaned forward so that the officers could see discoloration on his scalp, visible through his thinning hair. Everyone, including his lawyer, frowned at his eagerness to show his "war" wound. His eyes darted again, and he sat up straight.

Andy could take no more. "Poor baby."

"There was nothing I could do!" Malone screamed.

"Can you give us a description?" Ed said, softening his already velvet voice even further.

Malone pressed his hands to his eyes.

"You're not a very big guy," Ed said. "How big was he, compared to you?"

Malone's face lit up, eager to get off the subject of his cowardice. "Yes, he was huge, maybe six-six, and wide. He had these big hands like baseball mitts. When he grabbed her hair, his fist was nearly as big as her head. Oh, god!"

Malone dissolved into a blubbering mess, slobbering and wiping snot into the crook of his sleeve.

Ed interrupted. "What was he wearing?"

"That was the strange part." Malone closed his eyes and tilted his head back. He opened them again and looked at Ed. "He was wearing this light-blue pinstripe uniform with a matching cap. He was carrying this lantern, one of those old ones with a red, green, yellow, and white light on it."

"Are you kidding me?" Andy forced air between his lips and stood. "For god's sake, chief. Do we really have to listen to this?"

"It's all right, Andy, sit down," Ed said calmly.

Andy plopped onto the metal bench.

Kay-Smith turned to Malone. "Are you sure about that description?"

"Yes, I know it sounds crazy, but that's what happened. I could see him as plain as I can see you, now," Malone said.

Ed stared at him for a moment, remembering lessons from body-language school. Malone showed no signs of deception. "Hair color, eyes?"

"Uh." Malone looked down, his eyes searching. "Dirty blond and brown, I think."

"What happened next?" Ed asked.

"He began to drag her, and I—" He trailed off, but Andy finished for him.

"Ran."

"There was nothing I could do for her," Malone said to the floor.

"So you ran right out and called for help, right?" Andy said, his face red.

"No," Malone whispered.

"I didn't hear you!" Andy shouted.

"No!" Malone began to sob again.

Sandra Kay-Smith spoke quietly. "He didn't kill Meghan. You can see he was honest about that."

"He may or may not have killed her, and I'll talk to the DA," Ed said. "But he may not get any cooperation points unless he also talks about the sex crimes."

"Fair enough. I'll deal with the DA on the distribution allegations. I just don't want to see him scapegoated out of convenience."

"That's not what this is about," Ed said. "If his story checks out, he'll get a fair shake from me, but he's going to have to dance for the kiddie porn, so you might want to get him to come clean about that."

Outside, Andy turned to Ed. "I don't know how you can stand that guy."

"Whether or not you can stand him is irrelevant. If your goal is to get information, you need to show empathy, no matter what the suspect is accused of," Ed said.

Andy frowned. "It's hard."

"Obviously, but that's what you're going to have to learn to be a good investigator."

"I'm sorry, chief," Andy said, looking down. "These kinds of things get to me."

"They get to all of us, but we always remain professional, okay?" Ed said.

"Okay, chief."

**Ed and** Andy arrived at the office early the following morning. Nancy was hunched over her keyboard, typing reports from the night before. The wire-rimmed glasses she wore made her look like a college student desperately scratching out a term paper due later that morning. Ed noticed that most of her hair was a red, orange, and brown mix, but close to her face, it was almost blonde.

She removed her glasses and, taking the temple tips, brushed gossamer-like strands from her eyes and tucked them behind her ear. In the light of her computer screen, Ed noticed for the first time that her eyes were green. Then he became aware of himself staring and turned away. She put her glasses back on and pulled her hair back into the familiar bun. *She has no clue how gorgeous she is.*

"Hey, Nancy," Andy said. "The chief and I wanted to brief you on our talk with Malone."

"Oh," Nancy said. "What did he say?"

"Tried to say the boogeyman got her," Andy said.

"The boogeyman?" Nancy blinked.

"His story reeks to high heaven!" Andy sat at his desk. "He didn't want to accept responsibility for what he'd done."

Ed walked to the refrigerator and took out a can of Nature Boost. He hadn't slept the past few nights, and it was beginning to affect his concentration. He popped the lid and took a sip.

"Chief, do you think Malone killed Meghan?" Nancy asked.

Ed rotated the can in his fingers, studying the pastel colors. "He didn't do it."

"What?" Andy threw his arms in the air. "You believe that perv, chief?"

Ed took a slow pull of the energy drink and turned to the window. "I believe he's a pedophile."

"But you don't think he killed her?" Nancy finished.

Ed felt the pleasant tingle around the edge of his brain. When he was in school, his mother used to put caffeine tablets in his backpack. In emergencies, and only emergencies, he could get Mountain Dew from the vending machine.

"David Malone is the type of man who would start a social media rumor to get back at a colleague or to get ahead at work. He's the type of guy who drinks all the coffee and neglects to fill the pot. If a mouse got into his house, he'd call an exterminator rather than bash its head in with a broom, and yes, he's the type of guy who would take advantage of a vulnerable high school girl. But dragging a girl into a field and mangling her body beyond recognition? No. I've seen that type of person, and he's not it. Not by a long shot. Besides, you saw him, Andy. A strong wind could blow him over. Didn't that girl say Meghan would have kicked his ass if he got physical?"

"Chief, with all due respect, you didn't buy all that sniveling, did you?" Andy said.

Ed looked down at Andy. Apparently, in his haste to get dressed, he had pinned his tie too far to the right, making it slightly askew. Ed wasn't a stickler for tidy uniforms, but he knew if the tie remained crooked it would continue to draw his attention.

"I didn't buy anything. It would make it so much easier if it was Malone. We could find out how *he* pulled this fake train business, but I'm afraid it's more complicated than that."

"You told us to follow the evidence. Well, the evidence points to Malone," Andy said.

"The evidence points to Malone as a deviant and a coward. I've seen no evidence that indicates he has the wherewithal, or stomach for that matter, to pull off a crime like that." Ed paced about the room, sipping his energy drink.

Andy's shoulders slumped.

"We're expanding our investigation to include the man described by Dave Malone." Ed walked toward his office and paused at the door. "Andy, straighten your tie."

Andy looked down to see that his uniform tie was indeed off-kilter.

# Chapter 7

**The following Wednesday night**, Ed sat in his cabin preparing his nightly ritual. Restful sleep had always eluded him, and the Anthony Deavers shooting exacerbated the problem. Ed filled his potbelly tea kettle from the sink and placed it over the flame. His walls were bare except for the generic painting of a fruit basket that came with the place. No dirty dishes cluttered the sink and no clothes hung haphazardly over the couch or chairs. It wasn't that Ed was a neat person by nature. Like many who suffered from ADHD, he could be quite comfortable in clutter.

To keep his environment from falling into chaos, Elizabeth Freemen had taught Ed the "rule of the four." Ed had four changes of clothing, suits, hats, coats, and pairs of shoes. Similarly, he had four dinner settings, pots, and pans. Limiting his possessions to "the rule of the four" allowed him to clean up any mess in under five minutes.

In contemporary culture, Ed's mother would be ridiculed or even canceled for "normalizing" him, but Ed saw it as key to his success as a detective. The ability to control his racing thoughts while still accessing his keen observation skills helped him maintain a high clearance rate.

Toward the end of her short life, Ed's mother seemed to have a change of heart. She called him to the side of her bed and took his hand.

"Your mama did the best she could," she said. Her eyes fluttered as consciousness slowly slipped away. "Nobody can say different. But, son, I'm afraid there's going to be a cost." Ed's mother died before explaining this cost, leaving Ed to ponder the sword of Damocles hanging over his head.

Ed had two cups of extra-strength Sleepytime tea and got into bed. On his nightstand sat a globe-shaped diffuser containing one drop of lavender oil. He closed his eyes and allowed his mind to slip away. On a good night, he could keep all thoughts at bay for five minutes. After a half hour, he would drift away and prepare for the dream.

Since the night of the shooting, Ed had the same dream. It was not a nightmare populated by a phantasmagoria of spectral horrors. As a lucid dreamer, Ed never had nightmares. If he wanted to, he could control the dream and apprehend Deavers without a shot. Instead, Ed allowed it to play out as it had in reality.

He saw Deavers, long-legged and skinny, sprinting down Ivy Court. The kid had speed, but frequent drug use had sapped his endurance. He stumbled, as he had that night. The firearm—which resembled a Smith & Wesson 5906, two-toned with chrome plating on the slide and dark gray on the bottom—in his right hand.

This was the part Ed wanted to see, the chrome. As Deavers fell forward, rolled over, and brought the gun to bear, Ed used his power of lucid dreaming to zoom in and focus on the chrome plating—plating that was, in fact, not chrome but cheap plastic.

Ed ignored the two bursts shot from his Sig Sauer 226 that sounded like the coughing fit of a baby dragon. There was something wrong with the chrome. He knew it now as he had known it that night, but even zoomed in, he couldn't tell what it was.

He knelt next to the dying Deavers, applying pressure to his wounds—a tight grouping of two hits center mass. He could see the tiny imperfections in the faux chrome, black streaks where the paint had rubbed off. It was a BB gun. The question he kept asking himself was when he knew it. Was it just before he pulled the trigger or after? His mind compelled him to relive it over and over until he was sure.

**The following** morning brought bad news. Andy pressed his flushed face against Ed's office window.

"Malone is in the wind," Andy said. "Didn't show up for his preliminary hearing."

Ed came out of his office. "I'm sure the county checked his residence."

"Empty. And his car is gone."

"As a schoolteacher, he doesn't have a lot of resources. He won't get far without help." Ed walked over to the coffee pot, poured a cup, and added cream.

Andy sat at his desk. The cheap swivel chair creaked. "They shouldn't have given that perv bail."

"They couldn't deny him bail, Andy." Ed folded his arms. "He hasn't been charged with a felony of violence, and I'm sure his attorney argued that he was a pillar of the community and not a flight risk."

"Yeah, I know. Just burns me, is all."

"Okay. I'm sure Vinton is coordinating with Athens and Hocking counties. On our end, send out a bulletin to all state park offices. I want his picture and vehicle up in every office and ranger station. Let Sheriff Potter know anything he needs, he's got."

"Copy, chief. I guess this settles the question on the murder."

"Not necessarily." Ed sipped his coffee. Coffee had a similar effect as the Nature Boost but made his hands shake.

**The break** in the Malone case came four days later. A sharp-eyed ranger in the Hocking Hills spotted a man only vaguely fitting Malone's description. The photograph on the bulletin showed Malone as he had been apprehended, with short brown hair and a slightly receding hairline. Ranger Tony White spotted the man chopping wood at one of the private cabins sporting long blond locks and a three-day beard. White became suspicious because the cabin was normally used only during hunting season. Two days of surveillance confirmed the man's identity as David Malone. Follow-up investigation revealed that the cabin belonged to Douglas Henderson, who'd roomed with Malone in their first year of college at Ohio University. Henderson had of course denied knowledge of Malone being there.

They decided to execute the arrest warrant in the early hours when the subject was likely still asleep. Ed ordered all hands on deck with Andy, Nancy, and Doug from his office, and several rangers from Hocking Hills, including Tony White and Art Robinson of the Vinton County Sheriff's Office.

Leaving their vehicles down the road, the squad approached through a dense morning fog. The cabin was a single-room structure with overlapping wood paneling, large windows, and a slate roof. Ed saw smoke rising from the chimney and looked around at the other rangers. Fire wasn't needed for heat this time of year, but Tony had reported that the cabin was equipped with a wood-burning stove. As they got closer, Ed caught the distinct aroma of bacon.

The group separated left and right, surrounding the cabin. Ed, Andy, Nancy, and Doug remained in front. Before everyone was in position, the door banged open and David Malone appeared, holding a scoped hunting rifle.

Ed knelt behind a pile of wood. Nancy, Andy, and Doug stood behind trees. The rest of the team took up positions at the rear of the cabin. The officers covered Malone with their weapons. Nancy and Andy were equipped with AR-15s, while Doug and Ed held their service pistols.

Ed leveled his Glock at Malone. "State police! You're under arrest. Drop the weapon and walk toward me with your hands up!"

"I'm not going to prison," Malone said.

"What do you think is going to happen here?" Ed tried to reason with him. As a teacher, a logical argument should persuade him. "You're just going to shoot your way out and go about your day? You've got one choice."

"I'm not going to prison," Malone repeated. "You know what they're going to do to me there."

"It's not like that. They can put you in the secure housing unit."

"Yeah, right," Malone said. "The guards are in on it."

Malone had done his research, and Ed was running out of arguments. Out of the corner of his eye, Ed saw Nancy's head tilt to level her eye with the scope.

"It doesn't have to be like this. Drop your weapon," Ed said.

To his surprise, Ed heard Andy's voice. "Hey man, it ain't worth it. You can come back from this—a lot of people do. You're still young and with your teaching experience, you can help others find their way back."

Despite the situation, a small smile spread across Ed's lips. It must have been hard for Andy to try to talk the teacher down. Ed was proud. He didn't think it would do any good. Malone was determined to go out this way.

As if in response, Malone grabbed the bolt handle and slid it up, forward, and down.

Ed closed his left eye, bringing his focus through the tritium night sights and onto Malone's center mass. He allowed his finger to slip inside the trigger guard.

Malone heaved a huge sigh and brought the weapon to his shoulder. Ed exhaled slowly and put pressure on the trigger. His finger crooked but stopped just short of firing.

Before he could analyze what was wrong, he heard a loud crack to his right. Malone's body flinched. Malone lowered the muzzle and looked down at his chest as if a bee had just landed there.

Another crack. Malone flinched again, dropped the rifle, and placed his hand over an expanding crimson pool on his checkered shirt. He looked up, then dropped to his knees before flopping onto his face.

Ed moved in quickly, grabbed the rifle, and handed it to Doug who had moved in behind him. He holstered his weapon, knelt, and turned the teacher over. Rangers and officers came forward, their weapons still aimed at the fallen suspect.

Ed put pressure on the area. Malone opened his mouth and allowed a long moan to escape as if saying "ah" to allow a doctor to look at his tonsils. The teacher moved no more. Ed looked up at Nancy, who stared down blankly. The AR-15 hung from a sling on her shoulder.

# Chapter 8

**That night, Ed, Andy**, and Nancy sat around the firepit in Ed's backyard. Doug had volunteered to take Nancy's shift. The day's warmth gave way to a cool night, so Ed made a fire for the first time since moving there. The burning wood popped, sending tiny red-orange embers into the air that quickly lost energy and dropped back to the blaze.

Ed loved the smell of an open flame, and in a local faux pas bought seasoned hickory rather than chop his own wood. The pit had been constructed of pink paving stones. Four handmade wooden deck chairs were arranged around it on decorative gravel.

Ed thought the backyard was the best feature of the cabin and sometimes used it for his mindfulness meditation. He had gotten a great deal on the two-bedroom cabin. His rent was low, and utilities were included. In addition to a gas furnace, heat came from a large fireplace in the living room.

"I guess Malone was not as smart as we thought," Andy said.

"Why?" Ed put his energy drink down on the extra

wide arm of the chair.

"Well, he stayed right under our noses, just over in the Hocking Hills."

Ed picked the can up and took another sip.

"That was smart. Most people get caught trying to flee the state on planes, buses, trains, or even get pulled over for some random traffic offense. If Tony wasn't so persistent, Malone would still be there. He could have easily ignored a guy who didn't quite fit the description. Malone probably had people gathering resources and planned to leave the area when the heat died down."

They sat in silence for a while before Ed said, "You tried to talk him down."

Andy gulped his beer before responding. "I didn't want to, and it didn't do any good."

"I know, but you still tried."

"You think he would really have shot us?"

Ed looked at Nancy, who continued to stare at the fire. She was drinking Coors, and he wondered how much she'd had. Ed had steered the conversation clear of the shooting itself, preferring to focus on Meghan Haynes and if Malone's death ended that inquiry, but he knew this wouldn't last forever.

"You doing okay, Nancy?"

Her only answer was to tilt the neck of her bottle toward Ed. Though she looked at the fire, her gaze seemed to go right through it, to some faraway land where all conflicts are peacefully resolved. Ed understood. Most law enforcement officers went their entire careers without ever using their firearms in the line of duty. Ed had to use his weapon four times during his twenty-five years on the job. Anthony Deavers was the only one to die from his wounds.

"Suicide by cop. He knew he didn't have a chance in a shootout," Ed said.

Andy lifted his can to his lips. "You know you didn't have a choice, Nancy. He chambered a round. I would have shot him myself, but I didn't have a good angle, and Doug was behind me. I thought the chief was going to light him up."

*So did I.* "Nancy was faster," Ed said.

Ed wanted to ask her again if she was okay but knew from experience that it was better to let her initiate conversation.

Andy leaned back in his chair. "Nancy, you were in the Army, right? I mean you've killed before?"

Nancy turned the bottle up and drained the rest of the Coors before answering. "Artillery—Support—Specialist."

"What's that?" Andy asked.

Nancy went to the cooler and grabbed another Coors. Ed watched her. She was already listing to port.

"I told them where to fire and *boom*." She raised her hand, opened it, then wiggled her fingers and brought it down.

"Well, you did a good job. Don't beat yourself up over that scumbag." Andy slapped both knees and stood up. "Well, that's my limit. Nancy, you need a ride?"

Nancy sat again.

"Chief, you got her?" Andy fist-bumped Ed.

"I've got her. You take care, Andy. You did a great job with Malone. I know you would've liked to see it through to prosecution, but he took that out of our hands."

As Andy walked around to the front of the cabin, Ed walked over to Nancy and took the beer from her hand.

She looked at him but didn't resist.

"Let's let this soldier live," he said.

"That's a really messed up thing to do," she said.

At first, he thought she was talking about the beer. He stopped and looked at the bottle, trying to figure out how to respond.

"Suicide by cop! Why didn't he just shoot himself? Perv, coward, bastard."

Ed put the unopened beer back in the cooler. She must have seen the ugly side of war, interacted with soldiers wounded on the battlefield, and even entered villages devastated by artillery fire she'd directed. Still, her kills were impersonal, her enemies tiny figures on a drone video one minute and still the next. If Shakespeare was correct about the eyes being the windows to the soul, looking through those windows as the soul vacated the host was unnerving, especially if you were the authority who enforced that eviction.

"Come on. Time to go home." Ed helped her to her feet, and she leaned on him as they walked. He knew she worked out but was surprised by her muscularity.

She stopped walking and turned to him. "I'm sorry, chief. I'm a little drunk."

"It's all right." Ed smiled down at her. "You've had a rough day."

Nancy reached up and patted Ed's chest, then slipped her arms around his waist. "You're a good boss. You take care of us."

Ed turned her around and began to guide her toward the car. She stopped again, then angled toward the cabin.

"Sorry, chief. Gotta go bathroom."

Ed watched her make her way to the door, swaying

like a deckhand on a yacht. At the door, she turned back, smiled, and pulled it open. Ed took the opportunity to clear the backyard of paper plates, bottles, and cans. He heard the toilet flush. Ed knew the dangers of self-medicating with alcohol. He had seen many cops go down that rabbit hole and never come out. Nancy would be okay, though. She just needed to decompress.

When she didn't come out after a few minutes, he went in to investigate. Nancy's torso lay on the sofa, her face awkwardly twisted to one side. Her arms hung limp at her side, knuckles facing the floor. The poor thing had tried to make the sofa and flopped just shy of her destination.

Ed hooked his forearms underneath her armpits, dragged her to the chair, and propped her against the legs. Her head lolled back on the seat. Ed pulled the handle that converted the sofa to a bed, knelt, and lifted her off the floor.

She leaned into him and mumbled, "Sorry."

After laying her on the bed, Ed pulled off her shoes and sat next to her. Nancy's breath was slow and steady. Hair obscured her face like a ginger veil. Ed reached up and gently pushed the hair back, undid the two top buttons of her uniform, and tossed her clip-on tie to the side. He watched her until she turned on her side and pulled her legs to a fetal position.

Ed rose and quietly began his nightly ritual. He stopped, looked at his shooting hand, then opened and closed it. *It's just a lack of sleep. Nothing's wrong.* He went to the kitchen and prepared his tea.

**Nancy's eyes** popped open. The mattress underneath her felt flat and hard. As her eyes adjusted, she saw a foreboding wooden beam instead of her inviting mauve ceiling. For a moment she panicked, her hands frantically frisking her body. Except for her shoes, Nancy was fully clothed. She put a hand to her head. It felt numb. Then she realized that she was still at the chief's house.

Nancy struggled to remember the details. She must have fallen asleep. *Did the chief have to carry her to bed?* The thought should have embarrassed her. Getting blotto in front of her boss was not the best way to a stellar evaluation but the chief would understand. He was kind and genuinely cared. He could have called an Uber or Lyft, but he had taken care of her.

A naughty smile spread across Nancy's face and she bit the tip of her thumb. She wondered if the chief had felt her up as he put her to bed. Nancy knew he liked her. She had caught him looking at her when he didn't think she noticed. Of course, he wouldn't do that. He was a gentleman. A thought occurred to her. *Had she felt him up?* Nancy remembered patting his chest and her hand lingering on his pec. Now, she *was* embarrassed.

Nancy heard stirring in the bedroom. She lifted her head to look over the armrest of the couch bed. His door was slightly ajar, and she saw him turn over. Was the chief tossing and turning, thinking about her as she thought about him? Maybe he would come in and slip into bed with her. Nancy slapped her hand to her mouth as if she had said this aloud. The chief would never make the first move. Damn these stupid regulations, anyway. They were two consenting adults. What they did with their bodies was no one's business.

Nancy had no problem taking the initiative in a relationship. For most of her life, she had no control over the things that happened to her. She had determined not to live the rest of her life that way. Some men needed a nudge, others a push, and a few needed to be shoved right off the freaking cliff. That thought lingered in her head as she drifted back to sleep.

# Chapter 9

**Joshua—never Josh—P.** Morton and Samuel Wharton Green trekked through the Zaleski State Forest, cradling their prized possessions. Providence had been kind to them. After a day of panhandling, they had scraped together enough money for not one, but two bottles of Old Crow straight bourbon.

Joshua and Sam had once been promising musicians in the band The Faded Toads. The promising part had mostly been in their minds, but they both dropped out of Ohio University in their sophomore year to "make it." They, along with Sam's little brother, William "Wild Bill" Green, had made it only to local dive bars where the patrons were too plastered to care how good or bad, the band was.

What money they earned went to drugs and women, the former of which took Wild Bill's life thirty years ago. The latter had produced Joshua's only heir, a daughter named Praline. Her mother had a fondness for pecan ice cream.

No longer able to afford even low-end drugs, they turned to cheap whiskey, which had probably prolonged their lives. Now in their seventies, they roamed the area panhandling and doing the occasional odd job for money. When things got desperate, they would call on Praline in San Francisco to send them a little money. They had no illusions. They were bums and always would be until the day alcohol or drugs exacted their ultimate toll. Their autopsies would reveal livers with the consistency of beef jerky. At least, that's how they thought they would die.

"That Old Crow will melt your pecker like a boiled noodle," Sam said. He laughed a high-pitched *"hee hee"* that blasted spittle through what was left of his teeth.

"Well, I'll worry about that if I ever find anything to put it into," Joshua said.

They laughed together, staggering and bumping into one another.

The last light had slipped behind the trees as they moved along the familiar path. Soon, the forest would be alive with the nocturnal creatures of the woods, screeching, howling, rutting, and preying upon one another. These sounds had long ago ceased to frighten Joshua and Sam. They had camped out here for more than twenty years.

"Think we gonna get some action?" Sam asked.

"Most likely. Warm enough," Joshua said.

The "action" in question was one of their favorite pastimes. Starting in August, college kids from Ohio University or Ohio State would converge on the Moonville Tunnel to conjure the Moonville Ghost. It was often a ruse by the guys to get girls alone in the woods. After sufficient quantities of alcohol or drugs were consumed, the ritual would devolve into group sex with nubile coeds spread out on blankets like vegetables at a farmers' market.

Joshua and Sam watched all the action from the overgrown ledge overlooking the tunnel. Sometimes, true LaVeyan Satanists would visit the tunnel—not that these rituals were always free of orgies—but long black robes left too much to the imagination.

When they arrived at the shelf, Joshua and Sam sat with their feet dangling over the side like two schoolboys.

Joshua tilted his bottle. The scantily aged whiskey burned his throat, and he winced. He stuck out his tongue in the warm night air. "Hmm, if you hold it on your tongue long enough, it'll numb it like Novocaine."

Sam drank, pressed his eyes shut, and wagged his head like a wet dog. "Then don't hold it on your tongue."

"No, no," Joshua said. "I like it. I like my whiskey to fight back a little."

They continued to drink and scan the darkness for the night's entertainment. Two empty bottles later, Joshua saw points of light bobbing in the distance. "Hey, think we got something."

Just as he said the word "something," he was struck on the side of the head. He didn't know what hit him, but it was hard enough that when he regained his senses, he heard a loud ringing in his left ear. A large, meaty hand pulled him to his feet. He looked up to see a reject from a Li'l Abner casting call. The man had to be six foot five. He had smooth features that belied the malice Joshua saw in his face.

"What do you want?" Joshua croaked out. "We ain't got no money." Then a thought occurred to him. Where was Sam? "Sam!" he called. "Sammy!"

The big man dipped his left shoulder and sent a club-fisted punch into Joshua's stomach. The punch was hard enough to activate his diaphragm. Air shot out of him in a long "*ooooh*," and he couldn't pull the air back into his lungs. He started to slump to the ground, but his assailant yanked him to his feet again and hit him with a rib-splitting strike to his side. Joshua opened his mouth, but without air, he made no sound.

The ritual continued with Joshua trying to fall and the big man keeping him upright enough to pummel him. When he regained his breath, Joshua tried to plead with him, to find out what transgression he had committed to warrant such a vicious beating. But the man said nothing, just made grunting sounds as he sent blow after blow into Joshua's body. Joshua tasted iron and was sure he was bleeding inside.

"Help," Joshua moaned feebly. "Sammy, please, help me! I don't want to die."

He managed to look at his attacker. He had been wrong about the look of malice on the man's face. There was, in fact, no expression. No joy, no hate, just the grim determination of a man who had a job to do and was just gettin' to it.

Joshua felt something beating against his back. He turned and realized the man had an old lantern in the hand that held him. It hooked around the man's wrist and swung back and forth as the man dug into Joshua with his left. He never hit Joshua in the face—not once— just hammered every blow into his body.

Most of the punches made a thudding sound, but every once in a while, Joshua heard a sharp crack. He knew it was the sound of bone breaking. If he had been a boxer, the man would've had one of those catchy nicknames like James "Bone Crusher" Smith. Joshua wondered why he was thinking about boxing. He must be going into shock.

"I'm dying," he said, not to the man who was hitting him but to himself.

It was just an observation, not a plea for mercy. He

knew the man had none. Finally, the man let Joshua collapse to the ground. He stooped over and held his lantern out to look into Joshua's eyes. Joshua stared back, wincing at the final blow that would surely come to take his miserable life.

Joshua looked at the man's overalls. They weren't the generic kind worn by farmworkers all over the area but, instead, were some kind of uniform. Recognition poured into Joshua's face. He looked at the lantern and back at the man.

"No," Joshua said.

For the first time, his attacker changed his expression. He smiled as if to confirm Joshua's suspicion, then reached down and lifted Joshua over his head as easily as another man might lift a potato sack.

That's when Joshua saw Sam. His body was illuminated by the flashlights of several young people moving down the path toward him—the same group that Joshua and Sam had hoped to catch naked a little while ago. Sam's body was twisted in a manner that made it impossible to believe he was alive.

Joshua wriggled, but this sent shards of pain slicing through his midsection. He hoped that the killer would let him go and flee into the woods in fear of discovery by the youngsters. Those hopes were dashed when the big man lowered Joshua a few inches in preparation to hurl him over the edge as he must have done to poor Sam. It wasn't that far down. Depending on the angle, Joshua could survive.

He didn't know why he clung to life so hard. He was a derelict who begged by day and camped in the woods at night. His brain was so pickled most of the time he didn't know the day of the week, but he wanted to live, dammit.

He wanted to live! In spite of the pain, Joshua made one last mighty effort to free himself as the man threw him over the side. The last thing Joshua P. Morton saw that night was one of the boys looking up in surprise.

**To Ed**, Holt Potter sounded like the name of a B-movie Western star, but Potter had been elected Vinton County sheriff last November. Being six foot two, square-jawed, and long-legged, it was easy to see why Potter had defeated the incumbent, Carl Morrison, with more than 60 percent of the vote.

The twenty-eight-year-old had been one of the youngest men elected to office. He had run on a platform of revitalization. In his first weeks in office, Potter brought in a slew of young, enthusiastic deputies languishing as guards at the county jail and put them on the street. The move riled veteran deputies who were rotated to the jail to pick up the slack. One of these new deputies, Art Robinson, had called Nancy when he heard about the attack on Joshua Morton and Sam Green.

"Thanks for coming, Ed." Potter spoke in a rich baritone that complemented his Western movie-star image.

"Thank your deputy for calling us," Ed said.

"Art's a good cop. Always keeps his eyes open."

They crossed under a sign that read "ICU." A nurse came out of a door to the right and pulled it closed. When she saw the police coming, she turned, pulled it open, and held it as they walked in. As with many hospital rooms, the ICU was poorly lit, with one large bed surrounded by machines that displayed the patient's heart rate, blood pressure, and respiration.

At first glance, Joshua Morton gave the impression of an aged hippie. His emaciated arms and blotchy, leathery skin were the telltale markers of a person who had lived a life of deprivation and self-inflicted abuse. His hair was mostly silver with a few black streaks, but his beard was pure white.

In the same Western in which Holt Potter would play the lead, Morton would play a toothless, wisecracking prospector shot to death while trying to cash in his claim. Or he would play the equally wisecracking town drunk who hung around outside the saloon and warned Potter that the bad guys were waiting to bushwhack him.

A biowaste container distracted Ed. Some kind of bandaging hung out on the side. It should've been all the way inside. He forced his focus back on Joshua.

"Is he awake?" Holt whispered to the nurse.

"For now. He goes in and out."

Morton looked up. He had a haunted expression that Ed had seen many times. It was the look of a man who knew his time was near.

Morton waved for them to come closer. They moved to either side of his bed. It caused him to wince as he turned his head to follow them. Ed and Nancy moved to his right side and joined Holt.

"Mr. Morton," Holt said. "Do you remember me? I'm Sheriff Potter."

The old hippie's head went up and down.

"When we brought you in, you told us that you and your friend Sam were attacked and thrown off the ledge," Holt continued.

Frustrated, Morton pointed at the tube shoved down his nose and terminated into an ominous looking machine that hissed and whirred.

"It's okay. I know you can't speak. These people are from the state park, and there was another incident similar to yours there," Holt said.

Morton looked at Ed and Nancy and waved.

"You told us that the man who attacked you was big like me," Holt said, holding his hand near the top of his head.

Morton raised his own hand high above his head.

"Bigger than me?" Holt duplicated the gesture.

Morton moved both hands apart.

"And wider?" Holt said. "You also said that he was wearing overalls."

Morton pointed to Ed's badge.

"A uniform?" Ed asked.

Morton became as animated as his ravaged body would allow. He pointed to Ed and waved his hand back and forth. On the monitor, Ed could see his elevated heart rate. The nurse, who had stood quietly in the corner, straightened.

"Maybe we should stop now," she said, but Morton waved her off with a furious thrust of his hand.

Holt picked up the questioning. "My deputies told me you were trying to tell them something, but you kept passing out, and they couldn't understand you."

Morton forcefully pointed and pantomimed the lantern again.

"I don't understand." Ed looked around the room, but no one could interpret Morton's frantic mime act.

Morton pounded his fist on the bed and leaned back. The nurse came forward and ushered the investigators out.

**In the** hospital cafeteria, over a dark liquid masquerading as coffee, Ed sat with Nancy and Holt. Joshua's doctor would join them soon. The cafeteria was mostly empty at that time of night. The only food left revolved in a glass display case. Ed had eyed a ham and cheese sandwich, but Holt warned him off, lest he swap his visitor status for a patient wristband.

"What do you think that was about?" Holt said.

Ed rubbed his chin. "It was almost like he expected us to know what he was talking about."

"Yeah," Nancy said. "He seemed pissed that we didn't get it."

Holt watched his coffee but didn't drink. "Do you think the attack on Morton and Green is related to Meghan Haynes?"

Ed looked past Nancy and Holt as something caught his eye. A patient was shuffling across the floor in slippers. The open gown flashed his very white buttocks. The nurse at the central station didn't notice. Ed was about to call out when Holt got his attention.

"Ed?"

"Sorry." Ed looked back at Holt and blinked in embarrassment.

"You okay?" Holt asked.

"Yeah. Sorry about that."

"Morton and Green," Holt reminded him.

"It's certainly similar to what Dave Malone told us. Frankly, I've always had my doubts about Malone's guilt."

"What if Malone had an accomplice?" Nancy asked. "Lured Meghan out to the lake so the big guy could take care of her."

Ed paused to consider. "That's a possibility, but it would seem easier to tell Meghan he would meet her there, then establish a solid alibi for the time of the murder."

Nancy dumped four containers of cream into her

coffee to mute the flavor, sipped, winced, and put it back down. "If Malone is innocent, we've got a serial in the area."

A short, balding man in a white lab coat approached the table and extended his hand.

"Mr. Freemen, I'm Dr. Tremaine. I treated Mr. Morton. The sheriff said you had some questions for me."

Ed stood, shook his hand, and invited him to sit. Tremaine slid into the chair, grunting as his butt made contact with the seat.

"Doctor, is Morton going to live? I'd sure like to ask him some questions without that tube in him."

Tremaine puffed out his cheeks. Already a portly man, it did nothing for his appearance. "He's a tough old goat. Took quite a beating, though, and that double gainer off the ledge didn't do him any good. He's got some broken ribs and damage to his spleen and kidneys."

He stopped and cupped his forehead in his palm. "It takes a lot of rage to keep hammering at a man like that."

"So he was definitely trying to kill him, not just beat him up?" Ed asked.

"Oh yes," Tremaine said. "But only after he suffered."

Ed felt his focus slipping and told himself, *Here and now.* "When do you think we'll be able to talk to him without that tube down his throat?"

Tremaine scratched his chin. "It'll be a while. His surgery is tomorrow. When we step him down from the ICU, he should be good to go. We'll give you a call."

**On the** way back, Nancy stared at Ed.

He glanced over at her. "What?"

"Chief, I'm sorry about the other night. I don't really have an excuse."

"Stop it. You think that's the first time I've had to put a cop to bed? Please. In my third year in the department, I had to carry my sergeant to his apartment after a party at the Fraternal Order of Police lodge. He had no clue. When I went to pick him up the next morning, he asked where his car was."

"How bad was I?"

Ed chuckled. "Let's say you were feeling no pain."

Nancy turned away and looked at the road. "It's harder than I thought. With artillery, you know the people on the other end are dying, but it's different."

"You'll get through it. He put you in an impossible position. You had to take the shot. Andy was right. That coward is not worth beating yourself up over."

"Chief, can I ask why you came down here? I mean, I read about the shooting. If you don't want to talk about it, I understand."

Ed still wasn't ready to talk about Deavers, but Nancy was hurting and only a jerk would remain silent. He shifted in his seat.

"I was coming back from an interview and a call went out about an armed robbery. I was nearby and spotted the suspect running between houses. I got out and chased him. He got tired, fell, rolled over, and pointed what looked like a semi auto at me. I shot him twice, center mass, just like you did the other night. By the time I got to him, he was dying. Turned out it was just a BB gun."

"Wow."

Ed's head bobbed. "There was no video, so the media had a field day for a while, but the department ruled it a good shoot, and nothing ever went to trial. When Deavers's background came out, the jackals backed off. I still had a hard time with it, though. Lost my appetite for chasing bad guys. I was still young, but I had put enough time in, so I took early retirement."

"How did you end up here?"

"My old sergeant was in headquarters. Told me Waddell was retiring, and I put in for it."

Nancy leaned against the window and was quiet for a while. After a couple of minutes, she straightened, leaving an impression of her cheek on the window.

"As soon as you come here, people start dying."

Ed kept his eyes on the road. He wasn't ready to tell Nancy about Charlie's ten-year cycle theory. She would have to wait until Andy was present for that.

"You sound like my training agent. He used to call me 'shit magnet.'"

Nancy laughed, a high-pitched cackle that shook her whole body. Ed smiled. It was good to hear her laugh. They fell silent, and as he drove on, he was aware of Nancy's gaze on his profile. He decided it was better not to look back at her.

# Chapter 10

**The ranger station had** been converted from a lodge. The reception area had been the lobby in the original building and still boasted fluffy couches, oversized chairs, and a large fireplace. Ed couldn't wait until wintertime when he could light it and sit by the fire. Morning light gleamed off the mahogany table with legs like claws digging into the hand-tufted rug. The smell of fresh coffee seeped in from the break room. The three rangers sat around the table, Nancy and Andy clutching coffee cups and Ed with his Nature Boost.

"The investigation has taken an unexpected turn," Ed said. "I know none of you signed up for this. I didn't sign up for this, but it appears that David Malone is innocent of the murder of Meghan Haynes, and with the death of Samuel Green and the attack on Joshua Morton, we have to consider that we have a serial killer on our hands." He paused to allow it to sink in. Andy and Nancy looked on in silence.

"Our next step is to find out as much as we can about the killer, starting with what the victims have in common."

"They don't seem to have anything in common, chief," Andy said. "Meghan was a high school student, Green and Morton drunks and derelicts."

Ed spread out his arms. "You don't see anything in common?"

Nancy snapped her fingers, left the room, and came back rolling a presentation board with a map of Lake Hope State Park and the surrounding area affixed to it. "Proximity!"

Ed gave her a thumbs up.

"Meghan was killed miles from where Green and Morton were attacked," Andy said, knitting his forehead. "The chief and I walked it."

Nancy went to her desk and came back with a box of colored pins. "Meghan Haynes was killed here, and the two men were attacked here." She placed a red dot at the site of Meghan Haynes's attack and a green one where the two panhandlers were ambushed. "Miles apart, but both along the Moonville Rail Trail."

"So we need to know what the killer's connection is to the Rail Trail." Andy went to the map.

"When I talked to Charlie Cook, he had a map like that. Only his went back decades." Ed sipped his energy drink. Charlie had sounded like a crackpot with his map and spiral notebook, but looking at their own map made it seem much less crazy.

Ed related his conversation with Charlie about the ten-year cycle and Waddell's connection to it. When he stopped, Andy and Nancy stood in silence for half a minute, and Ed thought he had made a mistake telling them. He imagined them calling their friends and telling them how crazy the new chief was.

Andy broke the silence. "Chief, that sounds a lot like

the Moonville Ghost."

"The what?"

"The Moonville Ghost. It's an urban legend around these parts. I was going to brief you because you've got to tell the story during campfire night in October."

"This Moonville Ghost is supposed to kill people every ten years?" Ed rubbed his head.

"I don't know about killings, but the Moonville Ghost is supposed to be the spirit of a railroad worker who was killed by a train back in the early nineteen hundreds. He had his signal lantern and tried to wave the train off before it hit him. The legend is that sometimes you can see the lamp swinging at night. My Bubbe used to talk about it to try and scare me. There was a saying, 'When the Lantern Swings—' only I can't remember the rest."

"Bubbe?" Nancy asked.

"Grandma," Ed said.

"Good, chief." Andy smiled.

"Well, I don't know if this has anything to do with the Moonville Ghost, but it was real enough for local law enforcement to pass on to their successors," Ed said.

Nancy sat again. "Chief, you remember that report on the two boys who claimed to have been chased through the woods?"

Ed's head bobbed. "Yeah, the dad thought it was their imagination."

Nancy pointed to show that the chief was thinking of the right case. "The guy was supposed to be carrying an old lamp."

"As I recall from your report, there wasn't much of a description, but that's not too far from the Rail Trail. Could be our guy. Interesting that he didn't make much of an effort to catch them. Maybe that's the killer's MO.

He only attacks people who are flawed in some way."

"Wait a minute," Andy said with a frown. "Green and Morton were two drunks, but what was wrong with Meghan Haynes? She was an innocent girl."

"I agree," Ed said. "But remember, serial killers and psychopaths don't think the way we do. From his point of view, Meghan may have been the problem, tempting Malone to sin."

"That's sick." Andy shook his coffee cup. Once satisfied that it was empty, he went to the break room for another.

"What's our next move?" Nancy said.

"We have to find out how the killer selects his victims, how he made it look like Meghan Haynes was run over by a train, and what is going on with this ten-year cycle business."

Andy walked back in. "That means you're going to have to talk to Waddell."

"Or get shot trying," Ed said.

# Chapter 11

**The second time Ed** visited Jeff Waddell's quaint farmhouse, he was not greeted by the barrel of a shotgun. Thank the heavens for small wonders.

"Been expecting you," Waddell said.

Ed froze. "Let's not have any gunplay this time."

"Depends."

A hand, gnarled by rheumatoid arthritis, reached out and pushed the screen door open. Ed went inside, eyeing Waddell suspiciously. Waddell motioned for Ed to sit on his brown leather couch. He shuffled to a recliner. A border collie with gray whiskers padded in from the kitchen and peeked around the corner. Waddell waved his left hand, and the dog obediently turned and went back into the kitchen.

The shotgun that Waddell had shoved in Ed's face leaned against the wall next to his recliner. Ed wondered what the hell was up with that. Did Waddell really think he could get away with shooting him, and if so, was he in possession of all his faculties?

"Why were you expecting me?" Ed asked.

Waddell reached to the left of his chair and retrieved a

bottle of Bud Light sitting on the floor. He held the bottle out as if to offer Ed a drink.

"No, thanks."

"Figures," Waddell said.

"I have the occasional beer," Ed said. "But that's not why I'm here. So why were you expecting me?"

"I don't like you," Waddell said.

"I'm devastated." Ed looked at the mantle above Waddell's head. He saw a faded picture of Waddell standing with friends in what looked like someone's man cave. Clearly visible on the wall was a red flag bearing the crisscross stars of the Army of Northern Virginia.

"Not because of *that*," Waddell said. "It's because you big-city cops come down here thinking you know it all, then find out you don't know shit."

"Maybe this was a mistake." Ed started to get up.

"Sit down," Waddell said, waving his arthritic appendage up and down. "Don't get your panties in a bunch. Tell me what you want to know."

"I think you were supposed to brief me on something when I came down here."

"You mean the Moonville Ghost." Waddell leaned back in his chair.

"Whatever."

"You want to know if he's real."

"Is he?" Ed leaned forward.

Waddell gulped his beer and grinned. "It don't matter."

"It matters to me."

"What matters is that you got lucky. You got somebody just made to order," Waddell said.

"If you mean Malone, he didn't kill Meghan Haynes."

"Yeah, but he did her seven ways to sundown, and

don't think she's the only one either. Of course, I don't blame him for that one. Did you see the hooters on that girl?" His hand indicated a newspaper clipping on the table in front of him. It showed a smiling Meghan at the top of a VCHS cheerleading pyramid. Next to it were articles about Malone, Morton, and Green.

"Why do you still have that?" Ed said. When Waddell opened his mouth to answer, he held up a hand. "You know what, I don't want to know. I can't listen to this." He got up and started for the door.

The last image of Meghan in his mind was a pile of meat on Charlie's table.

"You better listen, and you better heed! You go poking into this mess too much, things are going to get bad."

Ed stopped and turned. "You might have noticed things are already bad."

Waddell waved a hand across his face and chuckled a hoarse laugh. "You're talking about those two winos? Forget them. Malone made it neat and tidy."

"Just blame it on the dead man, and it will go away?"

"Yes!" Waddell said. "You don't know what a gift you got when y'all popped Malone. Now there won't be any questions. Malone couldn't face what he done, so he took the coward's way out. Suicide by cop. Wrap it up and put it under the tree."

Ed leaned against the door. He couldn't understand why Waddell was being so cagey. He was a racist—Ed got that loud and clear. But he was obviously willing to share in spite of that, so why not give Ed everything? "Why can't you just tell me?"

Waddell laughed. "'Cause you ain't ready to hear it. Soon, but not yet."

"What does that even mean? You keep talking in

circles!"

When Waddell didn't respond, Ed yanked the door open and went out.

**Back at** the office that evening, Ed tried to figure out how he should report his conversation with Waddell. He decided upon a confidential memo. Ed didn't give a flip about Waddell's reputation, but if he reported that half the law enforcement agencies had conspired to cover up murders, Charlie would be caught in the crossfire. This was the second time someone had mentioned a ghost — well, third if he counted Charlie's cryptic reference back in the morgue. Was Ed really prepared to consider a supernatural explanation? He didn't think so, not yet. But there was the question of that train. The office phone rang.

Ed crossed the room, reached into the reception window, and picked it up.

"Mr. Freemen, it's Doctor Tremaine. Joshua Morton has sufficiently recovered to answer your questions, now."

"Thank you, doctor. I'll be right there," Ed said.

He called Nancy to pick him up. On the way to the hospital, she turned to him and said, "I thought Morton had one foot in the grave and the other on a banana peel."

"Yeah, that's one tough old rummy," Ed said.

"Rummy?" Nancy chuckled. "That's something my grandpa would say. Do you mind if I ask how old you are, chief?"

"Fifty-two," Ed said. "And that expression is about as old as a foot in the grave and the other on a banana peel."

"Yeah, but I got that from my grandpa. Don't worry, chief, you look good."

"Thanks."

When they arrived, Morton sat up in bed plucking a tune that Ed thought was "A Summer Song" by Chad and Jeremy. Talk about old school. Unlike most recovery rooms Ed had seen, Morton's room was void of get-well cards, flowers, or baskets of fruit. Ed had grown up poor but had escaped the despair of homelessness. He wondered what circumstances had brought this obviously talented man so low.

The nurse sat next to Morton's bed, tapping a foot.

"How's he doing?" Ed asked.

She stood. "Well enough to try to grab my ass this afternoon!"

"Mister Morton!" Ed said.

Morton grinned a rot-toothed smile.

"Oh, I missed on purpose."

"Haven't you ever heard of 'Me Too'?" Ed said.

"Me what?" Morton handed the nurse the guitar, and she left the room. He slumped a little, showing Ed he was more fragile than he pretended to be.

"You're one tough old dude," Nancy said, "but if you try to grab my ass, I'll put you back in the ICU."

Morton laughed and held his hands up.

"Mr. Morton, I want to get more details about the night you were attacked." Ed sat on the windowsill. "What happened to your friend?"

Morton lowered his head and shook it slowly. "I don't know what happened to poor Sammy. I think the sucker threw him off the ledge like he did me, but I didn't see it. He put my lights out with the first blow. If I landed headfirst like Sammy, I wouldn't be talking to you now."

"What about a more detailed description?"

"Forgive me for saying so, sir, but why don't you stop

screwing around?" Morton folded his arms and stared at Ed.

"Excuse me?" Ed said.

Morton huffed. "You know as well as I do. It was Jackie Hudak."

Ed looked at Nancy, who stared at him wide-eyed.

"You're saying you recognized him?" Nancy said.

"I don't know if recognize is the right word, but you know it too," Morton said. "The old train worker's uniform, the oil lantern from a hundred years ago. It was Hudak. Don't try to fool a fooler."

"Okay," Ed said. "I recognized the description the night we questioned you, but I don't know what you think I know about this Hudak."

"I never believed it myself. Just something your mama told you to keep you in line. Wander off, and Jackie Hudak will get you. That kind of stuff. There've always been mysterious deaths in these parts. We used to say it was Jackie Hudak, come to get his revenge. But I never thought it was true until I saw him. Now I know."

"Revenge for what?"

"Jackie Hudak was a railroad worker killed by a train sometime between the wars. You sure you don't know this story?"

"You mean the Moonville Ghost," Nancy said.

"Uh-huh," Morton said. "Ghost, demon, spirit, boogeyman, whatever you want to call him. He was once a real fella named Jackie Hudak."

"How did he die?" Nancy came closer.

"Nobody really knows. Some say he was walking home drunk through the tunnel and the train came along before he could get out. Some say he got jumped on top of the ledge by three men, and they knocked him off in front of the train. But no matter who tells it, one thing is always in the story. He had time to wave his lantern, frantically signaling the train, but it was too late. When I was a kid, we used to say, 'When the lantern swings, Jackie Hudak is coming back.'"

"Did he say anything to you?" Ed asked.

"You mean give me a reason why he was beatin' the hell out of me? Naw, he was just doing his thing. Didn't seem like he was mad, nor got no 'thank you please' from it. He could've been choppin' wood from the look on his face."

"The uniform — did it have any kind of insignia?" Ed asked him.

Morton scratched where his beard used to be. "It had some kind of patch on it, but I didn't pay no mind. I was busy gettin' my ass beat."

"What about the lantern?"Ed furiously scribbled notes. "Can you describe it?"

"I'll never forget. It was one of those that had four sides — red, yellow, green, and white, kinda like a traffic light. And old. They don't make 'em like that no more." Morton slumped back.

"You look like you could use a little rest," Ed said. "We can come back."

"I'm fine!" Morton said. "Let me get this out before that monster hurts anybody else."

"Okay. Could you see his features? Can you describe him further?" Ed said.

"Just a big ol' corn-fed country boy — and strong."

Ed looked up from his notes. "How strong?"

"He wasn't like Superman or nothin' if that's what you're getting at, but he tossed me around like a rag doll on a stick."

Ed looked at Nancy to see if she had any questions, but she remained silent.

"Thank you, Mr. Morton. I'm glad you're feeling better. Let me know if you remember anything else." Ed motioned to Nancy and started to leave.

"Mr. Freemen." Morton held up a hand to stop them. "If you catch up to him, you put him down. None of that 'you're under arrest' shit." He put a finger to his forehead. "This ain't that kind of situation. You know what I mean?"

Ed left without responding.

**Ed pulled** out his laptop when they returned to the office. After a while, Nancy came over and sat on the arm of the chair opposite him. She had taken off her glasses again and reached up to pull the tie that held her hair in a bun. It fell around her shoulders and appeared to ignite in the light of the lamp. He watched her surreptitiously then looked down at his screen.

"Chief, are you going to tell me everything you know?" she asked.

When he failed to answer, she leaned forward. "You can trust me."

Ed looked into her eyes and smiled. She was far more perceptive than he thought. In the short time they had worked together, Ed had found her to be smart, fiercely loyal, and, at times, impulsive. She struck him as the kind of woman who knew what she wanted and would let nothing stop her from getting it.

"When Meghan Haynes was killed, Charlie Cook told me that there's this conspiracy among area law enforcement officers to cover up certain odd crimes. Everyone's predecessor is supposed to brief them, but Jeff Waddell—"

"Is a racist, misogynist pig," Nancy finished. "It's okay, chief. Everyone knows it. If he hadn't been on his way out, there's no way they would have put a woman here. I can't tell you how many times he called me 'honey.'"

"It was hard to believe, as you might imagine, but however impossible it may seem, Meghan Haynes *was* run over by a train," Ed said. "I'd stake my reputation on that."

"Chief, do you believe in the supernatural?" Nancy shifted uncomfortably.

Ed closed the laptop. "My dad does."

"That doesn't answer my question."

"I'll tell you this," he said. "It's getting harder and harder to come up with another theory."

"Could it be someone dressed up like Hudak? Someone trying to keep the legend going?"

"Could be," Ed said. "But someone would have to impersonate him for many years, then pass it on to a successor. I doubt a centenarian is beating and killing people. And then there's the matter of the train. We can't get around it. We need Banacek."

"Bana-who?"

"Banacek." Ed smiled. "It's this old TV show I used to watch with my mom. It was a 'how dunnit.' Banacek was an insurance investigator whose specialty was figuring out seemingly impossible crimes."

"Well, what would Banacek say?"

"He would spout some old Polish proverb, then provide an elaborate explanation." Ed chuckled. "In fact, there was an episode where a train car in the middle of two other cars disappeared. I think the solution was that some people had used a wire to flip the car in the middle off the track, then used the wire to pull the other cars back together."

"That doesn't help us, chief," Nancy said. She yawned, flopped her head to one side, and smiled at him.

Ed cleared his throat. "You'd better get some coffee before you make your next round."

"Yes, sir." Nancy got up, then paused. "One more question."

"Yes?"

"Why do you always drink energy drinks?" Nancy asked. "If it's too personal, I understand."

Ed picked up the can and tilted it. "I have ADHD. It helps me focus."

Nancy threw her head back. "That explains it."

"Explains what?"

Nancy pressed her lips like she was hesitant to answer. "Well, why you notice things that other people don't pay attention to."

"It's my superpower," Ed said.

"Excuse me, sir?"

"When I was little, they had me on Ritalin. It made me loopy, so my mom made them take me off it. She read this study that said ADHD wasn't a condition to be treated but a genetic adaptation. When man lived in a hunter-gatherer culture, a small number of children would be born with this adaptation. They would be able to spot anomalies in the environment where game or predators were hiding. When man began to live in cities, this adaptation became a nuisance. According to the theory, it's not that we can't focus. It's that we focus on everything at the same time. My mom called it my superpower. I don't know why I'm sharing all this. I must be tired."

"Relax. Bosses are human too." Nancy started for the coffee machine.

# Chapter 12

**A week after Ed** and Nancy visited him in the hospital, Joshua Morton returned to his campsite in the Zaleski State Forest. In his hand was a large plastic bag containing medication and instructions on how to change his dressings and clean his wounds. The doctors didn't want to release Joshua and he had to sign a waiver to get out. He was under strict orders not to drink until completely healed. Joshua had no desire to drink, and the thought of panhandling without poor old Sammy made him sick to his stomach.

Joshua had an appointment to visit the doctor in four weeks but thought he would make his way out to San Francisco to see his daughter. Maybe get a job. Joshua looked at the bedroll on Sam's side of the tent but flopped down on his own. He rolled to his side, put his face into his blanket, and sobbed. His body painfully convulsed with each sound, but he didn't care.

He must have fallen asleep because the next thing he knew, it was dark outside. He would have to wait until morning to start out. Joshua decided to make it as long as he could before asking Praline for money. The staff at the hospital had taken a collection for him, and he had enough to feed himself for a while. He thought he would hike up to Athens, hop a freight, and go as far as he could on his own. Maybe she would be impressed by his perseverance.

Something caught the corner of his eye, and Joshua looked in time to see a yellow flash of light outside of the tent. He crawled across the synthetic floor and rummaged through Sammy's bag until he found what he was looking for — an old Bowie knife a fan had given Sammy years ago. Joshua passed a finger carefully over the serrated blade. Still sharp. He got out of the tent, the butt of the knife held close to his chest. He was puzzled. It was dark as pitch in the woods. Any light should have been easily visible for a mile. He turned around in a slow circle and leaned over to look behind the tent but saw nothing.

"Shit." Joshua went back inside and got his own kerosene lantern. He hung it on a hook attached to a tree just outside and looked around again.

"Come on, big boy! Let's see how you do when somebody is looking at you."

Joshua felt a puff of air then a twig broke behind him. He turned and stabbed in the air. When he did, a light flickered on behind him. He turned again and saw Hudak, his lantern held high. Joshua ground his teeth. He wasn't scared this time, just pissed off. He pointed the blade at the bigger man's stomach.

"All right, then. Let's dance, fat boy!"

Hudak raised the lantern higher and turned the green light toward his face. Joshua lunged forward. A sharp pain tore at his chest where the stitches strained. Just before he struck, Hudak vanished. Joshua stumbled

114

forward and turned in a circle.

"What?"

Hudak appeared again, this time several feet away. That should have frightened Joshua, but it just made him angrier.

"Oh, now you want to run. Come on and fight me! You like jumpin' old men when they got their backs turned, but when you got to fight, you got all kinds of tricks."

Hudak swung the lantern again and disappeared, this time popping up right behind Joshua. The old man, body ravaged by years of neglect and the recent beating, was slow to react. By the time he turned around, Hudak was sending a left hook into his ribs. Joshua's scream was loud and drawn out. He sank to his knees. Hudak stepped closer, and Joshua saw one opportunity. He lashed out with the knife and struck home. The blade sunk a half-inch into Hudak's thigh, and he roared in pain. Joshua grinned.

Joshua tried to bring the blade to bear again. Punches rained down on him, and he flopped back over his own legs, hyper flexing his knees. Joshua screamed again, but it came out as a pitiful whimper. Hudak straddled him and continued to pound. The lantern lay on its side where the big man dropped it. Joshua's hand opened involuntarily, and the knife rolled onto the grass. He looked at it in despair and tried to make his hand move, but it refused to obey.

"I'm coming, Sammy. I'm coming."

**Ed and** Andy received the call about a dead body in the woods the following morning. Heavy clouds threatened rain, and Ed was anxious to collect evidence before nature washed it into the earth. They followed the early-morning hikers who had discovered the body.

Todd and Meredith Bronsky had been hiking the woods for years. Normally, they hiked a more challenging trail but picked that one because it was closer to the road. If the rains came, they could beat a hasty retreat. The couple, who Ed guessed were in their mid-twenties, bounced up the incline with ease while Ed and Andy struggled to keep up.

Ed breathed a sigh of relief when the trail leveled off, but his heart sank when they broke into the clearing. Lying supine a few feet from a tent made from blue tarpaulins was Joshua Morton. His arms and legs were splayed. Blackened blood fanned out from his nostrils and covered both cheeks. His plaid flannel shirt appeared to be soaked with water, but Ed knew it was an optical illusion. In fact, it was coagulated blood that blended with the dark red and blue of the fabric. As he got closer, Ed saw a Bowie knife next to Joshua's right hand.

"We didn't touch anything," Todd assured Ed. "There was no need to go near him. We could tell he was dead from over here."

Ed turned around. For a moment, he had forgotten the couple was still with them. "Thank you, Mr. Bronsky. How long did it take you to call after you discovered the body?"

Todd frowned. "No more than a few minutes. We just had to move around until we got a signal."

"That gives us a good timeline," Ed said. "My deputy has all of your information, right?"

"Yes."

"Okay, we'll contact you if we need any further information. Thank you for your prompt notification, and

I'm sorry that your hike ended like this." Ed extended a hand, and the two returned to the path.

Andy stepped forward. "Is that—?"

"Yes," Ed said. "Joshua Morton."

"Killer came back and got him?"

"That's what it looks like. We're lucky that most of the scavengers in these woods are diurnal. A few hours later, they would have licked the blood and gnawed on his flesh," Ed said.

"That's a nice thought to go with breakfast," Andy said.

Ed walked around the corpse. "He couldn't have lasted too long after the beating he took."

"You think he was stabbed?"

"Doesn't fit the MO. This guy beats his victims to within an inch of their lives and drags them onto the trail."

"Why didn't he take Joshua to the tracks?" Andy asked.

"That's a good question," Ed said. "It means that his motive for killing Joshua was different—maybe personal."

"He didn't drag them to the trail the first time."

"In a way, he did." Ed walked to the edge of the clearing and looked out in the direction of the Moonville Rail Trail. "He threw them off the ledge down onto the trail. If those students hadn't come along, maybe Joshua and Sam would have been mangled as well."

"Good point, chief. Still don't explain why he came back after Joshua."

"Maybe he thought Joshua knew something that could help us catch him, or maybe he was just plain pissed off that he got away." Ed came back to the body. "In any case, we might have caught a break this time. You see this knife?"

"Uh-huh." Andy knelt and examined the Bowie knife. "It's got blood on it. The attacker could have used it on Morton."

"Can't find any cuts on him," Ed said. He unbuttoned Morton's shirt. He looked like a dummy held together by a zipper someone had ripped apart. The wound was similar to the Y incision Ed had seen in so many autopsies. "The only blood is where he busted his stitches. Let's roll him over."

They rolled Joshua Morton onto his stomach. Andy lifted the old hippie's shirt. "Nothing on the back. The old bastard put up a fight. Good for him."

"Good for us," Ed said. "Let's send this knife to the lab in Columbus. See if they can get DNA. Maybe we'll get lucky and this guy is in the database."

"Right, chief."

"And Andy, look through Morton's things. See if there's a next of kin."

"Yes, chief. You think this was the Hudak impersonator?"

Ed looked at the gathering storm clouds. A targeted killing meant they weren't dealing with a crazed maniac, killing only victims of opportunity. He had tracked, stalked, and killed Morton, maybe because he had the audacity to get away. This killer was on a mission. Ed wondered if ghosts had DNA. "Not exactly," he said.

**When Ed** arrived at the coroner's office that afternoon, Charlie was still examining the body of poor Joshua Morton. He waved Ed over with a twirl of his wrist.

"Hey, Ed," Charlie said.

"What's up?"

Charlie rolled his eyes. "Well, at least you didn't say 'doc.'"

"Thought about it." Ed looked at Charlie's clothes. This time, Charlie was wearing a paisley tie and multicolored tennis shoes.

"What's going on with this eccentric doctor's getup?"

"What eccentric?" Charlie said, and Ed couldn't tell if he was sincere.

Ed gestured to his clothing and said, "You look like you're auditioning for a remake of *Back to the Future*."

"Very funny," Charlie said. "You want to know what killed this man or is there a two-drink minimum?"

"I know what killed him. He was beaten to death. I need to find out how."

"Well, he had a ruptured spleen from the first beating, which the doctor repaired nicely, but it doesn't matter if you're going to go out and go another ten rounds with —"

"With what?"

"I was going to say, Mike Tyson." Charlie said. "Anyway, it ripped open his sutures, and he bled out into his abdominal cavity."

"Gruesome," Ed said.

"He was on borrowed time anyway."

"How so?"

Charlie walked to a counter and retrieved a stainless-steel container. "This is Morton's liver."

Ed looked at it. To him, it looked like a thick piece of flank steak that had been rolled in crumbs to prepare it for frying. "I take it that's not how it's supposed to look."

Ed wondered what Charlie's liver looked like.

"No, the surface should be smooth and the color more consistent. It takes years of serious, dedicated drinking

119

to get your liver like this—and not the good stuff. The kind that will melt the glue off your dentures," Charlie said.

"What if he had stopped drinking?"

"Too late. The damage was already done. The Grim Reaper would have been knocking on this guy's door by Christmas."

"He didn't have a door," Ed said under his breath.

"What?"

"Nothing. What about Meghan Haynes? Do you have your updated report?" Ed stepped close. Unlike Meghan Haynes, Joshua looked as if he were asleep. If someone could sleep with his chest cracked open like a walnut.

Charlie went into the next room and came out with a file. "I hope you know what you're doing. She was, as you said, run over by a train going forty to sixty miles per hour."

"Thank you, Charlie."

"Don't thank me. This is public record now. If somebody from the local paper gets ahold of this new report, it's going to be front page." Charlie handed him the report.

"It's the truth, Charlie," Ed said. He flipped through the file.

"Yeah? Well, what truth are you going to tell the press when they ask how a girl was run over by a ghost train on a path with no tracks? You should have thought about that before going around saying people are corrupt."

"I didn't say you were corrupt, Charlie."

"Well, you implied it."

Charlie turned back and replaced the organs in the empty chest cavity, minus the liver and spleen. He dropped these into large formalin jars.

"Why did you say ghost train?" Ed said.

"Did I say that?" Charlie kept his back to Ed.

"You know you did."

"I was just saying ghost, 'cause we don't know what it is."

"Well, anyway, the killer is not a ghost." Ed pulled out his phone and showed Charlie the bloody knife from the Morton crime scene. "Ghosts don't bleed."

"How do you know? You ever meet one?"

**The following** morning, Ed got to the office early to brief Nancy on the latest murder. She looked like she had a rough night. Heavy bags tugged at her eyes, and her skin was the color of an old newspaper. The right side of her collar was flipped up, and Ed reached over to adjust it. She smiled.

He filled her in about Morton's murder and the bloody knife. When he finished, she leaned back in her chair and stifled a yawn with her hand. Ed understood. The night shift was rough on the body. Ed worked the 11 p.m. to 7 a.m. shift for three years as a patrol officer. Most days, his body could handle it, but it seemed that on the last day before his day off, his body would rebel, and he would spend the entire shift in a running battle with the sandman.

Most people who worked nights returned to a normal schedule on their day off. A veteran officer told him that was the problem. He advised Ed to sleep during the day and stay up all night on his days off. It worked, but there was a cost. Two or three times a month, even more than fifteen years after working the night shift, Ed's body would return to that schedule, and he struggled with daytime sleepiness.

"So why did Hudak—are we saying it's Hudak?—come back to get Joshua after he came out of the hospital?" Nancy asked.

The morning sun was just starting to slice through the horizontal blinds, painting stripes on Nancy's face and uniform.

"I don't know if we can definitively say who it is at this point. Certainly, someone wants us to believe it's Hudak, so it's as good a name as any at this point. Andy and I talked about revenge as a motive. The one who got away. It's rare but has happened before."

"Do we know it's the same killer? I mean, could be someone else, right?" Nancy said.

"If not, someone totally unrelated trekked through the woods, found Morton, and decided to beat him to death for no apparent reason. We found a few hundred dollars in his tent. A worker at the hospital told us that they had taken up a collection for Morton. He was planning to go see his daughter. So that eliminates robbery as a motive."

Nancy turned as the door opened. Andy hurried in. He ran to his desk without speaking. His arms seemed to move twice as fast as his legs, like an old lady hurrying to get across the street. Andy's trembling hands fumbled to get a flash drive off his key ring and into his computer.

"Chief, you're not going to believe this!"

Ed looked at Nancy. "You'd be surprised what we would believe, but what are you talking about?"

"I've been working on Meghan's phone. It was in pretty bad shape, and the file was corrupted, but I—"

"Skip to the punch line," Ed said, his arms folded.

Andy seemed disappointed that he couldn't go through the technical aspects of his accomplishments. "Aww, chief, I think I got the killer on video."

"What? You're a freaking genius!" Nancy jumped out of her seat, ran to Andy, and squeezed his cheeks.

Ed kept his arms folded but smiled. "Let's see the video."

Andy's fingers played over the keyboard like a virtuoso pianist. A few seconds later, blurry images appeared on the screen. The phone violently whipped back and forth. A scream sounded, so full of abject terror that even the veteran cop felt a chill. Nancy looked at Ed with all the dread of someone watching the events unfold in real time but was powerless to do anything to stop it. The sound of Malone's voice gradually got farther away.

"Leave her alone! Oh my God, Meghan! Oh, my dear God!"

They heard Meghan continue to scream. Then the first clear images appeared as Meghan tried to steady herself and the phone.

"Brave girl," Ed whispered.

First, all Ed could see was the night sky. Then the camera panned to a large man in railroad workers' overalls. He had been holding Meghan's left arm. He let go of it and grabbed for her bare legs. She kicked at him furiously, her screams becoming more and more panicked. The phone dropped when blind terror took control of her. Everything else that happened was off camera.

The man roared something unintelligible. Perhaps it was "shut up!" There were two dull thuds—the sound of the bastard pounding her with his fists. After a couple of seconds, the screams abruptly stopped. The sound of dragging could be heard, but nothing showed on the screen except the moon in half crescent. The killer began mumbling a chant. Soon they heard the distinct *chugga-*

*chugga* of a train engine.

The sound was familiar to Ed. As a child, he lived near train tracks. The afternoon train would come by just around his nap time. To this day, the sound of an engine or train whistle made him sleepy. But not this time.

"Please don't let her wake up," he whispered to himself.

There was no screech of metal on metal as there would be if the train were desperately trying to stop. Wherever, or whenever the train was, it must have been completely unaware of its pending victim. The pitch changed as if the train were inside a vault, and someone was closing a vacuum-sealed door. The pitch continued to rise and speed up until it was just a rush of air suddenly swallowed up. Nothing but silence followed.

"Woo-hoo!" Andy threw up his hands and spun around in his chair.

With eyes locked on him, Ed and Nancy's mouths hung slightly open. Andy beat on the side of his desk like a drum.

"Andy," Ed said.

"We got it on video, chief. A genuine ghost!"

"Andy!"

Andy stopped drumming his desk and looked from Nancy to Ed. His hands came down slowly and color flooded into his cheeks.

"We just heard the last moments of a young woman who was violently murdered," Ed said, his voice quiet and even.

Andy lowered his head and put his hands in front of him. "I'm sorry, chief. I got carried away."

"You did a good job with the video, but this is not a time for celebration." Ed sat on the edge of the desk opposite Andy. "Do you understand?"

"Yes, chief. Sorry."

"Okay," Ed said. "Let's talk about what we just heard. Everyone agrees that *was* a train on a track. No mistake, right?"

They both agreed.

"And when it went away, it sounded like some sort of portal being closed." Ed gestured with his hands, starting wide and then closing them.

"Yeah," Nancy said. "It was like the sound was being compressed as the hole closed. Does that make sense?"

"Yes," Andy said. "I got that sense, too, but not when it opened. It's like it opens suddenly but closes gradually."

"Okay, here's the money question," Ed said. "Is there any way to explain this by any science known to man?"

"I don't know, chief," Nancy said.

Andy squinted and looked at the ceiling. "Chief, did you ever hear of the Coral Castle?"

"I think I saw a documentary once." Ed scratched his bald head. "Something about levitation?"

"Yeah, I've been there," Andy said. "It was built by this man named Edward Leedskalnin out of blocks of stone weighing ten, fifteen tons. The castle had a nine-ton stone gate so perfectly balanced that a child could push it open. When they asked him how he did it, he said something vague about magnetic fields. He died before he could reveal the secret. Maybe this is something like that."

"That's pretty far-fetched," Nancy said.

Andy's eyebrows shot up. "The whole damned thing is far-fetched."

"Well, however he was able to do it, Leedskalnin had stone blocks available to him," Ed said, standing up. "But

125

that sounded like a moving locomotive. Even if you've figured out how to levitate objects, it's not something you can just pick up off the ground."

"You're right, chief," Andy said, his voice dejected.

"Okay, I just want to be clear that we all agree that what we're dealing with is, by definition, supernatural." Ed moved closer to the two rangers.

"You said that out loud." Nancy took off her glasses and cleaned them. "I never thought I'd hear that word spoken in a police station."

"No way 'round it," Andy said.

"We have another problem." Ed went to his office, retrieved a file, and tossed it on Andy's desk.

"What's this?" Andy asked.

"Coroner's report on Meghan," Ed said. "Charlie Cook wrote a watered-down report to keep publicity to a minimum. In my infinite wisdom, I guilted him into doing an addendum with full disclosure, which includes the conclusion that Meghan was run over by a train."

"What's wrong with that?" Nancy stood and came over to Andy's desk.

Andy looked up. "If it hits the paper that there was a train involved, this place becomes a three-ring circus. Everybody knows that there are no tracks down there."

"Exactly," Ed said.

"When you saw Waddell, he told you to blame Malone for it, didn't he?" Andy said.

"Yeah. How'd you know?"

Andy shrugged. "He seemed the type."

"Is there anyone around who was here ten years ago?" Ed asked.

"No," Andy said. "I've been around the longest— seven years. It's been six for Doug, and Nancy came last year. Why, chief?"

"According to Charlie, this thing runs in ten-year cycles. If we can find someone who was here, we can get some insight."

"We could talk to Waddell again," Nancy said. "Maybe he'll be in a more cooperative mood."

Ed looked at the ceiling. "I'd like to avoid that if at all possible. Anyway, let's deal with the matter at hand. I've got a plan. We show Sheriff Potter the video."

"What?" Nancy and Andy said together.

"Hear me out. We show him the video and leak to the media that we have video evidence of another suspect. Potter will agree to keep the other details quiet. He won't want to answer questions about that anyway. The media will be in a frenzy to get the video, and no one will think to go back and look for an updated autopsy."

"I get it," Nancy said. "Show them a brighter object, and they'll follow that one."

"Exactly. We'll say we can't discuss an ongoing investigation and that releasing the video would reveal too much information to the suspect. The media will sue for the video. If they win, we appeal to the sixth circuit. By the time it goes through all the legal challenges, we will have bought ourselves a year."

Nancy's head bobbed. "You're good at this stuff, chief."

"All right, Andy and I will brief Potter. Nancy, you go home and get some sleep."

# Chapter 13

Holt Potter greeted Andy and Ed with a big smile and invited them to sit. Holt's office was three times the size of Ed's and had a sitting area with a leather couch and matching chairs. The walls were adorned with classic movie posters, many starring Humphrey Bogart.

Ed pointed to the poster of *Casablanca*. "Great movie. Shot in a few weeks, mostly on the Warner Brothers' lot."

"My favorite," Holt said. He sat on one of the U-shaped chairs while Ed and Andy sat on the couch.

"We've got something to show you, Holt. It's a game changer." Ed motioned for Andy to set up the video on his tablet.

"Oh, how so?" Holt said.

Behind him, photographs of a young Holt Potter in various athletic uniforms, including track, football, and basketball adorned the walls.

"We have another suspect in the murder, and we're pretty sure Malone didn't do it," Ed said.

"I assumed he pulled a weapon on you because he was guilty of both the murder and child porn." Holt leaned forward in his chair, studying Ed.

"That's what we thought at first," Ed said. "But we've run across something that can only be described as…bizarre, and I wanted to give you a heads-up."

"Okay," Holt said. "Now you have me intrigued."

"Andy." Ed signaled.

Andy played the recording for the sheriff. His face went through a gambit of emotions—horror, curiosity, and utter confusion. He asked to view it again. Andy complied. When it was over, Holt stood up and walked around the room, his jaw set in a grim expression.

"So this is why you were so interested in what Joshua Morton had to say?" Holt said.

Ed walked over to Holt and handed him a copy of the revised autopsy report. "I didn't even have this. Just a watered-down version concocted by Charlie Cook. In the past, all area law enforcement leaders had an unwritten agreement to keep all of this under wraps."

Holt took the autopsy form and turned to Andy. "Is there any way the video could have been faked?"

"No way. The same file was backed up to the cloud and hadn't been altered. It's the real deal," Andy said.

"I assume Joshua Morton's death is related to this?" Holt said. Both men sat again, but Holt leaned back. "What do you make of the train?"

Ed turned his palms up. "You saw it, Holt. There's no way to explain this by science or any natural law known to man."

"How does this tie in with your suspect?"

"Have you heard the story of Jackie Hudak or the Moonville Ghost?"

Holt blinked on the word *ghost*. Ed was afraid they had lost him, but after showing him the video, there was no turning back.

"No."

"Your predecessor never briefed you on the ten-year cycle?"

"No."

Ed took a deep breath and told Holt the story of Jackie Hudak and the ten-year cycle of deaths.

Holt held his hand up. "I'm sorry, but I don't think I want to know about that, Ed."

*He's shutting down.* Holt's brain wouldn't let him accept what was happening even though he understood it intellectually.

"In any case, we can't let that version get into the press." Ed pointed to the autopsy. "This area would be flooded with reporters and conspiracy nuts from all over the country. We won't be able to get anything done."

"I agree," Holt said and handed the report back to Ed. He avoided eye contact as he did so and looked out his office window as people walked up and down the street going about their daily routine, completely unaware that their world had just changed forever.

"I'm going to leak the existence of the video to the press," Ed said. "Get them chasing their tails, so they don't go after the autopsy."

"Good idea." Holt's voice sounded mechanical. "I'll refer all queries to your office."

"Thanks," Ed said. He understood Potter's reaction but hoped he hadn't just lost a friend.

Potter finally turned to look at Ed. "Let me know if you need anything."

"Sure," Ed said, extending his hand.

Holt's eyes didn't match his words. What he probably wanted to say was that he never wanted to hear about Jackie Hudak again.

*The genie is out of the bottle and can't be put back.*

**The press** conference was scheduled for the following morning. Ed had asked Charlie to leak to a friend in the press that law enforcement was in possession of a video recording showing the killer. Ed, Nancy, and Andy stood at a podium in front of the main lodge. Some guests came out of their cabins to witness the spectacle.

The event was sparsely attended, which was okay with Ed. He recognized reporters from the *Vinton Jackson Courier* and radio stations in Athens, McArthur, Huntington, and Point Pleasant. The one who concerned him was a woman whose name tag read Savannah Hughes. She held a microphone with the Associated Press logo. If something noteworthy happened, she would feed it to all their affiliates around the country.

"Good morning, everyone," Ed said. "Based on new evidence, the late David Malone has been cleared of the murder of Meghan Haynes."

"What new evidence?" Stan Collins from the *Courier* asked.

"We have identified another suspect. I have provided a description of this suspect in your briefing packets."

"Has the Haynes family been notified?" Stan followed up.

"Yes, the family was notified last night and is satisfied with the direction of the investigation."

In fact, it had taken quite a bit of persuasion to convince Henry Haynes that the creep Malone wasn't responsible for his daughter's death. They were forced to provide evidence that Joshua Morton and Samuel Green had been killed by the same man. They then had to swear

Haynes to secrecy.

"Why isn't Sheriff Potter here?" the same reporter asked.

*That's a good question.* Ed did his best to minimize his reaction. "Sheriff Potter had other pressing matters. With the death of David Malone, the Vinton County case is closed."

The real reason was that Holt had made up an excuse not to be here and declined a request to send a representative. He was distancing himself from Ed in case everything went sideways. Ed was somewhat sympathetic. Potter would have to run for re-election one day, and his opponent would have a field day with an incumbent who chased ghosts during his term.

Savannah Hughes raised her hand. Ed braced himself.

"Can you confirm the existence of a video showing the killer?"

Ed went into autopilot mode. "This is an ongoing investigation, and we're following several leads, not all of which can be disclosed to the public for obvious reasons."

Hughes continued to press. "Wouldn't releasing an image of the killer help your investigation?"

Ed smiled pleasantly. "I haven't confirmed the existence of such an image."

Hughes took out a notebook and held it in front of her eyes. "Were the deaths of Samuel Green and Joshua Morton related to the death of Meghan Haynes?"

Ed glanced at Andy. "The manner of death in those cases were dissimilar, and there was no relationship between Miss Haynes and the other two men."

"You didn't answer my question, chief."

"That is not something we can assume," Ed said.

After the news conference broke up, Savannah Hughes walked up to Ed. She had dark brown hair accented by a few strands of gray. She wore a knee-length black dress designed to show every curve. Savannah lowered her sunglasses and smiled, shocking Ed with electric blue eyes. Then the smile flattened to a thin line. No doubt, she was used to making men roll over and kick all four paws in the air. Ed wanted to but had to remain strong.

"You're a slippery one, chief."

"I don't mean to be."

"I want that video," she said. "If it's something that needs to be enhanced, we have equipment that can help with that. Maybe we can help each other."

"What video?" Ed relaxed his facial muscles revealing no expression.

She stepped close and stared up at him. Despite himself, he looked down into her eyes, which seemed to have an incandescence all their own. Her lips spread into a satisfied grin, and she pushed a card into his hand.

"If you change your mind, give me a call." She turned and walked away. Modern women weren't supposed to use their looks to get what they wanted but good reporters used every weapon in their arsenal, and Savannah Huges was armed to the teeth.

"You okay there, chief? We can get you a bib," Nancy said, turning away.

"Whoo wee, chief," Andy said. "You're a stronger man than me. If she looked at me like that, I'd have given her the keys to the kingdom and thanked her for the privilege. You think she took the bait?"

"She's smart," Ed said, watching Hughes climb into

the Associated Press minivan. "Don't be fooled by that femme fatale routine. That first salvo was the carrot, tomorrow we'll get the stick in the form of a lawsuit. Then she'll contact us again with another carrot. If she calls the office, refer all inquiries to me."

"Copy that, chief," Andy said.

Ed looked around. "Where's Nancy?"

"Guess she was tired after her shift." Andy pointed toward the parking lot where Nancy was entering her cruiser.

"I guess," Ed said.

**At work**, Monday morning, Ed had a message from the Columbus crime lab. He called the number, and they picked it up after the second ring.

"Gordon," the voice on the other end answered.

"Walter, this is Ed Freemen from Lake Hope. You left a message," Ed said.

"Ed, yes. Thanks for getting back to me." He sounded excited. "You sent me an interesting one."

"You have no idea," Ed said. "What can you tell me about my guy?"

"Quite a lot. What do you want to know first?"

"Well, let's start with the basics. Gender, age, and ethnicity," Ed said.

"Okay, we have a male of European descent. We can make a guess at age but don't take it as gospel. My best guess is that your guy is between twenty and thirty."

Ed hesitated. He didn't want to sound crazy. "Is there anything...unusual that you found?"

"That's a funny question," Gordon said. "Unusual in what way?"

"Umm..." Ed stammered. He had hoped Gordon

would make it easier. "Is there...anything to indicate that he's from somewhere...uh, other than here?"

Gordon was quiet for a long time on the other end of the line. "You mean like an alien?"

"What?" Ed said.

"I'm just messing with you, Ed. I've been waiting to tell you this."

"You did find something unusual," Ed said, relieved.

"Unusual, yes," Gordon said. "Is your suspect some kind of health nut?"

"We don't really know at this point."

"Well, from what we can tell from his lipids, your guy has never ingested processed foods. Does that help?" Gordon sounded like he was smiling.

"I take it that's out of the ordinary," Ed said.

"If your guy lived his whole life in a monastery, is Amish, or grew up in a hunter-gatherer society, it's not unusual. Otherwise, I'd say it's pretty damned odd. Do you have an explanation for this?"

"No," Ed lied. "Do you have a theory?"

"Maybe," Gordon said. "If he were a subsistence farmer and never shopped for food — basically lived like it was a hundred and fifty years ago. You sure he's not Amish? Even the Amish go into town every once and a while."

"He's not Amish, but that does explain some things," Ed said.

"Sounds like you can't tell me the whole story, Ed. I'm curious as hell. I hope you get back to me when this is all over. Come up to Columbus and have a beer."

"That sounds good," Ed said. Walter Gordon sounded like a nice fellow. Ed hated to keep him in the dark, but no good would come of telling him.

Ed heard a rap on his office window. Andy stood at the edge of his door, and Ed motioned him in.

"Chief, there's one thing we didn't discuss."

Ed waited.

"If Hudak is not a ghost, how does he come back every ten years? It makes no sense."

"It's a fair point, Andy," Ed said. "If we don't know what Hudak is, we can't develop a strategy to deal with him."

"I don't even know who we could ask," Andy said.

Ed cocked his head, pulled out his phone, and opened his contacts. "I might."

# Chapter 14

"How's my worst student?" Roland Donegal maneuvered his bulk around a large desk in his office at Ohio University. His stomach brushed the polished walnut as he moved to his chair as if taking even one extra step would require too much energy. His tie dragged across a small chess set, threatening to tumble the pieces. It was set to a problem Donegal probably got on the internet. He and Ed occasionally played online. Ed always won. He lowered himself slowly into his chair until his knees surrendered and he plopped down. A grunt escaped his lips. Many years earlier, he had taught Ed statistics at the University of Akron. Math was not Ed's best subject, and to this day, Donegal referred to him as his worst student.

For years, Donegal regaled his students about the day Ed barged into his office desperate to find an "easy" class to complete his modern university math or MUM module. Donegal, then a lowly math professor, had told him that he could substitute statistics for the final two courses in the series, although that wasn't something the math department advertised. Ed worked feverishly, completing every extra credit assignment issued and passing with a D. Now head of the quantum physics department at Ohio University, Donegal liked to tell this story to his students who were convinced that math would be the end of them.

"You're not still telling that story, are you, Roland?" Ed reached across and clasped Donegal's meaty hand.

"Of course," Donegal said, motioning for Ed to sit. "I still marvel at how such an intelligent man can be such a blithering idiot when it comes to numbers."

"I've always appreciated how you got me through, and your advice over the years," Ed said, sitting across from Donegal.

Donegal waved his hand. "I didn't get you through, Edward. You got yourself through with hard work and persistence. The story I tell is one of triumph, not ridicule."

"Now your worst student has an even bigger problem."

Ed told him about Jackie Hudak, the murders, and the DNA results. When he finished, Donegal leaned back against the leather desk chair, which protested with a whine.

"So you think this Hudak can travel through time?" Donegal said.

"That depends. Is time travel possible?"

Donegal chuckled. The buttons on his shirt appeared to dance as they caught the light. "There are theories that demonstrate that time travel is possible, but each is fraught with a set of insurmountable obstacles. Take the wormhole theory. In order to create a wormhole, you would need some kind of special matter not currently in existence, and even then, the wormhole would be highly unstable, minuscule, and of such short duration that it would prove useless. Of course, now they're talking about this exotic matter, which is supposed to repel gravity, but it still doesn't solve the stabilization problem."

"I heard something about traveling to a black hole as a way to time travel," Ed said.

Frowning, Donegal snorted, blowing a burst of air through his nose. "That's a load of crap. Hawking said that you could skim around the event horizon of a black hole, and the gravity would be so great that, according to special relativity, time dilation would slow you down relative to your counterparts on Earth."

"That's not correct?" Ed said, leaning forward in his seat.

"Yes, but that's not time travel any more than putting someone in suspended animation is time travel. You haven't gone anywhere. You've just found a way to slow your aging process. You wouldn't call Rip Van Winkle a time traveler."

"I take it you don't believe in time travel." Ed grinned.

"I don't believe that you can travel in time because there's no place to go. My theory is that time is dynamic, like light—and it can only exist in its dynamic form. It's like Einstein's thought experiment where he imagined riding on the end of a beam of light next to another beam of light. If you were riding on a train and looked at a friend riding a parallel train at the exact same speed, the friend would appear stationary. Light is different. If you looked at a parallel beam of light, it would hurtle away from you at the speed of light." Donegal's eyes lit up as he spoke.

"Some of the stars you see at night no longer exist, but you're not looking into the past. It just takes that long for their light to reach us. Just like light, you can bend and manipulate time, but it doesn't exist on some line that you can visit at any point. The only time that truly exists is right now. The big bang didn't happen thirteen-point-eight billion years ago. It's happening now." He laughed. "Well, now you've got me going. This is all to say that I don't think this Hudak character is popping around in time."

"It's okay. I miss our talks," Ed said. "What *do* you think?"

"I think that some person or persons have found a way to fool you into thinking that they're some boogeyman from a century ago, although I'm at a loss to explain the train. Didn't David Copperfield make the Statue of Liberty disappear using forced perspective?"

"That really doesn't help me," Ed said.

"Sorry, but time travel theories aren't going to help you with this one either. Your guy is just some costume-wearing serial killer determined to use this Jackie Hudak legend to terrorize."

"Still not helping."

"Well, maybe this does," Donegal said. "You're asking the wrong question. Does it really matter where he came from? What you have to deal with is you have a man who is killing people in your area, and you need to stop him, right?"

"But how do I stop him if I don't know what he is?"

"It doesn't matter what he is, Edward. Think about it. You have the answer right in front of you."

"Okay, well, while he's here, he can be hurt," Ed said. "Joshua Morton proved that."

"Yes!" Donegal said. "So no matter what he is—even if I'm wrong, and he's a time traveler, magician, wizard, ghost, or whatever—while he is here, he has to obey the same physical laws that you and I do."

"And if he can be hurt, he can be captured," Ed said.

"Only if I'm correct," the professor said.

"Why?"

Donegal put a hand on his stomach and groaned. Ed worried that his indulgence in food and drink was beginning to exact a terrible toll.

"Using your theory," Donegal said, "the killer has the capability to travel through space-time. You don't know how he does it. Theoretically, he can escape any custody by temporarily returning to his own time. If you're correct, then you will have to kill him."

Ed's face twisted into a frown. "I can't just drop him on sight."

"Then you'd better hope that I'm correct," Donegal said.

"Roland, I want to thank you for your help." Ed stood. "I'd appreciate your leaving this out of the stories you tell your students about me."

Donegal laughed and held his hands out. "Who would believe me? Besides, I've got plenty of material."

**"What does** your old professor think?" Nancy asked. She sat at her desk holding an oversized coffee mug.

"He thinks we're after David Copperfield." Ed sipped his energy drink.

Andy, who was reading the newspaper, looked up. "What?"

"He doesn't see anything supernatural here," Ed said.

Andy folded the paper and put it on his desk. Ed caught a glimpse of the headline. It was about a home invasion in McArthur. He had been scouring the news every day looking for references to a train and was glad not to find any.

"Didn't you tell him about the train, chief?" Andy said.

"I think it's different if you actually hear it. Anyway, I have a new strategy. I'm afraid it involves extra hours."

"I'm good with that," Nancy said.

"I could always use overtime," Andy said.

"Good. Nancy, you'll come in at nine and go to seven a.m. Andy, you take three in the afternoon to one a.m., and I'll come in from one to eleven a.m. That way, we have two units on duty in the hours the killer is most active."

"What about Doug?" Andy said.

"We'll put him on days. He'll like that."

"What do we tell him?" Nancy smirked.

"The truth, at least part of it. We tell him we're hunting for the killer. We don't have to say anything about Jackie Hudak."

Andy looked away and brushed imaginary dust off his desk. "You know Doug tells Waddell about everything you do, chief."

"I know," Ed said. "I can't worry about him now. We start tomorrow night."

"There's another little problem." Andy wheeled his chair up to his computer and turned it on.

"What is it?"

"I've been looking on the dark web, uh, just to sort of keep my hands in." Andy's voice stammered, but Ed didn't interrupt so he continued. "I ran across some chatter about Lake Hope. Nothing big, just some of the fringe groups, but there's some interest."

"Okay," Ed said slowly. "And this means...?"

"Well, we might get a few extra visitors," Andy said.

144

"You mean ghost hunters. Nuts."

"Can we really call 'em nuts now, chief?" Nancy turned away when Ed gave her a mock look of disapproval.

"But you haven't seen anything on the more mainstream sites, the regular web?"

"No, sir, not yet," Andy said.

"All right," Ed said. "We'll have to be extra careful. We don't want to shoot some yahoo running around with an EMF meter. Anything else, we'll have to deal with as it comes."

Nancy and Andy both looked at him, their eyes wide with surprise.

"What?" Ed said.

They both shook their heads.

"What?" Ed repeated.

They both pretended to look at something on their computer screens.

"You don't think I've ever watched the History Channel?"

# Chapter 15

**Night three of their** vigil started out like the previous two. Ed met Nancy and Andy near the boat rental. They both responded negatively to Ed's query about activity. Andy's shirt was not quite tucked in on the right side. Ed resisted the urge to point it out. It was Friday night, and new arrivals poured into the cabins.

Cabin rentals had been down most of the summer, but the park was at capacity this weekend. Ed thought it a miracle his officers hadn't received multiple reports of Hudak sightings. The stress of additional hours had begun to wear on them. Andy, who usually eschewed the green baseball cap, had it firmly smashed down on unruly hair. Nancy had given up on her bun and sported a simple ponytail and the bare minimum of makeup.

"You guys be careful. Alcohol is flowing tonight," Andy said. He got in his cruiser and, with a weary wave, drove off.

Ed turned to Nancy. "Well, just you and me."

"Same routine?" Nancy said.

"Yeah. I'll patrol the cabins close to the lodge and the Hope Furnace. You take the outer cabins and the road leading to the Moonville Rail Trail. Then we'll switch."

"Okay, chief," Nancy said. "Be safe."

Ed drove south on Park Road 9, then turned northeast on 278, skirting the east side of the lake. Points of lights floated on the water from night fishermen taking advantage of the glassy still water, lamps affixed to the bows of their aluminum boats.

He turned left on Park Road 1 and into the cul-de-sac containing the large family cabins. Most of the time, the sound of crickets and owls dominated the night, but when Ed pulled in, he heard music, loud voices, and the occasional clink of glasses. He drove slowly, scanning the areas between cabins for any anomalies.

The family cabins had large screened-in back porches with picnic tables. Many were full of guests, some playing cards or board games, others consuming copious amounts of alcohol. Ed continued back up the park road and circled the smaller cabins near the lodge. These cabins held a maximum of four guests, while the larger family cabins could sleep up to eight. Most of the lights were out.

Ed circled back, intending to go back down Park Road 1 and turn left toward the Hope Furnace. As he passed the road leading to the family cabins, something caught his eye. He stopped his cruiser and looked into the rearview mirror. A man stumbled toward him. He wore a long bathrobe, pajama bottoms decorated with some kind of animal, and no shoes. His large belly protruded from a white T-shirt, stretched at the bottom by his paunch and at the top by his man boobs. He waved his arms over his head like a man who had just missed his bus and was late to work.

Ed snatched his mic from its hook. "Nancy, we've got a situation by the family cabins."

He got out of the car and approached the man with his left hand held out and his right hovering near his sidearm.

"On my way, chief," Nancy's voice came back.

"Help, help!" the man said. He huffed the words out through gulps of air.

"What's going on, sir?" Ed asked. "Are you hurt?"

"What? No, I got away, but he's going to kill my wife. You've got to get there quick!"

"Sir, what's your name?" Ed asked.

The man shook his head in confusion. "My name? My name is Vince, but what does that matter? He's going to kill her."

"Vince, I need you to tell me what happened. Who's going to kill your wife?"

"Gary," Vince said. "My wife's ex. Gary Waverly. He found out we got married, and he came here to kill me. He's got a gun. Sue jumped him so I could get away, but now he's got her, and he's going to kill her."

"Okay, Vince, you're doing fine. Which cabin is it? Is there anyone there besides Sue and Gary?"

"The kids are there. Three of 'em. Gary was trying to get them to come out. He wants to kill Sue in front of them!"

"Okay, which cabin?"

"Cabin fifty-two," Vince said. "It's—"

"I know where it is," Ed said and pointed. "Vince, I want you to follow this road until you get to the main lodge. Wait in the lobby until I come back to get you."

"Okay, okay. You got to help her."

Ed got back in his cruiser and headed for the cabin. He had been in similar situations in Akron but never thought to see one at Lake Hope. He picked up the mic again. "Nancy, how far are you?"

Nancy came back, her voice sounding frustrated. "Still a couple of minutes, chief. I was halfway to the tunnel when the call came in."

"That's okay. We've got an active domestic with a firearm. I'm going to have to go in. Cabin fifty-two. Get here as soon as you can."

"Chief, wait for me," Nancy said.

"Can't. I'll try to de-escalate until you get here."

Ed didn't turn on his siren, fearing the noise might startle Gary into action. He parked his cruiser at the next cabin and, with his back to it, walked sideways until he got to cabin fifty-two. He heard rustling on the side of the cabin and moved to the edge of the building. With his weapon held at high ready, Ed did a quick peek. He saw Gary holding Sue against the side of the cabin near the back porch. In the dim light of the lamp over them, Ed saw a revolver sticking out of Gary's blue jeans. Neither could have been over five-foot-two. To Ed, they looked like two kids playing cops and robbers. Gary had an arm crooked around Sue's neck. She tugged at it without success.

"Boys, come on out! Daddy brought a present for you," Gary said. His tone was solicitous, saccharine in a way that belied any hint of humanity.

"Don't you move, boys. You stay right where you are," Sue said.

Gary increased the pressure on his chokehold. Sue kicked and stomped at his feet.

"I told you to shut up, you whore!" Gary said.

Ed switched his weapon to his left hand, exposing as little of his body as possible. He heard a car stop behind him. Nancy had arrived. Ed cut the pie, taking small steps in a semi-circle to minimize his exposure until he had Gary in his sights.

"Gary!" Ed said. "Put your hands up and walk toward me!"

"Who is it?" Gary strained to get a look at Ed while keeping the chokehold on Sue. She must have felt a slight release in pressure because Sue renewed her attempts to get away. "You think he's going to save you, bitch? You think I'm afraid to die?"

Ed heard Nancy get out of the car. Without looking, he signaled her to take a position behind a nearby tree. "State police! Now, put your hands up and walk toward me!"

"Shoot me!"

Gary reached for the butt of the revolver. Ed slid his finger into the trigger guard and exhaled. Nothing happened. He tried to make his finger squeeze, but it didn't budge. Ed's chest tightened. He couldn't fire! Why couldn't he fire? Nancy was too far away. Panic rose as Gary's hand closed around the handle, but Ed forced it down.

He took a deep breath and sprinted forward. Gary turned his head, pressed his eyes closed, and pulled the weapon from his belt. Before he could fire, Ed reached Gary, grabbed him by the collar, and flung him to the dirt. Gary rolled onto his stomach and tried to get up. Ed stomped him flat and stepped on the hand holding the weapon, forcing it open. Ed took the gun, stuck it in his waistband, and holstered his own. Nancy ran up, flopped on Gary, and cuffed him. When Nancy pulled him to his feet, a blast of alcohol hit Ed. He turned his head.

"You didn't have to put your feet on me," Gary said, glaring at Ed.

"I think that might be the least of your worries," Ed said. He signaled Nancy to take him to the cruiser.

"You didn't have to put your feet on me," Gary repeated as Nancy led him away.

Ed turned to Sue. "You're one tough lady."

"He really tried to kill me that time." She said mechanically. She seemed more surprised than scared. She looked past Ed as she spoke. "I can usually handle him when he's drunk, but he was like a maniac this time. He got me down, put the gun to my head, and pulled the trigger."

"He actually fired?" Ed asked.

Sue opened her hand and showed Ed the butterfly-shaped powder marks. "I pushed the gun away at the last second. The bullet must have gone over my head. That's when he made me get up and tried to call the kids out."

Sue clapped both hands over her mouth, then suddenly grabbed Ed's arm. "Vince. The kids?"

"He's fine." Ed put his hand over her small one. "He's at the lodge. We'll pick him up on the way to the station. We've got a long night ahead of us. Is there someone who can stay with the kids?"

"It's just us. I've got to check on them. I don't know how much of that they saw."

"We'll get someone to help you," Ed said.

**It was** one o'clock in the afternoon when Ed finally got home. He showered, put on pajamas — which in his case were an old T-shirt and gym shorts — then stood in front of the bathroom mirror looking at his reflection. He couldn't see anything but there was still a lot wrong, more than he realized.

He went to his bedroom, drew his Glock 40, removed the bullets from the magazine, and ejected the round in the chamber. Ed looked into the ejection port to satisfy

152

himself that the weapon was safe and empty.

He aimed at the wall and took turns dry firing with his right and left hands, racking the slide after each shot. He placed the weapon in the safe next to his bed and laid down. Ed was exhausted but sleep eluded him.

He got up, went to the fridge, and pulled out a bottle of blackberry Arbor Mist. He wondered what the hell was wrong with him. Why couldn't he fire? He drank straight from the bottle, put it down, and pinched the bridge of his nose.

"I'm going to have to resign."

He drank some more. A cop who couldn't fire his weapon wasn't a cop. Ed could really retire this time. He had enough money.

Maybe he should have stayed in therapy longer after the Anthony Deavers shooting. It was, after all, the "precipitating incident." He laughed humorlessly and looked at the bottle. It was halfway gone. Ed didn't remember drinking that much. His head was already starting to buzz. Ed could never hold his alcohol, and it made it difficult to control his symptoms. He shrugged and drank more of the sweet, fruity liquid.

Ed rubbed his bald head. How could he resign with Jackie Hudak running around mashing people up with trains?

*Yeah, and what are you going to do about it?*

Ed looked around but there was no one there. Had the voice come from him?

*A cop who can't shoot his weapon. What are you going to do, throw rocks at him?*

"Hello?"

He got up and searched the cabin, looking in closets, cupboards, and even laundry baskets — places impossible for a human to hide. He poked his head out of all the windows to ensure no one was outside.

Defeated, he came back and sat on the chair. Ed picked up the wine bottle and examined the label. What did he expect that it would say, "Laced with LSD?"

"Great," Ed said.

That was it. Now on top of everything else, he was bat-guano, stark-staring, howling-at-the-moon mad. He thought of his aunt who spent her final days in a mental hospital. Was schizophrenia hereditary? Was that his future?

He leaned back in the chair and closed his eyes. Maybe he just needed rest. He sat in silence for a while, his eyes closed. He tried to block out all thoughts and concentrate on his breathing. He wasn't aware how long it took, but the line between wakefulness and sleep blurred. His last conscious thought was of the 1931 Universal Pictures classic *Dracula*. It was the scene where Renfield, played brilliantly by Dwight Frye, was discovered by authorities as the only survivor of Dracula's ship. Only instead of Dwight Frye, Ed saw himself clinging to the railing, grinning madly and laughing through his teeth, "Ah, huh, huh, huh, huuuh." Ed slipped into unconsciousness.

A knock on the door woke Ed hours later. His head flopped to the right. Drool had collected in the corner of his mouth. Ed raised his wrist, but he had taken off his watch when dressing for bed. He looked out the window. It was dark outside. He got up, hurried to the kitchen, and splashed water on his face. There was another knock, more insistent.

"Just a minute," Ed said and winced.

His head hurt. He glanced at the Arbor Mist bottle. There was about half a liter left in the 1.5-liter container.

*Lightweight*, the voice chimed in.

Maybe ignoring it would make it go away, though he knew that was irrational. He made a mental note never to drink again. He walked to the door and pulled it open. Nancy stepped in, sliding sideways to squeeze through the small opening through which he intended to address her. Ed thought he saw a flash of light in the woods and paused at the door, but decided his hallucinations must be visual as well. What would he see next, Oompa Loompas dancing on his counter?

"Come on in," Ed said sarcastically.

He watched her walk into the living room and turn around, taking it in. Did he smell alcohol on her breath? She wore a clingy denim skirt and a gray hollow-out tank top that left only a little to the imagination. Her ginger hair was combed, styled, and layered. Thin, gossamer strands formed an oval around her face, and she wore the full spectrum of make-up, including a luscious shade of medium brown lipstick.

*She's beautiful*, the voice said. Ed had to agree.

"Yep," Nancy said. "This is a man's place."

"What are you doing here, Nancy?" Ed asked, still standing by the open door.

"I wanted to see you."

Ed cocked his head and stared at her, trying to figure out if she was being deliberately flirtatious. He closed the door and followed her in. She circled the couch and paused at Ed's chair.

"May I?" Nancy said, indicating the wine.

When she grabbed the bottle by the neck, Ed thought she would drink out of it as he had done. Instead, she took the bottle into the kitchen and began to hunt for glasses. Ed sat in his chair. He was tired and still buzzed from the drink. Ed could hear Nancy puttering around in the kitchen. He thought he should tell her to leave, but part of him didn't want her to. Ed waited for the voice to add some witty insult, but it was silent.

"You have to work tonight," Ed warned.

"You gave me the night off," Nancy said.

She came back with two glasses. Ed sat his glass down on the small table next to the chair. He didn't want to drink anymore, afraid that his new friend would manifest itself anew, perhaps this time in the form of a talking dog who would order him to kill couples in parked cars. She sat on the low table across from him. At this angle, her skirt slid right up to the border.

*Hell-o-o-o,* the voice said, dragging the word out.

Ed's gaze snapped up, stopping right between her breasts, her cleavage exposed by the opening in her top. He raised his eyes again, finally settling on her soft green eyes. She had a slight smile on her face as if amused by his discomfort.

"I'm rescinding that. Go to work."

Nancy chuckled, put her drink down, and leaned forward, looking into his eyes. "I need to talk to you, chief. You don't have to tell me anything if you don't want to."

"Glad I have your permission," Ed said.

Nancy pushed on. "At the cabin last night, you looked like you were going to shoot Waverly, but—"

"I don't have to justify my actions to you, Nancy," Ed said.

"I know. That's not what this is about, I promise you." Nancy put up her hands. "I'm just concerned."

Ed turned his head. "You should go now."

"Chief, please." Nancy slid off the table and grabbed the armrest of Ed's chair. "How can I make you understand?

I want to help."

Nancy's eyes told Ed that she was sincere and genuinely cared about what happened to him. His inhibitions were down. He wanted to trust her and talk to someone other than that sardonic voice.

*That's not all you want to do to her.*

He pressed his eyes shut.

"Nancy, you can't help. Let it go."

"Chief, what is it?" Nancy straightened.

"I said, let it go," Ed repeated. He sounded subdued — weary. "It's not something I can discuss."

"Chief." Nancy grabbed his hand.

Nancy wasn't wearing her glasses, and as she leaned forward, her hair fell just around her eyes. Her beauty was not incandescent but understated, like a soft persistent glow, and the longer he looked at her, the more he noticed. He wanted her, God help him. The voice was right. He wanted her.

Ed looked away. Tried to put it out of his mind. His control was slipping, and he had to rein it in. Ed conjured up the stream of marigolds, but instead of dropping onto the flower, her image grew.

"Chief?" She got even closer.

"I tried to shoot him. I couldn't." He continued to look away, but she gently cupped his chin and pulled him back.

"That's all right, chief. Taking a life is a hard thing, even for an experienced cop. It all worked out."

"That's not what I'm saying. I mean, I *tried* to shoot and couldn't."

"I don't understand." Nancy pulled back. "You mean you physically couldn't pull the trigger?"

"I think it happened with Malone as well. I just thought

I was tired."

"You've been under a lot of pressure."

"No, I've been under pressure before. This is some kind of block." Ed hated the way he sounded, vulnerable and not in control. He hadn't felt like this since he was a kid and had just been taken off the Ritalin. At the same time, he felt he could be vulnerable in front of her.

*Oh, you've got it bad.*

Ed wanted to scream *shut up*, but he was hanging on by a thread. If he started shouting, he wouldn't stop. "I'm a liability."

Nancy put her hands on her hips. "What I saw out there was pretty badass."

"No, there's something wrong." Ed wagged his head from side to side.

Nancy slid back so she was all the way on the table again. She looked away from him to the kitchen.

Ed welcomed the release in tension. "What is it?"

She looked back at him, her eyes searching his. "Do you think this has something to do with the shooting you told me about?"

"I don't know. I really don't want to talk about this."

"It might help," Nancy said, smiling. "I'm a wonderful listener."

Ed leaned back in his chair, looked at her, then down at the floor.

"Okay, here's the thing. I should have known it was a fake gun."

"How could you possibly know that?"

"Observation. It's kind of my thing."

"Your superpower," Nancy said.

"Exactly."

She looked at the ceiling in exasperation. "You set

standards for yourself no one can meet. Sometimes I see you struggling to maintain control. If you don't stop winding yourself so tight, you're going to break."

"Too late," Ed said.

Nancy lowered her gaze, stared at Ed for a long moment, then seemed to resolve something in her head. She pushed off the table and came forward. Ed's heart quickened. Nancy leaned over him and stretched out her arms.

*Here we go*, the voice said with glee.

Ed hesitated.

*Do it! We're in the asshole of Ohio. No one will care. She came to your place looking smoking hot. No one will blame you. DO IT!*

When Ed didn't move, Nancy climbed into his lap and pulled him into an embrace. Ed's fingers dug into the arms of the chair and his face heated up. He smashed his eyelids together to get rid of the imp.

"It's okay," Nancy whispered. She smelled of sweet almonds. Almond butter lotion.

Ed felt her pull back a little and turn her face, her lips, toward him. He grabbed onto her and pulled her back into a hug.

"Thank you, Nancy. I'm okay now."

*Awww! Come on!*

"I'll see you tomorrow."

Nancy moved back, studied his eyes for a moment, then got up to leave. "Okay. I'll see you at work, chief." She turned away but hesitated at the door. "You're going to be okay."

*You punk! You wimp! She was right there. She wanted it and you let her go. We both know how long it's been since you had some.*

159

Ed held his head and groaned. There was some truth to what his tormentor said. It had been a long time since he was intimate with a woman, since he broke up with his girlfriend, Connie, around the time of the Deavers shooting. He got up and headed for the shower, uncharacteristically dropping his clothes as he went.

*Cold water, I presume?*

"Shut up!"

# Chapter 16

"**Chief, I'm with you** a hundred percent, but I'm getting a low-bat signal here," Andy said.

He, Nancy, and Ed were on their seventh night of patrols.

"I understand, Andy," Ed said. They couldn't keep this up much longer. There had been no activity since the Waverly incident, and they were on the brink of exhaustion. Perhaps Hudak could see their activities, or maybe he had killed to his satisfaction for this cycle. "And I realize this is a Whack-A-Mole approach, but this is all we have."

"Okay, but I'll need stock in a coffee company."

The night began just as the previous ones. Ed and Andy investigated a lantern bobbing up and down along the Wild Cat Trail. It turned out to be two teenagers gathering worms for fishing the following day.

**Later, Andy** parked near the picnic tables at Oak Point. To his left, he saw flashlights bobbing up and down near Grouse Point. This was normal as Grouse Point was the terminus of the guided tour known as the Beaver Walk, where guests watched beavers build and reinforce their lodges.

The group gathered at the bank and crouched to watch the beavers go about their chores. Andy turned back toward the water, which shimmered with the light of the half-moon. Andy checked his watch. He had only an hour to go before the end of his shift. He blinked once, twice, three times, each blink slower than the previous one. By the fourth blink, Andy's eyes remained closed. He wasn't asleep, not yet, just in that pleasant dozing state that Rod Serling would say exists between light and shadow. Something—he didn't know what—caused his eyes to flutter open.

Andy looked at the lake where people were gathered for The Beaver Walk guided tour. He scanned left. About a hundred yards away from the guests, a light flickered in and out as if someone moved through the trees. At first, he thought someone from the tour group had slipped off to answer nature's call in the woods. Then he remembered there were bathrooms near the dock only twenty feet away. Plus, the light wasn't the steady directional beam of a flashlight. It swayed back and forth as if—oh god— as if someone was holding it by the handle, and it was swinging. *When the lantern swings—*

Ripping off his seat belt, Andy gripped his shoulder mic and tilted his head. "Chief, this is Andy. We got a situation here. Grouse Point." Andy slid out of the cruiser, pushed the car door closed with the heel of his hand, and sprinted perpendicular to the lake in long, loping strides.

"On our way, Andy," he heard the chief say over the radio. "What've you got?"

Andy spoke between gulps of air. "Lantern— swinging— woods near Grouse Point."

Entering the woods, Andy had to slow down considerably in the thick foliage. He took out his flashlight and cautiously weaved through the trees. If he wasn't careful, he could get jacked up by a low branch or fallen log.

About forty feet away, Andy saw an outline of the man holding the lantern continuing in the direction of the guests. Suddenly, the lantern turned in Andy's direction, the amber side facing him. Andy stopped and drew his weapon.

"I'm gonna need you to stop right there, sir," Andy said.

He rested his gun hand on top of his left, which held the flashlight. Andy stepped forward. He could see a little more now. The man wore the blue striped overalls, just like the legend said.

*Holy shit!* Andy struggled to hold his hand steady, the flashlight beam vibrating in his shaking hands. Still, he pressed forward. If he could just hold the man until the chief and Nancy arrived, they could take him down together. The man held the lantern, so it obscured his face.

"Now, why don't you just lay that old lantern down and put your hands up." Andy quickly pointed the flashlight beam down and up. Though he couldn't make out features, Andy saw the man tilt his head. Then, in a sudden movement, he turned and walked briskly away from the lake.

"Stop!" Andy ordered, but the man continued.

Andy holstered his weapon. The fleeing felon rule did not apply, and Andy had no cause to shoot him.

"We're almost there, Andy. What's your status?" the chief said. Andy looked and saw two cruisers rounding

163

the lake near the boat rental office.

"Big man, carrying an old-style oil lantern, heading southeast from Grouse Point. He's not obeying commands," Andy said. He noticed the man negotiated the trees much better than he did. He casually stepped around and over things in his path. Although the man wasn't running, Andy found it difficult to keep up. He ducked branches and stumbled forward, but the man was gaining ground.

Out of the corner of his eye, Andy saw the chief and Nancy pull into the parking lot and run across the open field toward the woods. The man, Hudak or whoever it was, paused, knelt, and the light went out. With no light, Hudak was utterly invisible.

Drawing his weapon again, Andy aimed the flashlight beam at Hudak's last location. There was nothing. Andy turned slowly in a circle, expecting him to jump out of the woods and hammer him with the same blows that had broken the bones of poor old Joshua Morton. Nothing.

"Andy," the breathless voice of the chief said.

Andy turned and saw the chief moving toward him. "Where is he?"

"I don't know. He was here, turned off his lamp, and that was it," Andy said.

Nancy ran up to them, then bent forward and put her hands on her knees. "Did you see him, Andy? Was it Hudak?"

Andy threw his hands in the air. "I don't know. Seems like it. Disappeared, though."

They searched the woods for about fifteen minutes and were about to give up when something caught Ed's eye. He started to pull his attention back, thinking it was his ADHD again, but something held his gaze. What appeared to be a small red dot was visible in the distance. "Got him. He's right there, see?"

Andy followed Ed's finger with his flashlight, sounding confused. "I don't see anything, chief."

Ed pushed the flashlight away. "You can't see it with that. He's up by the road."

Nancy leaned forward and squinted. "I don't see it either."

"It's right there," Ed said. "That point of red light by Park Road 9 and 278."

"Damn, he must have backtracked. He could have walked right past us, and we wouldn't have seen him in this darkness," Andy said.

"I don't know, chief," Nancy said. "It's not even moving."

"That's because he's watching us." Ed continued to stare at the light.

"Why would he be watching us?" Nancy said.

Ed turned. "He wants to see what we're going to do next."

They walked together to their cruisers, occasionally glancing at the red light in the distance.

"Couldn't that just be one of those reflectors on the side of the road to tell drivers where the edge is?" Andy said.

"Reflectors need light from a car's headlamps. It's Hudak," Ed said.

When they reached their vehicles, the light turned amber and began to move.

"Damned if you weren't right, chief," Andy said.

"Let's drive up the road." Ed pulled his car door open. "See if we can close the distance on him."

They lost sight of him while driving through the

parking lot toward Park Road 9. They turned right and headed to the area where Ed spotted Hudak. Ed stopped his cruiser south of Cabin Ridge. They all got out and looked around. Hudak was gone.

"You sure this was the spot, chief?" Nancy said.

"He was here," Ed said, staring into the darkness.

"Should we split up again? Check all the cabins and roads?"

"I've got a hunch." Ed jumped back into his cruiser, made a U-turn, and headed back down Park Road 9. Nancy and Andy followed.

Ed followed the road past the boat docks and left onto State Route 278. He drove so fast Nancy and Andy could barely keep up with him. He turned right onto Shea Road where he stopped his cruiser and sprinted toward the old rail line.

Hudak held an old-style oil lantern in the exact spot where Meghan Haynes's body was found less than two weeks ago. He looked up at Ed, turned the lantern so that the green side faced him, and swung it in a wide arc. A bright flash of light followed. When it dimmed, Hudak was gone.

Nancy and Andy ran up to Ed. He felt a very light touch on his hand and knew it was Nancy. He did not react. Instead, he turned to Andy. "Did you see—"

"Yeah," Andy said breathlessly. "Yeah, I did."

**"I don't** know if I'm up for this, chief," Andy said when they returned to the office. "I'm having a little trouble wrapping my mind around this."

"You knew we were dealing with the supernatural," Nancy said. "I mean, you said you believed us about Hudak."

"I know, I know," Andy said. "I *did* believe you. It's just seeing it outright like that. That's something different. I mean, what did we even see out there?"

"I think we have to consider that Hudak has the ability to, uh, dematerialize," Ed said.

"Dematerialize?" Nancy said. "Wait a minute, chief."

"I don't know what else you call it. He was there, then he wasn't," Ed said. "He turned the lantern around and swung it. It must hold some kind of power, like a talisman."

"You see, that's what I'm talking about, chief. We're saying that a man who was born a hundred years ago is running around conjuring trains out of thin air!" Andy threw his hat down on his desk and ran his hands through his hair. "We're just a few cops. How're we supposed to handle this?"

"I don't have the answer, but we're the only ones standing between him and more death," Ed said. "If you want me to reassign you to the day shift, I understand, but I'm not going to pretend that we don't need you, because we do."

"No, I'm in, chief. This is just a little overwhelming, that's all."

"So this dematerialization thing," Nancy said. "How does it work? Can he pop up anywhere? Can he just appear in our bedrooms? Kill us in our sleep?"

"I don't know." Ed squinted. "I would think that he has some limitations, but that brings up another question. Where does he go when he's not—hunting?"

"Where does he go?" Nancy said.

"Yeah. I talked to the lab tech in Columbus. According to him, the sample was from a person who has never consumed processed foods. How many people today don't consume processed food of some kind?"

Nancy scratched her head. "When he disappeared at the railroad tracks, maybe he didn't just go to another location? Is that what you're saying?"

"Exactly," Ed said.

"You think he goes back to the past?" Andy said. "How would that work? Would he always return back to the same point that he left, or is he living back there and ten years for him in the past is ten years here?"

"Or does he go into some kind of limbo?" Nancy added.

"I think that answers some of our questions about his limitations. If he could go into the past and pop back here at any point in our present, he could have gone back in time, popped up behind us before we spotted him, and killed us one by one."

Andy rubbed his chin. "What does that mean?"

"It means that he's not all-powerful. And we know he can be hurt." Ed walked to the window and looked out into the darkness.

"Hurt or killed?" Andy asked.

Ed continued to stare out the window but did not answer.

# Chapter 17

**The following afternoon, Ed** and Andy arrived at Jeff Waddell's home. Waddell had requested another meeting through Doug Weems. When they walked in, Waddell took a seat in his favorite chair. A fifth of bourbon sat on the small table next to him. Ed made no greeting, just stood across the room with his arms folded.

Waddell grinned widely. "Where's that little hottie. Still working nights?"

Ed stared at him, unblinking.

"I didn't bring you here to fight." Waddell held both hands in front of him. "I'm really trying to help. Well, that's not exactly true. I could give a shit what happens to you. I just don't want the community to suffer needlessly."

"What do you mean 'needlessly?'" Ed said.

Waddell tipped the bottle into his glass, paused, and held the bottle out to Ed, who didn't react. "I know about your nocturnal activities."

"Nocturnal," Ed said. "Did you learn that word on the Discovery Channel?"

Waddell glared then softened his gaze. He pointed

his index finger at Ed while still holding on to the glass. "You see, I'm gonna let that go. Like I said, I don't want to fight."

"So what do you want?" Ed sat on the couch.

"Pardon?"

"You said you didn't want to fight, so what *do* you want?" Ed said.

"I told you once to back off, but you didn't listen. Now I'm telling you again before it's too late," Waddell said.

"He's killing people. What difference does it make?" Ed said.

"He's gonna get his due," Waddell said. "There's nothing you can do about it."

"How would you know?" Ed cocked his head. "You didn't even try."

Waddell jumped out of his chair with surprising speed, whiskey flying across the room. "I *did* try, and it cost me. It cost me big! That's why I'm telling you to stop!"

Ed held his ground. "Just let him kill his fill, mark it down as animal predation and freak accidents, huh?"

"You don't know shit." Waddell turned, grabbed the bottle of bourbon, and drank from it. When he turned back, his voice was calm.

"Then tell me!" Ed said through clenched teeth. "You keep talking around it. Just tell me what you know!"

Waddell put the bottle back on the table and sat. He turned to the window, his eyes looking even older than before.

"It was his last killing cycle. I set up a task force with the county sheriff's department. We staked out his favorite locations, just like you're doing now. It pissed him off. Early one morning, I was returning to my house when I sensed something behind me. I pulled my weapon and turned. He smacked it out of my hand, grabbed me by the neck, and backed me up against the house. I thought, 'This is it. This is where I die,' but he just stared at me, his face inches from mine. He didn't say a word, but I knew what he wanted. *Don't mess with me, or I'll mess with you back.* I didn't listen, kept up the pressure, figured I was getting to him. That's when we found her. Stella. My Stella."

"I thought your wife's name was Dorothy." Andy looked confused.

Waddell chuckled. "Yeah."

Ed stared at him, expressionless. He was such a despicable human being that he didn't deserve Ed's sympathy, but Waddell looked so pathetic.

Waddell wiped his eyes with a shaky hand, and Ed saw moisture on his knuckle.

"We dragged her to the road and pretended like it was a hit-and-run." Waddell paused, sniffed and drank more bourbon. "He killed more people that summer than ever before. That night we made a pact — me, Sheriff Charlie Hickey, and Alice Camden, the county coroner. We'd give the devil his due, and he would leave us be." Waddell looked away.

The room was silent except for the gurgle of whiskey Waddell poured down his gullet. Waddell — tough guy and bigot. He got just what he deserved, but even bigots could have a soft spot for someone.

"How did he know to go after her? Or was it blind luck?" Ed said.

Waddell pushed his lower lip out. "He knew. He knew. That's why he got in my face. He wanted me to know that he could get to anyone I cared about."

"Why didn't he go after Dorothy?" Andy said.

"You a little smart-ass, always was." Waddell filled his mouth with bourbon, swished it around his mouth like mouthwash, then paused. For a second, Ed thought he would spit it at Andy, but he swallowed it with a gulp.

"How many more did he kill after you made your pact?" Ed asked.

"Two. A drunk and a prostitute."

"In other words, folks nobody would miss," Andy said.

"It's easy for you to sit back and judge what we did, but now that the lives are on your head, what are *you* gonna do?"

Ed got up without a word, walked out, and motioned for Andy to follow.

"Wow, that was awkward," Andy said when they got outside.

"Yep," Ed dropped his head and shook it slowly.

**I'm not** a fan of Waddell, but I think we have to consider what he said." Andy sat on the edge of the table near the fireplace. Ed sat on the couch, and Nancy in the oversized chair. The moonless night made the windows appear as if they'd been painted black.

"You mean just let people die?" Nancy said. "Cover it up?"

Andy turned to Ed. "I'm sorry, chief, but that's kinda what we're doing now. I mean, we hid that autopsy from the press."

Nancy gripped the arms of her chair. "That was just to buy us some time. I can't believe we're considering looking the other way."

"Andy's right," Ed said. Out of the corner of his eye,

he saw Nancy and Andy turn quickly to look at him. "The law of unintended consequences."

"What?" Nancy squinted.

"I mean, we have to at least talk about it." Ed reached for a water glass on the table. He sipped and continued. "Will more people die if we continue to pursue this?"

"It's our job," Nancy said.

The look of disappointment on her face made Ed's heart sink.

"And if this guy goes on a wild killing spree, what are we going to do then?" Andy said.

Nancy sat forward. "If we had a serial killer, a regular one, and he called in and said, 'Hey, just let me have a few more victims, and I'll stop killing,' would we say yes?"

"That's apples and oranges, Nancy," Andy said. "It's easy to criticize what Waddell and the others did, but you didn't see him. He went after Hudak, just like we're doing now. He got burned for it. He got burned bad. This guy has powers we don't understand. Hell, we don't even know if we *can* stop him."

They both looked at Ed. Nancy was good to go, but he was worried about Andy. His hand had been on the rip cord since his encounter with Hudak, and Ed thought he knew why. During the Malone investigation, Andy was in his element. Everything was black and white, ones and zeros, like computer code. But Hudak existed in the gray fog of the supernatural, and it frightened Andy.

Ed's instincts told him to continue to go after Hudak but, for Andy's sake, they had to have this discussion. He looked down at his shooting hand and was reminded that his instincts had been a little rocky these days.

*You got that right*, the voice said.

"Chief?" Nancy said.

Ed cleared his throat. "Say we back off and let him fill whatever his quota is for this cycle. Then in another ten years, he comes back to do it again. Is that something we can live with? I don't think I can."

"What about the hell he raises this cycle?" Andy asked.

"Then we will just have to stop him before he does that." Ed thought to himself, *before this thing gets any further, I have to get some help.*

*You need it,* the voice offered.

# Chapter 18

**Later that week, Ed** headed to Columbus and the office of Dr. Mary Spicer. Short and chubby, she wore loose-fitting jeans and a multicolored blouse that could have been from a bargain bin. She sat across from Ed on a green loveseat with thin black stripes. On occasion, she contorted herself in awkward positions, like hooking a leg over the oversized arm of the seat and lying back so that she had to look up at him.

"So what brings you here?" She tucked her legs under her knees and sat upright.

Ed inhaled the fresh scent of lavender and looked around. Behind Spicer's desk across the room, two scented candles burned, permeating the room with a soothing floral aroma. "Well, I'm having some issues, and it's affecting my job."

"I mean, were you ordered to come here? I see a lot of law enforcement types, and most aren't here of their own free will."

"It was my decision to come."

Mary Spicer's eyebrows rose, disappearing behind her dirty blonde bangs. "Good. What kind of issues?"

"Well, one thing is that I'm hearing things." Ed shifted in his chair.

"Hearing what?"

Ed scratched his chin. "Uh, a voice."

"What does the voice say?" Dr. Spicer moved closer to the edge of the chair. "A lot of things," Ed said.

"Mostly, it's being a smart-ass."

"Do you hear it now?"

"No."

Spicer leaned back, removed her glasses, and began to chew on the tip. "Can you be more specific about what the voice says?"

"It's mostly observations about myself and others that are derogatory in nature."

"'You suck?' Things like that?" Spicer asked.

"Yes."

"Do you hear the voice through your ears, or is it in your head?"

Ed wasn't sure how to answer that. "I don't know," he said with some surprise.

"It's not telling you to kill your neighbors, barbeque 'em up, and feed them to your friends, is it?"

"No." Ed put his hands up. "Nothing like that. Just smart-ass comments."

Spicer reached into a side pocket of the chair and pulled out a pad and pencil. She wrote on it while keeping her eyes on Ed. "Well, if you hear it through your ears, we're talking hallucination—audio or visual perception for which there is no appropriate stimulus."

"Okay."

"Do you have a history of schizophrenia in your family?" Spicer leaned back, trying to look casual.

Ed's Aunt Pearline used to think that people were spying on her through the walls. When they were children, Ed and his cousin Duane used to play tricks on her, silently moving her furniture around when she was out of the room. Aunt Pearline would point to it as proof of the mysterious agency that kept her under constant surveillance. In retrospect, it was cruel, but they were children and didn't know any better. A thought occurred to him. Aunt Pearline spent a significant amount of time in mental hospitals in her later years. Was that where he was headed—the looney bin?

"Mr. Freemen?" Dr. Spicer prompted.

"My Aunt Pearline."

"On which side of your family?"

"My dad's."

Spicer scratched some notes. "Do you know how old she was when she first developed symptoms?"

"I don't know. I can't remember a time when she was...normal. Why? Is it hereditary?"

"No," Spicer said. "At least not in the way you mean. However, certain families can be predisposed to contract the disorder. It is rare, however, that a person develops symptoms in their fifties. How was your aunt treated?"

"She took medication." Ed pressed his eyebrows together. "And she was committed a few times."

"Did the medication help?" Spicer fidgeted with her glasses.

"Not as far as I could tell." Ed looked down.

Spicer jotted down more notes.

"Is this my future doc? In and out of mental institutions, medication?" Ed had seen Aunt Pearline deteriorate and become dependent on her brothers and sisters until her death. He didn't want that for himself.

"Let's not get ahead of ourselves. Tell me about the voice."

"Well, it's kind of hard to explain. It seems to manifest in stressful situations."

"It bothers you?"

"Yes."

"You don't like what it says?" Spicer continued to write.

"No."

"Why?"

"I don't know what you mean."

"I think you do know what I mean," Spicer said.

"I really don't." Ed leaned back.

Spicer checked her notes. "You said the voice was one issue. What's the other?"

"I can't fire my weapon." Ed clasped his hands in front of him. "Uh, at least not when I need to."

"You'll have to explain that one to me."

Ed told her about the Anthony Deavers, Dave Malone, and Gary Waverly cases and how he had come to Lake Hope. Spicer was writing furiously and looked up when he finished.

"You had mandatory counseling after the Deavers shooting, right?"

"Yes. It was kind of a check-the-box thing."

"And this mental block never came up?"

Ed shrugged. "I had no idea I had it. The doctor gave me some meditation exercises. I thought I was okay."

"Why did you quit?" Spicer asked.

"Pardon me?"

"You said you thought you were okay, but you quit and moved down to Lake Hope." Spicer pushed her glasses up on her nose. "That's a pretty drastic move for someone who thought he was okay."

"I just didn't want to..." *What didn't I want to do? What, be a cop anymore?* "...I guess it was a way of being a cop without being a cop. Does that make sense?"

Spicer didn't answer Ed's question. "Now circumstances have forced you to be a cop again, but you're not quitting."

"I thought about it." Ed turned to look out the window. It had begun to rain. Fat beads of water formed on the window. "It's not a good time."

"What is compelling you to stay?"

"It's complicated," Ed said.

"I do complicated." Spicer cocked her head as if dealing with a dull child. "It's kind of in the job title."

*I like her,* the voice said.

Ed blinked and turned away.

"It just happened, didn't it?" Spicer sat up straight.

"Yes." Even though it was why he was there, Ed was embarrassed. He thought again of his aunt talking to the mysterious government agency through the walls.

"What did it say?"

"He says he likes you," Ed mumbled.

"Of course he does." Spicer had a satisfied grin on her face.

Ed looked at the floor. "If I can't use my weapon—"

"You're not going to quit," Spicer said.

Ed looked up, his face twisting in puzzlement.

"If you wanted to quit, you would have driven right past Columbus and back to Akron. You came here because you can't do your job if you're unable to use your firearm, and you want me to fix you."

Ed had to admit she was correct. He was useless without the ability to employ his weapon, but the thought of passing on the responsibility to someone else seemed abhorrent.

"How are you sleeping?"

"Not like a baby."

"How often do you dream about the Deavers shooting?"

"A lot."

"Trouble concentrating?"

"Yes. But I have ADHD."

"Any hallucinations other than the voice? Objects or people that are not there? Noises or smells?"

"No."

Spicer wrote it down. Ed half expected her to say that he was really messed up and beyond hope. Instead, she put down her pad and slid back.

"One thing I will say is that while we can't rule it out, I'm not seeing schizophrenia. I think you may have Post Traumatic Stress Disorder that you never dealt with. Your hallucinations could be your brain struggling to deal with the guilt of shooting an unarmed teen. You're torn between flight—wanting to quit law enforcement—and fight—your sense of duty that won't allow you to run away when you're needed. You law enforcement types are a stoic bunch. Never share your feelings. Never admit weakness until something snaps. I'm lecturing now. I don't mean to."

"It's okay," Ed said. He liked Spicer as well. She wasn't the stereotypical so-how-does-that-make-you-feel doctor, and he preferred her directness. "What do I do?"

"I need to see you at least once a week," Spicer said.

"That might be tough."

Spicer's eyes narrowed. "You want to get better or not?"

**"We have** to find out where his hot spots are," Ed said.

They stood inside the station near the end of Andy's shift and the beginning of Nancy's.

Nancy went to the area map. "We know he can disappear from the tracks, and we can infer those same abilities exist at the Moonville Tunnel."

"Why the tunnel?" Andy sat on the edge of his desk, twirling a pen in his fingers.

"The Moonville Tunnel is where Hudak was supposed to have been killed." Ed joined Nancy at the map. "If his power to disappear or teleport is in any way dependent on areas of significance, then it stands to reason that the tunnel would be one of those areas."

"And if we're wrong about that?" Andy said.

Ed waved his hand. "Then we're going to die."

Nancy walked to her desk and sat. Dark patches marred her fair skin, and wrinkles creased her uniform as if it had been slept in. The last few nights were frustrating. A report of a strange man with a light in the woods reached their office, but it was nothing concrete.

Ed walked to the coffeemaker and poured Nancy a cup. He took it to her desk and set it down along with two small cups of non-dairy creamer. Nancy looked up gratefully, pulled the lid off, and added the cream.

A loud buzz made them all straighten up. Few visitors came to the office during the day and almost none at night. Had Hudak attacked someone while they were dithering about what to do? He rushed to the door and paused at the security monitor.

Savannah Hughes, looking resplendent in a clingy black dress and high heels, stood in the glow of the light over the door. She looked up expectantly at the monitor, wearing a broad, dimpled smile. Against her right leg, she tapped a cloth wine tote bag. Ed looked back at the others before pulling the door open. Savannah swayed past him and entered the room. Ed glanced at Nancy, who watched him intently.

*Keep your eyes up, or that one will cut you smooth*, the voice said.

"This is quaint," Savannah said, moving into the lounge area. She sat on the couch with a sweeping flourish of her arms.

"Ms. Hughes," Ed said, "we're in the middle of something."

Savannah feigned shock by putting her hand over her chest like a Southern belle. "Well, is this how you treat a guest?"

"Guest?" Nancy said with enough venom for Ed to silence her with a look.

"Yes, I just rented one of your large housekeeping cabins. A little rustic for my taste but comfy," Savannah said.

"Why?" Ed asked, dragging it out.

That time, the reporter used both hands to display faux surprise. "Can't a girl get out in nature?"

"Ms. Hughes," Ed said.

"All right." She put both hands up. "Believe it or not, I came here to help."

"Help us with what?" Andy said.

Hughes smiled, revealing brilliant teeth. "Oh, please, you guys didn't think for a minute I bought that bullshit at the press conference."

"I don't know what you're talking about." Ed looked at Andy and Nancy.

Hughes reached into her bra but paused to look

directly at Ed before pulling out a folded sheet of paper. Ed took it, perused it, and handed it to Andy, who in turn handed it to Nancy.

"Autopsy face sheet," Nancy said.

"The real face sheet," Hughes corrected.

"What do you want?" Ed sat next to the reporter. Nancy fidgeted. "We've been looking for the story online, and we haven't seen anything. You want me to comment first? You could have done that over the phone."

Hughes reached out and patted Ed's knee. "I'm not here to blow up your investigation. I'm going to help."

"And get yourself a nice, sensational story in the bargain," Nancy said.

Hughes leaned back against the couch. "Yes, I'm going to get a hell of a story out of this. National exposure, if I have my way, but I can also bring something to the table."

"What's that?" Andy tilted his head.

"Resources. Night cameras, motion sensors — state of the art." Hughes spread her arms. "Gentlemen, and lady, we're going to catch ourselves a ghost on camera!"

Andy's face turned pink. "We don't need you, lady. We can get that stuff for ourselves."

"Really? How are you going to do that? Order equipment from Columbus? Oh, but you haven't told them you've been out every night chasing ghosts."

"No one said anything about ghosts." Ed stood.

Hughes rolled her eyes. "If we're going to work together, and we *will* be working together, you have to be honest with me. No more BS."

Ed looked at the others. Andy nodded, and Nancy shook her head vigorously.

"He's not a ghost. He's flesh and blood," Ed said.

"And how do you know that?" Hughes asked.

"Because we have a sample of his blood."

"Well, now, that *is* interesting. It's going to be nice working with you, but a girl's got to get her rest. If you need me—" She paused and looked at Ed. "—I've rented cabin forty-eight. I'll have a surprise for you in the morning."

They all watched her walk out the door. When she was gone, Nancy turned to Ed. "Chief, you can't be serious about working with that—reporter!"

"I don't think we have a choice, Nancy."

"She's right about the resources," Andy said. "I don't trust her either, but if we put cameras all over the park, we won't have to kill ourselves with these long hours, hoping to be in the right place at the right time. We can set up monitoring right here in the station, and when something pops, we can be right there. Besides, she could have blown this whole thing up if she wanted to."

"It's a fair point." Ed looked out the window. "Tonight, we'll do our normal thing. Tomorrow, we'll get the cameras up, and I'll write a new schedule. Get you guys back on regular eight-hour shifts before you drop. Speaking of shifts, we'd better get out there."

"Right, chief." Andy picked up his radio and headed for the door.

Nancy grabbed hers as well but hung back after Andy left. "Chief, you can't trust her, and you know it."

"I don't know what your problem is with Savannah," Ed said.

"My problem is that all she had to do was come in here swinging her hips and you gave her the run of the place."

"That's not fair. She has value."

184

"Oh, you mean the cameras?" Nancy said. "Are you sure that's the equipment you're interested in?"

Ed took a step back. "Nancy, what's this about?"

"You know what it's about," she said. "Are we going to talk about what happened in your cabin?"

*Oh, this is going to be good,* the voice said.

Ed looked over his shoulder.

"Stop looking around," Nancy said. "There's no one here. Just you and me."

*Yeah, stop looking around.*

"We shouldn't talk about this," Ed said.

"When should we talk about it, after Hudak lays us out on the track and the ghost train spreads our intestines all over the place?"

"I-I can't deal with this now." Ed tried to walk to his office but Nancy stepped in front of him, getting on her tiptoes to press her face close to his. A crimson hue colored her features.

"Why can't you deal with it, because of rules and regulations? Bringing Savannah in is against the rules but you had no problem with that one!"

*She got you there, hoss!* The voice grew louder and louder in Ed's head, nearly drowning Nancy out. *It's about time somebody called you out on your self righteous bullshit!*

"Do you know what I think?" Nancy said. Ed tried to go around her but she moved right and left to keep him in front. "I think you're afraid. You use rules and regulations to avoid anything that might disrupt the neat little world you built for yourself."

"Nancy, please."

"Rules are fine, and everyone has to live by them. But anything taken to an extreme can be a trap, a prison—a place to hide. Now I want to hear you tell me you don't know what I'm talking about. Tell me you don't have feelings for me!"

*She's got your number and you've got nobody to blame but yourself. You led her on. Gave her mixed signals. And when she acted on it, you pushed her away. She's the best thing that could have happened to you and she's right. You're nothing but a coward! A sniveling coward hiding in your self imposed purgatory!*

Ed clamped both hands over his ears. "Oh my god, shut up!" he yelled.

Ed's eyes opened wide.

Nancy's jaw dropped. "Shut up? Shut up? That's where you want to take this. You're pulling rank on me?"

"No, no." Ed held his hands out, but Nancy was already moving toward the door.

She stopped, turned, and saluted. "Yes, sir, chief. I'll shut up!" She slammed the door behind her.

Ed dropped his face into his hands.

*That went well*, the voice said.

**"So, you** and Nancy?" Savannah Hughes said, sitting in the passenger's seat of Ed's cruiser the following morning. She wore tight blue jeans, a black tank, and Converse shoes. Ed noticed the left cuff on her jeans was turned up in the back but forced himself to look away.

"No." He waited for the annoying voice to step in with a vulgar witticism, but it remained silent.

Perhaps their fight, if you could call it that, had been a good thing. Whatever was happening between them only added more stress. Though he hadn't consciously intended to push Nancy away, his response to her outburst may have done just that. He waited for confirmation, but the voice remained silent. Ed pulled into the parking lot of Ellis Hall at the Ohio University Campus. Hughes had a contact there who might be able to shed light on Jackie Hudak.

Ellis Hall was a typical early-twentieth-century campus building with a brick exterior and Doric columns supporting a capital façade entryway. Though built specifically for classrooms and lecture halls, it could have been, as many of its contemporaries were, donated from the estates of Ohio's wealthy industrialists. Ed could imagine guests ascending the grand entrance to be introduced by uniformed staff who would usher them into the ballroom capable of accommodating hundreds of guests.

Associate Professor Audrey Mason's office was on the second floor. Small and windowless, Ed suspected that it had been converted from a storage room. At six foot two, she was an inch taller than Ed. She extended a bony hand and offered them each a chair. Mason's light brown hair hung loosely in no particular style. Stick a bandana on her head, and she could have easily passed for a flower child in the 1960s.

Ed's ADHD was in overdrive as there seemed to be no straight lines in the office. Books leaned haphazardly against one another on shelves that appeared too flimsy to carry the weight. Both Mason's IN and OUT mail organizers overflowed with handwritten notes, envelopes, and typed papers. Whenever Ed tried to focus on Mason, something else caught his eye. Finally, he closed them and placed the thought on the river of marigolds to refocus his attention.

*You're a mess*, the voice said.

Ed agreed. He just had to hang on until they got

Hudak. Then they could put him away in a nice 1930s-style sanitorium. The kind with large picture windows overlooking a vast plain. Orderlies in white jumpsuits would roll him out onto a wrap-around porch where they would read to him. There he would lean back, blissfully zonked out on Thorazine or Haldol.

"So what brings you to Professor Spooky?" Mason said jovially.

The word "spooky" snapped Ed back to reality. He wondered if he had looked out of it.

"Professor Spooky?" Savannah said.

"That's what the undergrads call me, affectionately of course. Early American superstitions is popular with the students, but I'm afraid my colleagues are less enthused." She opened her hands. "That's why I'm in here."

"That's why I contacted you." Savannah scooted her chair closer, which was hardly necessary in the tiny room, but Ed followed suit. "As I said on the phone, we're interested in the legend of Jackie Hudak."

"What can I tell you?" Mason reached into a desk drawer and pulled out a manila envelope.

"First, was he a real person, or is he a composite of some kind?" Ed asked.

Mason's eyes gleamed like a small child who was about to get her favorite treat. "Well put. The answer is both. He was a real person for sure, but whether others added or took away from his life story, that's another matter. Here's what I know. Hudak's family were West Virginia coal miners who moved to Moonville sometime between the wars. They had bad timing because this was around the time that the mines in Moonville began to decline, and they supposedly turned to subsistence farming. When Jackie was eighteen, he got a job at the railroad."

Mason's cell phone buzzed. She silenced it with a touch.

"There wasn't much to do in Moonville, so men passed their time by getting drunk on bootleg liquor. Jackie's favorite drinking spot was the ledge overlooking the tunnel. I'm sure you've heard the story of his death in the Moonville Tunnel."

"Only that he died there," Ed said.

"Supposedly, he was in a brawl with several men. He was knocked over the ledge onto the tracks and couldn't get out of the way before the train hit him. Or, he was walking home drunk, cut through the tunnel, and couldn't get out in time. In that version, he died desperately waving his lantern to warn the train."

"What happened to Hudak's family?" Savannah asked.

Mason pulled out an old black-and-white photograph. "They died one by one, all before their time. Freak accidents, mostly. One was run over by a train."

Ed and Savannah exchanged glances.

Mason looked back and forth between the two of them. "What?"

"Nothing. Go on," Ed said.

"I want you to look at this and tell me what's wrong." Mason stared at the photograph.

Ed squinted at the grainy image. He saw a white two-story colonial house near a creek and railroad tracks. The porch sat high, most likely due to the creek flooding during heavy rains. But the most remarkable features were the entry doors. On both the front and side, Ed could see two distinct doorways, one bricked up and the other immediately to its left, intact. "What the hell?"

Mason's eyes lit up with delight. "That's the Hudak house, and apparently, they believed they had an evil spirit in their midst."

"An evil spirit?" Savannah trapped the photo with a finger and slid it closer. "How can you tell?"

"In the superstitions of that time and area, people had several ways to deal with evil spirits. One was to brick up all doorways leading to the outside and put a new door next to it. They believed the evil spirit would become confused when it tried to reenter and go away." Mason retrieved the photograph from Savannah and placed it in the envelope.

"I don't think it worked," Savannah said.

"So no members of the family survived?" Ed said.

"Well," Mason said. "That's not certain. There was a little girl in the house, but there was no record of what happened to her. It's entirely possible that she survived to live out the remainder of her life."

"Do you know the girl's name?" Ed asked.

"No, I'm sorry. I don't. I could do some more digging and get back to you."

"Thank you. That would be very helpful." Ed stood to leave. "I wonder if I could take pictures of those with my phone?"

"Of course," Mason said. "But don't you want to see a picture of Jackie Hudak first?"

Ed's mouth dropped open. "You have a picture of Jackie Hudak?"

"We think so."

Mason pulled another photograph from the envelope. It showed seven children posing outside a one-room schoolhouse. Towering over the rest was a chubby kid with curly blond hair. From his features, Ed guessed that he was nine or ten, but big for his age. Ironically, he was wearing overalls. Mason stabbed the blond kid with her fingernail.

"We think that's Jackie Hudak."

"Holy crap." Savannah clapped a hand over her mouth.

As Ed took photos with his phone, Mason said, "Can I ask why you're so interested in Jackie Hudak?"

"Research," they both answered simultaneously.

They had agreed on the excuse, but botched the delivery so badly it was unlikely Mason bought their story.

"We're considering adding a Jackie Hudak ghost tour at the state park, and Savannah—Ms. Hughes—is covering it," Ed stammered.

"I see." Audrey Mason eyed them suspiciously as they left the office.

**That evening**, at the station, Ed and Savannah briefed Nancy and Andy on their trip to Athens. Nancy alternately stabbed Savannah and Ed with a dagger-like stare. Ed passed out blown-up copies of the photographs taken with his phone.

"So this is Jackie Hudak?" Andy said. "He was a cute fella. Hard to believe he would grow up to be the boogeyman."

"The more we understand about him, the more it will help us catch him," Savannah added.

"We? *Us*?" Nancy said. She turned to Ed. "You going to give her a weapon now?"

"Nancy," Ed said.

"No." Savannah stood. "Let her say what she means."

"We're not going to do this." Ed held up his hand.

"Savannah is here to get a story. She was straight up about that, but she has resources that we don't have access to, and not just the equipment she brought. So, we're going to help her get her story, and she's going to help us get Hudak. We go into this thing divided, and he'll chew us up. Is that clear?"

Nancy blinked, and quietly said, "Yes, chief."

"Good, let's get on with this." Ed looked around to ensure everyone was paying attention. "We know Hudak was at least, at some point, human and something happened that changed him fundamentally."

"And has given him powers we don't understand," Savannah said.

"But we know he has limitations. The blood from the Morton killing. He can be hurt," Ed said.

"Or die," Andy said.

"So that's our strategy. We just shoot him on sight?" The voice was Nancy's, but the tone was subdued. Ed didn't care. She was participating again.

Ed rubbed his eyes. He needed sleep. "I don't know. It's our job to bring him to justice, but what does justice look like for him?"

Andy laughed. "I can't see him sittin' in a jail cell waiting for trial. I can just imagine the judge asking him where he's from. 'Well, that's complicated, your honor.'"

They all laughed, even Nancy.

"I hear what you're saying," Ed said, still smiling, "but I think we're obligated to at least try to apprehend him. If he resists, that's another story."

"Okay, chief. But if he flinches, I'm going to send him on to glory," Andy said.

# Chapter 19

"**Nancy, you good?**" **Ed's** soothing voice came over the radio.

"Okay, chief," she radioed back.

Nancy knew Ed was watching the multiscreen display from his office.

Midnight was only a few minutes away, and Nancy's shift had been uneventful. She didn't know how Ed was doing it. Nancy and Andy had returned to normal shift hours, but Ed was operating on three or four hours of sleep every day. She admired his determination and dedication to duty. No, she *loved* him for it. A small gasp escaped her. It was the first time she had even thought of the L-word, and it scared her. She was sure he felt the same about her but wouldn't realize it until he dislodged that huge stick from his ass.

She supposed it was why she reacted as she did when Miss Savannah "look at my body" Hughes inserted herself into their little group. Nancy was ashamed at the thought of it. She was behaving like a teenager who had been dumped by her first crush. She had always worn her heart on her sleeve, and it sometimes got her into trouble.

Nancy should have been used to rejection by then. Her biological dad ran out on her family before her fourth birthday. Nancy moved around with her mother, Susan, who drifted from job to dead-end job. When Nancy was ten, Susan met Greg, a handsy, alcoholic contractor with long hair and a boyish smile. Despite his boozing, Nancy liked Greg, mostly because of the effect he had on her mother.

Greg always had a job, and when they lived with him, they had a nice apartment and plenty to eat. Nancy had no clue, at least at first, that the way he touched her was inappropriate. She had developed early, and his hands always found her breasts and buttocks. He never penetrated her, although she came to understand that he wanted to. Whenever his hands went "down there," she pretended to giggle and push his hand away.

The three of them played a delicate and dangerous game of chicken for three years. Nancy's mother pretended not to know while trying to keep Greg from going too far to fill some sick void with a little girl. And Nancy tried to hold their psychotic family together without paying too high a price.

In the end, Greg threw them out onto the street. Nancy's mother didn't openly blame her, but she became sullen and despondent. They drifted back into poverty. In the dark, when no one was around, Nancy told herself that if she had given Greg what he wanted—all that he wanted—their lives would have been easier. It didn't matter that she wasn't in the least to blame. That knowledge gave her no solace.

At seventeen, Nancy moved in with the first guy who smiled at her. She joined the United States Army two years later. During her multiple deployments, she learned that her boyfriend, Guy — *Freud might say it was no coincidence his name started with a "G" too* — ran around with everything in a skirt.

When she got out of the Army, she didn't even return to retrieve her belongings. She wanted a fresh new start. As she sat recalling the events of her life, she realized her fear of abandonment was affecting her.

"Damn," she whispered to herself, putting the car in gear. "I'm going to have to apologize."

**Ed sat** in his office reading reports on his computer screen. To his left sat a forty-two-inch monitor showing the six cameras Andy set up around the park. Andy had set the monitor to beep whenever the camera's motion sensor was activated. Ed could then select the camera he wanted, causing it to fill the monitor, rewind, or playback.

Because Hudak seemed to be nocturnal, the cameras were off during the daytime. So far, Ed had recorded only deer, squirrels, and frogs. He heard the front door open and, through the glass, saw Nancy come in.

*Here it comes*, the voice said.

Ed reached into his small refrigerator, pulled out a can of Nature Boost, and drank. Nancy walked with her shoulders slumped, looking at the floor in front of her. Ed relaxed. She wasn't prepared for a fight.

"Can I talk to you, chief?" Nancy said.

Ed motioned to a chair, and she sat.

Nancy's eyes looked like they were searching for the right words. "What happened between us, or almost happened —"

"We shouldn't talk about it," Ed said.

Nancy's shoulders relaxed even further. "I'm sorry about the way I acted."

"I didn't help." Ed smiled.

"You see, I have a hard time —" Nancy bit her lower lip. "I just need to know if we're good."

"We're good." Ed got up, walked to the front of his desk, and sat on its edge in front of her. "Nancy, when I yelled 'shut up' —"

"I was completely out of line. You had every right."

"No, that's not what I mean," Ed said.

*Don't*, the voice warned.

"I wasn't talking to you."

*Don't do it*, the voice repeated more forcefully.

Nancy cocked her head. "Who were you talking to?" she said slowly.

Ed looked away. "For the past few weeks, I've been hearing a voice. Hallucinating, really. Shrink says it has something to do with the Deavers shooting. I don't know. I'm just trying to handle it."

*I can't believe you did that. Do you* want *to end up in a lunatic asylum?* the voice taunted.

There was a long uncomfortable pause during which Nancy continued to stare at him, her head still cocked.

*You did it now. She's trying to figure out if she can get to the door in time*, the voice said.

"You need to say something." Ed slid off the desk and returned to his seat.

The silence hung between them for a few more seconds before she said, "And I thought *I* was messed up."

Ed stared into her eyes. Then, simultaneously, they burst out laughing.

"I can't pretend to understand everything you're going through, but I'll be here for you. Maybe you're not feeling all that confident now. All I can say is that I've been in combat, and I wouldn't want to be in this fight with anyone else. Look at how far we've come with this Hudak thing. *You* got us this far, chief."

Nancy touched Ed's shoulder as she left the office. Watching her walk away, Ed felt a sense of calm he hadn't experienced in weeks. He turned his attention to the voice. Fighting it hadn't been effective. He couldn't simply banish it downstream as he could with negative thoughts. Perhaps opening up to it was the way. But wasn't having a full-on dialogue with oneself the very definition of insanity?

Ed inhaled deeply and exhaled a slow count of ten. He cleared his mind and waited for the voice to come. Nothing. Another deep breath—

Ed stood. "Very funny."

# Chapter 20

George Riley sat outside a general store in Zaleski. His red beard hung between his legs like a ginger ZZ Top. Grabbing it just under his chin, he stroked it to a point where it fanned out again. He had no idea why he did this. It was just a habit, he supposed.

Two empty bottles of Wild Irish Rose Red sat at his feet. George briefly thought of taking them over to the dumpster twenty feet to his left. In his current condition, however, twenty feet seemed very far away.

He looked at his watch. It was a little after ten at night. In an hour, he would stretch out on the porch and go to sleep. Any earlier and Mark, the store owner, would come and roust him away. Mark said bums sleeping on his porch was bad for business. That hurt George because he wasn't a bum, at least not technically.

Bums were homeless, and George had a home. His girlfriend Zelda lived right up the street. He could go there anytime—well, not anytime. She had taken his key and forbidden him to come home drunk, mostly because he beat her when he was in this state. She always said something to set him off or refused to have sex with him when he was plastered. As he was drunk more often than not, he spent a lot of nights on the street.

A thought occurred to George. Did the fact that he spent more nights on the street than in his home make him a bum by default?

"It is a philosophical question," he said, holding his finger in the air like Linus in the *Peanuts* cartoons.

Unlike Linus, he slurred his words.

"Shut up, Georgie!" Mark called from his apartment upstairs. "And go home!"

George did shut up but he couldn't go home just yet. Maybe he could sneak a little nap and then go home after he sobered up a little. He stretched out on the porch and closed his eyes.

What seemed like only a moment later, George's breathing became restricted. A large hand had clamped around his neck and dragged him down the street.

George tried to pull the hand away, but it was strong. George dug at the fingers with his nails. The man didn't seem to notice, or maybe he just didn't care about the pain. George's eyes bulged and his mouth worked up and down, trying to catch a breath.

Swirls of light danced in front of his eyes, and his arms became heavy. He tried to look at his assailant, but a combination of darkness and the awkward angle gave him only a vague outline of the man's shoulder and profile.

George's feet dragged on the pavement. A desperate thought occurred to him. He reached into his pocket. His fingers found the Raven MP-25 pistol there. His father's generation would refer to it as a "Saturday Night Special." It was as likely to blow up in his hand as fire its .25 caliber bullets. George's vision blurred. He saw spots. He shoved the barrel over his head and fired blindly.

George's attacker snatched him off the ground and threw him. He was airborne a moment before he hit something hard and metal. His mind went blank.

**The following** morning, Ed sat at his desk reviewing footage from the night before. In the outer office, he saw the receding hairline of Doug Weems bobbing up and down and reasoned that he was on the phone. Perhaps he was talking to Waddell. Ed didn't like having someone on his squad he couldn't trust.

Weems was an experienced deputy, and they could use his help, but his relationship with Waddell made that impossible. Ed was already out on a limb. Utilizing resources without the full knowledge of his superiors could get him fired.

*And don't forget your little honey*, the voice said.

Ed gasped and looked around. For the first time, he thought he recognized the voice. It was Kevy, a foul-mouthed kid who used to hang around when Ed was a teenager.

He was a little smart-ass, and Ed would have beaten him up, but Kevy was always small for his age.

*Oh, you thought I was gone? You don't know me very well, do you?* The last part mimicked the voice of Bugs Bunny.

Ed reached into his desk drawer and pulled out a small bottle of naproxen sodium. His hands shook and pills shot out in all directions. Amazingly, Ed was able to catch three in his hand and popped them all into his mouth.

He didn't have a headache and didn't really know what he expected the NSAID to do. He waited for a smart comeback from Kevy. When none came, he bent to gather the wayward pills.

Doug Weems walked to the door and rapped on the frame. "Chief, you've got a call," he said.

Ed looked up. "Who is it?"

"Sheriff Potter."

Weems had been on the phone too long just to transfer a call. He must have been trying to pump Potter for information, but Ed was confident the sheriff didn't share anything sensitive.

"Put him through," Ed said, picking up the phone and putting it to his ear.

"Ed?" Potter said.

"Holt, what's up?"

"Can you come over? I've got something weird to share with you," Potter said.

"Weird is my department these days. I'll be right over." Ed put down the phone and headed for the door.

An hour later, Ed and Holt Potter pulled up in front of the Athens County Sheriff's Office, a quaint two-story brick building on Washington Street. Next door, a coffeehouse with the unfortunate name Donkey Coffee offered Wi-Fi, espresso, and music.

Sheriff Dirk Lambert had a gleaming bald head and meaty forearms. His office was spartan with just two cloth chairs that could have been ordered from an Ikea catalog in front of a large teak desk. Ed wondered how much a man had to work out before his lower arm bulged out further than his biceps but couldn't reach a satisfying conclusion. Holt Potter, pole-like in comparison, stood to his left, looking over Lambert's office. On the ride over, Holt had said there was something weird Ed had to see. Surely Dirk wasn't it?

Also, unlike Potter, there was little to indicate Lambert's

background. Just a photograph of an apparent wife and child, certificates from various academies, including a stint at the FBI National Academy for local law enforcement, and a pair of handcuffs in a frame.

"Well now, this should be interesting," Lambert said, motioning the two men to have a seat. His voice was one of those that, while not loud, must have carried a great distance. "Holt, why don't you tell us why we're here?"

Holt turned to Ed. "We were at our monthly sheriff's meeting where we normally share war stories. Dirk, uh, Sheriff Lambert—"

"Dirk," Lambert corrected.

"—told us about a case they were working on. A woman reported that her boyfriend had been murdered on the old Moonville Rail Trail." Holt hesitated. "Said she heard a train come through, and it looked like he had been run over by it."

"She was high as Mount Everest," Dirk said. "My deputies found her walking down the street bare-ass naked, and you do not, I repeat, *not* want to see this woman naked. Not only did she not know where she left her clothes, but she didn't remember how she got naked in the first place. Anyway, she had a warrant for passing bad checks, so my deputies ran her in. We didn't put any stock in it until a couple walking their dog found some remains, just where she said it happened."

Ed perked up. "What was the condition of the body?"

Dirk shook his massive bald head. He looked like a comic book character that Ed couldn't quite place.

*Juggernaut,* Kevy offered helpfully, and Ed had to admit he was right. His head was shaped like Juggernaut's helmet.

"Animals got to it. You could hardly tell it had been

human. No telling how long it had been out there. The couple wouldn't have found it if the dog hadn't started digging."

"Did you determine the cause of death?" Ed asked.

Dirk's laugh sounded somewhere between a wheeze and a cough. "Could've been measles for all we know. We found part of a pelvis, though. Looked like it had been pulverized."

Ed and Holt exchanged glances.

"What's going on?" Dirk looked back and forth between the two men.

"It just seems similar to a case I'm working on," Ed said.

"Nah, you're not getting away with that." Dirk smiled broadly. "There's something you two aren't telling me."

Ed looked at Holt, who shook his head slightly as if to say, *Don't tell him.*

"It's just that we had a death on the Moonville Rail Trail," Ed said.

"And?" Dirk moved his hand in a circular motion.

"That's it. We found a body there. Sounds like there might be a connection."

"Now, look," All of Dirk's features drew into the middle of his face and his mouth set in a flat, straight line. "You come all the way up here to get information, I lay it out for you, and you don't even have the courtesy to let me know what's going on."

"It's not that." Ed held up his hands. He glanced at Holt for help, but he stared straight ahead.

"There are some aspects to the case that may seem bizarre."

"We do bizarre here," Dirk said. "Go for it."

Ed started to say something, then pressed his lips

closed.

"Well, that's too bad." Dirk said. "If you were working on something, you could speak to the witness."

"She's still in custody?" Ed asked. "Did she see anything?"

"See what?" Dirk said deliberately.

"Okay." Ed dropped his head, pulled out his phone, and searched for the video that Andy found on Meghan's phone.

*He's going to laugh at you.*

Ed closed his eyes and tried to put the thought into the stream but couldn't concentrate. "We found this on the phone of a girl who was found on the trail. It looked — it looked like she had been run over by a train."

"A train?" Dirk said, taking the phone. "You realize that there hasn't been a train through there in forty years?"

"That would be the strange part."

After looking at the video, Dirk handed the phone back to Ed. "A fake video?"

"It's not fake. At least, not according to my guy."

"Come on, what are you saying here, Ed?" Dirk spread his hands out. "A train rolled down non-existent tracks and killed the girl? You can't be serious."

"We know that two things are true. First, the girl was killed, and second, this video indicates a train where there couldn't be a train."

"Well, you don't actually see a train." Dirk turned the phone as if looking at it from a different angle would make a difference. "It could be sound effects."

"To what purpose?"

Dirk grinned. "I don't know, maybe to frighten her."

"She seemed pretty damned scared already," Holt said.

"But a train?" Dirk leaned back and interlaced his fingers. "Really? There has to be some other explanation."

Ed leaned forward. "What about the pulverized bones? Doesn't that indicate that your guy was hit by something heavy as well?"

"Got to admit that we were stumped by that one, and there's more. When we did a neighborhood canvas, people living on Route Three-Fifty-Six reported hearing what sounded like a train a couple of weeks back. Not many cars travel that road at night, so it's pretty still out there. That's why the neighbors remembered hearing a train. Some of them were old enough to remember when trains still ran through there. Still, I can't subscribe to this train business, unless there's something else you want to tell me?"

"I apologize for my reticence earlier. You can imagine what it's like to talk to someone about this." Ed told him about the killings, leaving out the more exotic parts.

"Well, let's talk to our witness. I warn you, she's a doozy." Dirk pushed a button on his phone. "Stu, bring in that Julie what's-her-name they brought in the other day."

A voice came back. "Julie Rafferty. Yes, sheriff."

Dirk looked at his guests. "Cover your eyes. They're about to open Pandora's box."

Five minutes later, a deputy walked in with a woman so emaciated she had to hold up her orange jail bottoms with her left hand. She stepped soundlessly with the grace of a ballet dancer. Ed wondered what her life had been like before drugs took hold of her.

The deputy, Stu from the intercom, pulled out one of the outer chairs. Julie sat, folding her hands in her lap like a schoolgirl who was about to be scolded by the principal.

206

With a nod from the sheriff, Stu walked out of the room. Ed noticed his handcuff holder was unbuttoned but forced his attention back to the matter at hand. He had forgotten to bring his Nature Boost, and it was beginning to affect his concentration.

*Go ahead and chug that shit until it stops your heart like a dollar watch.*

*Shut up, Kevy,* Ed thought back.

*Uh-oh, you gave me a name. Now you're really crazy. In a week, you're going to look like that based-out whore, talking to yourself and scratching your arms.*

Ed closed his eyes and took a deep breath. He conjured the image of the stream and carefully placed each word on a marigold until it floated away, tumbling gently over the waterfall.

"Ed?" Dirk said.

Ed opened his eyes and everyone, even Julie, stared at him. He blinked twice and smiled.

"Okay, buddy? We lost you for a minute."

Ed rubbed the back of his neck. "Yeah, sorry. I've got a headache coming on. Been a long week. You were saying?"

"I was just asking if you had any questions for Miss Rafferty," Dirk said.

"Well, Miss Rafferty ain't agreed to talk about nothing!" she said. "What do I get out of talking to you, huh? You gonna drop these lame-ass charges, sheriff?"

Dirk leaned forward, his eyes closed to narrow slits and his Juggernaut head tilted toward Julie. "How about I drop your ass back in your cell and discontinue your methadone?"

Julie hugged herself and looked at the floor. Then she turned to Ed with an expectant look. Ed knew that a junkie's greatest fear was being locked up in a place without access to drugs. In many jails, drugs were smuggled in and could be obtained as easily as on the outside. Apparently, Athens County was not one of those places, and even the mild relief from methadone was better than withdrawals.

"That's what I thought," Dirk said. "Go ahead, Ed."

"Well, why don't you just tell me what you told the deputies?" Ed asked. He took out a notebook and pen.

She said, "Me and Wheel—"

"Wheel would be Gareth Cauthorne," Dirk said, squinting at his computer screen.

"Anyway, me and Wheel were, um—" Julie paused and looked at Dirk.

Dirk waved her off. "We already told your attorney we wouldn't charge you with anything you told us as long as you tell us the truth."

"Well, we were getting high, you see, and Wheel had to go pee—excuse me—urinate."

Ed wanted to laugh but held it down.

"He went outside, and he was gone too long. I thought he might have some more stuff and was keeping it to himself. That's when I heard what sounded like a train rushing right by the trailer. It even shook the ground a little bit, and that was the strange part 'cause there ain't even no tracks there anymore. I went up to the trail where the tracks used to be, but there was nothing there."

"Did you see anyone?" Ed asked.

"Not exactly."

"What does that mean?" Ed leaned forward.

Looking around, Julie's head moved in quick jerks like a bird. She already had the furtive eyes of a drug addict, but they had become even more animated, darting around like an animal that caught the scent of a predator. It was as if she expected someone to jump out and get her even though she sat with three law enforcement officers.

"I saw a light, a lamp or something. It was too dark to see what was holding it."

"You mean, *who* was holding it?" Ed said.

"I mean *what*. Even though I couldn't see who it was, there was something off about it—something not right." Julie rubbed her arms as if she had just been hit by a draft, or maybe it was just a junkie itch.

"Did you look for Wheel after that?"

Tears welled in Julie's eyes. "I found him, I mean what was left of him, on the trail. He was all smashed up. I went to look for some stuff, trying to forget. I never went back. Then I got busted. I tried to tell the cops what happened, but they wouldn't believe me. I know what you all think of me. Strung out meth whore! It doesn't matter what happens to us. Society will be better off without us."

"We're just trying to find out what happened to your friend, Wheel," Ed said. "Tell me more about this lamp. What did it look like?"

Julie turned to him. "I couldn't see it. It was just a light in the distance."

"How did you know it was a lamp?"

Julie rubbed her chin with a long, thin hand. It appeared so dry Ed thought that she could start a fire if she rubbed too hard.

"It looked like it was bobbing." She paused, thinking. "Not bobbing, swaying."

Julie rocked her hand back and forth, much in the way Joshua Morton had done, ages ago it seemed. Ed looked at Holt Potter and knew he had made the same connection.

"What?" Dirk said.

Ed didn't answer. "One more thing. How long ago did this happen?"

Julie looked at the floor in front of her. "I'll tell you the truth, mister. I'm not all that good with time."

Ed understood. From the many drug addicts he'd arrested as a patrol officer, he learned that chasing the dragon was a full-time occupation. Time meant nothing. The only thing that mattered was getting that next hit as soon as the high wore off, sometimes before. Many remained unaware of their changing appearance, only realizing the passage of time after they were apprehended. Ed wondered when Julie realized that her beauty, which once must have been considerable, had morphed into the gaunt haggardness before him.

Dirk called for the deputy to take her back to her cell. Ed thanked her on her way out. She smiled with rotten, ground-down teeth and went out the door.

"Whew, man!" Dirk said when she was out the door but not quite out of earshot. "Now that is ugly on a biblical scale!"

"I think she might have been beautiful at one point, maybe a dancer. Did you see the way she walked? I once dated a ballet dancer. She walked like that, kind of slew-footed and graceful. No matter how long they've been away from it, they always walk like that." Ed looked back and forth between the two men, who were staring at him with amused expressions.

"Well, must have been a *long* time ago," Dirk said. "Now, what were you two making googly eyes about?"

"The description fits with what we've seen on other cases," Ed said.

"What description? She said she didn't see anyone."

"The lantern."

"The light on the video?" Dirk asked.

"Yes," Ed said. Thankfully Dirk let it go, and Ed assumed that the legend of Jackie Hudak was not widely known this far east.

"Is it all right if I speak to your medical examiner?"

"Sure thing," Dirk said and picked up the phone.

**"Crushed, pulverized**—either of those would fit," the medical examiner's chief investigator, Reg Armstrong, said.

They met in a conference room at the County Clerk of Courts Office. The room, probably not originally intended as a conference room, was too small for a large meeting. The large faux-cedar table took up most of the space, and Ed's chair sat uncomfortably close to its side. If he tried to scoot the chair back it could hit the wall behind him, possibly damaging it. Small and stoop-shouldered, Reg Armstrong reminded Ed of the actor Rick Moranis, only he wore his hair close-cropped—a military cut.

"Like the pelvis had been run over by a train?" Ed said.

"I would have said a large vehicle, like a truck," Reg said, smiling. "But a train would do it too. Although there are no tracks there."

Ed held up one of the photos Reg brought to the meeting. It showed a V-shaped groove in the middle of the crushed pelvis. "How do you explain this indentation?"

"I don't. A vehicle is just one possibility. A killer may have hacked at the body with some heavy object. Though I admit that groove is not consistent with any tool or weapon I can think of."

"How did you rule?"

"Probable homicide." Reg slid his notes across the table. "It's hard to imagine, even if the victim were trying to commit suicide, that he would lie down on that trail. Vehicles are not even supposed to ride on the old rail trails, and in some places, it's too narrow for a four-wheeled vehicle to travel. No, if it *was* a vehicle, someone would have to render him unconscious and deliberately run him over."

"Was there any other trauma to the body?" Ed asked.

"What body? We're talking about bones. The animal scavenging was extensive. The pelvis would have been dragged off, too, if it hadn't been pressed into the soil when it was still partially wet and hard to dislodge when the ground dried."

"Can you make an educated guess as to the date of death?"

"Yes. It last rained about two weeks ago, so it would have been within a couple of days of that." Reg shifted.

"What?" Ed said.

"Why did you ask me about a train?" Reg looked back and forth between Holt and Ed.

"It came up in our investigation. Why?" Ed tried to sound nonchalant.

Reg lowered his voice. "When I was in Pittsburgh, a guy fell or jumped in front of a moving train. One of the wheels cut him in half at the pelvis. It looked a lot like this guy's. But, of course, this one couldn't be a train, could it?"

"No," Ed lied. "It couldn't be a train."

**"This changes** everything," Holt said on their way back.

"How so?" Ed turned to him.

"Your guy's hunting range is far more extensive than we originally thought. We can't bring other jurisdictions into the fold, or they'll throw us both in the loony bin."

Ed looked out the window. Holt knew the roads well. Ed would never have taken them as fast as Holt was driving. In some places, the road had a steep incline only to curve sharply on the other side. It was so steep you couldn't see what was coming until you were already over the hill. Streetlamps were sparse and ineffective. Ed wondered how many cars plunged down the hill and missed the turn entirely, ending up on someone's farm.

"I notice you rarely use the name Hudak," Ed said. Holt briefly turned away from the road to look at him, and it scared him a little.

"I know, intellectually, that the evidence shows that, Ed. I'm having problems wrapping my head around this, though. Maybe my coping mechanism is not to say it aloud."

"Like not saying the boogeyman's name?"

Holt shrugged one shoulder.

"I'm just glad to have an ally." Ed looked out the side window at the dark woods speeding by.

"Doesn't mean we're engaged or anything," Holt said.

Ed chuckled. "It does seem that Hudak stays within a few miles of the Moonville Trail."

"That's not much consolation. The trail runs from Zaleski all the way to Athens County."

# Chapter 21

**The following day, Ed** went to see Charlie Cook in his office instead of the morgue. Cook's desk was predictably scattered with paper, pens, and a plethora of sticky notes in more colors than Ed thought available. Ed handed the Athens County autopsy to Charlie. He perused it while snacking on pistachios from a large jar. Vinton County was lucky to have Charlie Cook. Most coroners were not forensic pathologists and had to farm out the work to other jurisdictions. When they elected Charlie, they got a twofer. Ed wondered what would have happened if they'd had to send the bodies elsewhere.

"Yep, this was a train, all right," Charlie said.

"How do you find anything in this place?" Ed looked at the piles of paper on Charlie's desk.

"What? I can find anything. Just ask me."

"Meghan Haynes's toxicology report," Ed said, quickly.

Charlie pulled five pages from the right side of his desk and stacked them on the left side. It seemed he'd sat them at an angle that served to offset the piles. From the remaining pile of documents on the right, Charlie pulled a sheet of paper and handed it to Ed.

"See?"

"Impressive." Ed gestured to the autopsy report. "The Athens County coroner said it could have been some other heavy object."

"Well, he didn't have the information we have, and thank goodness for it. See where the wheels cut right through the pelvic bone? I just hope to God he was out when the train hit."

"At least we have the surrounding counties on alert. Maybe heavy police presence will cause Hudak to make a mistake."

Charlie's laugh was humorless. "A mistake like coming up to someone in broad daylight?"

"You know what I mean."

"I do, and I want you to consider what your nocturnal activities might do. A desperate man is a dangerous one."

"Hudak is not a man," Ed said.

"You don't know that, Ed. That's just speculation. Speaking of speculation, you tell Holt Potter the whole story yet?"

"No." Ed exhaled. "He's hanging in there now but telling him Hudak can dematerialize may be a bridge too far."

"I think he has a right to know what he's getting into. You have to consider that even your combined forces may not be a match for Hudak."

"You're not agreeing with Waddell? Just let him kill his fill and pray he doesn't come after us?"

"No, that's not what I'm saying. I'm just saying that actions have consequences."

"Like keeping information from me?"

Charlie turned away. "I knew about the ghost. I didn't know about the Hudak story until you told me."

"Charlie."

"Ed, I'm sorry. I thought you'd think I was nuts. Or worse."

"Worse?" Ed crossed his arms.

Charlie reached down and picked up his pen set. "You might think it was the drink."

Ed looked toward the door.

"You think I'm proud of this?" Charlie said. "I palmed you off on Waddell, who pulled a damned gun on you!"

"I have to go, Charlie." Ed got up.

"Ed."

"It's all right. I'll see you later."

**Later that** night, Charlie slapped his hand down on the bar three times and requested another scotch, neat. The smell of hamburgers and fries caressed his nose, but ordering food was not on his mind. Rich, the bartender, watched Charlie. His tattooed forearm moved in a circle, drying a glass. Charlie rapped again, this time more insistently.

Rich walked to the end of the bar, leaned over, and whispered, "I think you're done, sir."

"I'll tell you when I'm done!" Charlie said. But he looked up into the bigger man's eyes and relented. "I— think I'm done."

Charlie pulled out his wallet and tossed two twenties on the bar. "Knock yourself out."

As Charlie headed for the door, Rich called out, "Let me call you a Lyft."

"I've got it." Charlie waved him off.

"Sir, I don't think you should drive!"

"Who's driving?" Charlie called back and stumbled out onto the sidewalk. He turned left where his Toyota Forerunner was parked, bracing himself against the side of the building. Though he drank often, it had been a long time since he was stumbling drunk. His head felt as if it were tethered to his neck by a long, thin string. If he shook it too hard, it might detach and float away, leaving his body standing on the street. Broadway was nearly deserted this time of night and poorly lit. He could just make out the outline of his truck between two other vehicles. He walked forward, overbalanced, and caught himself on a storefront.

"Whoa." He stopped. "If you can't even walk, how are you going to drive?" he asked himself.

Charlie returned to the Pub and looked in the window. The bartender chatted with customers as he served beverages and snacks. Maybe he was regaling them with the story about how he just chased the drunk away? He wouldn't give the bartender the satisfaction of having to call him a Lyft. Charlie sat on a bench and pulled out his phone.

He had never used one of those services in his life. His nephew and namesake, Chuck, had explained it to him once. He fought through the clouded brine of his pickled brain to remember. He would have to download the app and enter his credit card information. He opened the Play Store and typed "Lyft." An icon came up, and he hit install. A line near the top of the screen started to move to the right and then stopped. Charlie frowned at it.

"Damn." What did Chuck say? He would have to log in to the Pub's Wi-Fi, or it would take forever. That meant asking Mr. Burly Bartender for the password. *To hell with that.*

Charlie started to head south on Broadway when something caught his eye. It looked like a man stood next to his truck holding something glowing down at his side.

But when Charlie turned to see it full-on, no one was there.

"Hmm."

Charlie wondered how much scotch he'd had. He continued down Broadway. The humidity of the day had given way to a pleasant nighttime warmth, and a light breeze brushed his face. A walk might sober him up a little, though it never worked before.

Three years ago, his wife, Linda, had taken their fourteen-year-old daughter and left. Well, his drinking had driven them out, if he was being honest with himself. It wasn't that he had been a violent drunk, just a persistent one who embarrassed her in front of guests. If he had tried to beat Linda, she would have kicked his ass. She had twenty pounds on him, and physical prowess had never been his strong suit.

Charlie reached South Street and turned right. Across the street, a man stood behind a car, staring. He held his right arm straight down by his side as if a heavy weight pulled it down. In the dark, Charlie couldn't make out the man's features. Just his height—well over six feet. As he continued down the street, a thought occurred to him. *Could it be the same man who stood outside the Pub?* Charlie looked back again. He didn't see him. *Nah.*

His dulled brain finally made the connection. *Was it Jackie Hudak?* This thought should have caused icy fear to creep down Charlie's back, but in his current state of intoxication, he put his hand to his mouth and tried to stifle a laugh.

"When the lantern schwings, schwings, schwings." He laughed again.

"Schwings," he tried again, causing another giggling fit. "Gshackie Hudak's comin' back." Charlie burst into full-blown laughter this time. There was no way Hudak was way the hell out here in Jackson stalking him. He doubted Hudak knew who he was.

Charlie turned onto North Davis Street and went into his one-story brick home. He tossed his keys and cell phone into the wicker basket near the door and went straight to the kitchen. He had to get something to eat. Charlie pulled out a plastic container of spaghetti, cracked the lid, and sniffed. *Good enough.* Charlie opened the microwave. He saw a reddish-orange stain at the edge of the turntable from the last time he heated the spaghetti and briefly thought about using the cover. Screw it. Linda wasn't there to yell at him about it.

Charlie heard a thump at the door. He looked through the kitchen into the living room and saw a man, the same man, looking through the window of the front door. He could clearly see the lantern in the man's right hand.

"Ahh!" Charlie jumped back so hard, he crashed into the wall and slid down.

He scrambled to his feet and ran to the living room. The idea that he could barricade the door occurred to him. Running out the back door did not. A double-cylinder lock secured that exit, and his keys were by the front door. His foot speed also left something to be desired. No doubt Hudak would bring him down in short order.

Charlie got behind the couch and started to push, but his feet slipped on the area rug. He turned and put his back against the couch. It finally moved. Then he heard a loud, wrenching crack. Splinters of wood flew over his head and landed in the dining room. Charlie got up. Jackie Hudak, in all his railroad regalia, stood at his doorway.

Charlie opened his mouth, then closed it. When he was nervous or scared, he usually talked, but what could he say? "Uh, uh. I got nothing."

Hudak just stared with a blank expression. As Charlie stared back, he had an odd sensation. As if he knew what Hudak wanted or, more accurately, needed.

Charlie's mind raced. Damn his drinking, anyway. He couldn't think clearly. His keys and phone were within Hudak's reach, but maybe he could surprise Hudak with a sudden movement and snatch them. Charlie remembered Ed saying something about action beating reaction. He grabbed the back of the couch and jumped over. Hudak turned casually, grabbed the phone, hurled it into the street, and looked back at Charlie.

"Come on, man!" Charlie backed away. The coffee table had crashed into the couch when Charlie pushed it. In his panic to get away, he backed into it and sprawled backward onto the couch. He tried to stand on the cushions but fell backward over the backrest. Charlie looked up in time to see Hudak coming forward, his knees pushing the table and couch toward Charlie. Their eyes locked again, then Charlie looked around for something to hit Hudak with. *The Mossberg! Idiot!* He had forgotten about the loaded Mossberg 12-gauge shotgun he kept in the closet. At least he thought it was still there. Charlie hadn't seen it since they'd moved in.

There was no particular reason he kept a shotgun, but he was a country boy at heart, and it seemed kind of obligatory. He didn't know if it was loaded with slugs or buckshot. If it was buckshot, it might just make Hudak mad, but if it was slugs, he could end this thing. With Hudak on the other side of the couch, he thought he could get to it. Hudak stopped pushing and squinted. He looked left toward the closet and back to Charlie. Charlie hesitated. There was no way the maniac could read his mind, but he had looked to the closet as soon as Charlie thought of the Mossberg.

No time to wonder about it. Charlie and Hudak moved at the same time, but Charlie was closer. He reached the closet, grabbed the Mossberg, and yanked the forearm. His heart sank when he watched a red shell fly out of the ejection port and tumble through the air. A round had already been chambered and Charlie had just ejected it. Still, he pulled it forward, chambered another round, and slid his index finger to the round safety button. He pressed it too late.

Hudak smacked the shotgun out of his hands as easily as a parent might snatch a dangerous object from a child. The smack threw Charlie against the wall, his head dented the drywall and gray swirls danced in front of his eyes. He took advantage of the distance and ran to the bedroom.

Charlie tried to close the door, but Hudak shouldered it. His superior weight sent Charlie flying onto the bed. He sprang up, scrambled to the windowsill, and yanked the window open. Charlie put his arms out like superman and dove. Relief washed over him as his head and torso entered empty space but melted away as Hudak caught his ankle and snatched him back into the room. Charlie's chin cracked the windowsill and his eyes filled with water. Hudak flipped Charlie onto his back, put the lantern down and brought up his fists.

"Oh no," Charlie said.

**Ed arrived** at Holzer Medical Center at 3:10 a.m. Holt Potter met him in the hallway, and together, they went in. Charlie's daughter, Mary, stood next to the bed, holding Charlie's good hand. The other was in a cast up to the triceps. Both eyes were blackened, and his nose sat at a strange angle.

*Damn*, Kevy said.

"Charlie, how are you doing?" Ed asked.

Charlie's smile revealed a missing incisor. "I'm alive, Ed."

"Of course you're alive," Holt said. "You don't get off that easy."

Ed turned to his daughter. "Hi, Mary. Would you mind giving us a minute?"

Mary touched Ed's hand and left the room.

As soon as the door closed, Charlie said, "It was Hudak. I gave the locals a correct description but nothing else. They think it was a botched robbery attempt."

"That's perfect," Ed said. "We can't bring anyone else into this."

"I don't understand. Why try to kill Charlie? He's no threat to Hudak, and he's nowhere near his hunting ground," Holt asked.

"What do you mean 'no threat?' I got my punches in." Charlie looked at the two men staring at him and said, "Well, you should see his fists. I gave them a good working over."

"Hudak didn't try to kill him," Ed said to Holt.

"What? He tuned me up something good. I got a concussion, broken arm, broken nose, and two bruised ribs to prove it." Charlie struggled to lean on his good elbow.

Ed looked at him. "If he wanted you dead, you'd be dead."

"Why take the trouble of beating him up?" Holt asked.

"It's a message. He's telling us he can reach out and touch us anywhere."

Holt turned to Charlie. "We've got to get you some protection."

With a wince, Charlie lay back on the pillow. "Locals got it covered. Thanks, though."

Ed grabbed Charlie's shoulder, the only place that didn't seem to hurt. "We'd better let you get some rest."

As the two men started for the door, Charlie called out, "Ed, hang back a minute." He pointed to his water glass. Ed walked over and handed it to him.

After taking a drink, Charlie said, "Ed, something happened that I can't explain."

"What?"

"I think he could read my mind."

"Read your mind?" Ed said.

"No, that's not right," Charlie said. "But he knew I was going for the Mossberg right after I thought of it."

"You must have had some non-verbal cue. Maybe your eyes darted over there, just for a split second."

"No, I'm sure I didn't. He knew, Ed. Somehow, he knew."

"Okay, but what am I supposed to do with that?"

"I don't know, but when you look at him, it's like you become—linked or something."

"You mean telepathy?"

"No, not telepathy, just intentions."

"So he knows everything you're about to do?"

"That's not the impression I got. Only when you're locked in with him. I know I'm not making any sense," Charlie said.

"We've been saying that for the past few weeks. What did he want?"

"What?" Charlie said.

"You said you could read his intentions when you were connected. What did he want?"

"Not want, Ed. *Need*. He needs to hurt, maim, and kill."

224

In a way, it made sense. Some serial killers were compelled to kill, or in the case of David Berkowitz, instructed by a dog.

"That's what I wanted to tell you." Charlie reached out with his good hand and grabbed Ed's wrist. "You can't handle this guy. You need to get a high-powered rifle, lie in wait, and pop him from a distance."

"I can't do that. Frankly, I'm not sure it would work."

"You've got to, Ed. Or he's going to kill all of us."

**"Andy, I** want you to take Ms. Hughes into town and get her a weapon," Ed said.

Andy and Nancy were in Ed's office. The smell of brewed coffee wafted into the open door. Ed was proud of the way the two of them had held up under the stress. Of all the law enforcement jobs, this assignment was supposed to be the least stressful, yet they had endured changes to their routine and accepted ideas well outside of their training and experience.

"You sure about that, chief?" Andy asked.

"Yes."

"And if she doesn't want it?"

"Then she has to leave," Ed said.

Nancy uncrossed her legs and planted her feet on the floor. "You really think Hudak would come after her?"

"He's going to come after all of us."

"How did he even know where Dr. Cook was? Or who he was, for that matter?" Andy asked.

"I don't know. I suspect it was me."

"Why would it have been you?" Nancy frowned.

Ed fidgeted.

*That's right, hoss. It was your fault,* Kevy said.

"Charlie said that Hudak knew he was going for the

shotgun."

"You sayin' he's telepathic, chief?" Andy said.

"No. More like he can read intention but only if you're locked in, according to Charlie."

Andy sat back in his chair. "I still don't see how that can be on you. You never even got close to Hudak."

"We don't know that. With his abilities, he could have tracked me into town."

"He's not omniscient," Nancy said.

"No," Ed agreed. "If he knew everything, he wouldn't worry about us enough to bother with warnings. He's doing this because we're boxing him in, surveilling his hunting ground. But still, he knows things he shouldn't."

"That could make him even more dangerous," Andy said. "You know the saying about the cornered animal."

"I do. But the fact that he's warning us means that he's trying to eliminate the threat without taking us on directly. That means he's worried, and if he's worried, he can be beaten. Do you remember our conversation with Waddell, Andy?"

"How could I forget?"

"They were using similar tactics, but Hudak backed them off by coming after someone Waddell cared about. He's using the same strategy here."

Nancy furrowed her brows. "And you think he'll go after Savannah because—"

"Because she's the most vulnerable among us," Ed cut her off. "That's why I want her armed. Also, the two of you need to start carrying your weapons wherever you go—the grocery store, even the shower. Sleep with it under your pillow if you have to."

# Chapter 22

**Ed slept in for** the first time in a week. He had been wrong about Hudak going after someone else. In fact, there had been no activity, at least none they were aware of. Perhaps Hudak was done, and his beating of poor Charlie Cook was meant to warn the next set of investigators when he returned in ten years. He showered, dressed, and checked his email and phone messages. One email jumped out. It read, *Mr. Freemen, I would like to meet with you concerning my grandson.* It was signed, *Phyllis Brandt.*

Ed froze. Phyllis Brandt was Anthony Deavers's grandmother. Ed sat on the edge of the bed, reading the message over and over. Deavers's mother was in prison, and Ms. Brandt had been his primary caregiver. He wondered for a moment how she had gotten his email, then remembered that it was on the State of Ohio website.

This wasn't the first time she'd tried to see him. She had come to the station and left a note at the front desk inviting him to Anthony's funeral. No way in hell would he have attended that. He had ignored her. Now, a year later, she wanted to see him again. Why? Did she want to spit in his face or get an explanation as to why he had cut down her grandson in his youth?

*You don't owe her anything*, Kevy said.

Ed wondered if that was true. He certainly had no legal obligation to contact her. All litigation matters had been settled. Ms. Brandt had received a tidy sum from the city, which stipulated that it was not an admission of responsibility for the boy's death.

Ed switched screens and began to dial the number at the bottom of the email.

*What are you doing?* Kevy asked.

The phone rang twice before an elderly voice answered. "Yes?"

"This is Ed Freemen."

"Detective Freemen." The voice sounded relieved. "I'm so glad you called."

"It's not 'detective' anymore, Ms. Brandt."

"Oh, so formal. You can call me Phyllis."

"No, ma'am, I can't. That's not how I was raised."

"Then you was raised right. Miss Phyllis, then."

"Okay, Miss Phyllis." He struggled to find the words. "I just called to tell you that I won't be coming to see you."

"You'll come." Her voice sounded insistent but not harsh. She reminded Ed of his late grandmother. She never raised her voice, but when she told you to come, you came. "You'll come soon."

"Ma'am, the city already settled with you. I don't see what I could do."

"You think this is about money?" Miss Phyllis said.

The hurt in her voice made Ed feel like a jerk. "No, no, I'm sorry. I didn't mean that, Miss Phyllis. I just—there's a lot going on here. I can't get away."

There was a long sigh on the other end. "This ain't Christian of me, and I'm going to have to ask the Lord's forgiveness, but you better come see me. You killed my boy, the boy I raised like my own, and when I tell you to come see me, you come."

"Ma'am, I'm sorry. I can't." Ed doubled over and clutched his stomach with his free hand. "Maybe — maybe in the fall, I could get away."

"There ain't no fall, boy!" Miss Phyllis said. Her voice softened. "I'm dying. Now you come see me, and you come soon."

The phone went silent.

**"I think** Hudak might be gone, chief," Andy said. Ed had called a meeting with Andy, Nancy, and Savannah to discuss their next steps.

"Yeah, but is that a good or bad thing?" Nancy said.

They were all sitting around the coffee table in the lounge area. Ed fingered his energy drink. "Well, if he *is* done, we don't have to worry for ten years, but how many more would die then? The best-case scenario is that we stop him now, so he doesn't return to terrorize the next generation. Who knows what crew will be here in ten years? I hope to be sipping margaritas on a beach somewhere."

"I don't know if it's within our power to stop him," Savannah said.

"Should we take the video equipment down?" Andy asked.

"No," Ed looked out the window at an owl perched on a lamppost. "We maintain status quo. Nancy, I'll have you take over reviewing the video in the mornings before you leave."

"You going somewhere, chief?" Nancy asked.

"I have something to do back home." Ed stood.

229

"In Akron?" Nancy sounded surprised. "What if something pops off?"

Ed looked back and forth between Nancy and Andy. "Don't either of you try to take him on without the other. Wait for backup. If necessary, back off, and report his whereabouts."

He turned to Savannah. "Keep working your sources to see if we can find out more about Hudak. Even if we get a hold of him, we don't know how to stop him."

Savannah gave a parodied salute.

"And keep that gun at your side." Ed stabbed a finger toward Savannah's purse, which had a side pouch containing a Smith & Wesson Model 10 revolver.

**On Copley** Road in Akron, Ohio, Ed passed his Alma Mater, John R. Buchtel High School, now Buchtel Community Learning Center. The complex was three times the size of the school Ed had attended and housed students from grades seven through twelve. What would it have been like in his day if the school had middle-school students attending with high school juniors and seniors? There had been guys in his school that he wouldn't want to see around young kids.

Ed continued east on Copley and turned left on Noah Avenue. Ed had made numerous arrests here in his days as a patrolman, but Noah Avenue looked better. No crack dealers hung out on street corners waiting to flag down motorists. No gang members tagged houses and fire hydrants to mark their territory. The yards were neat and the street clean.

Ed stopped in front of a two-story colonial with vinyl siding and a large screened-in porch. He walked up the stairs and was about to push the doorbell when he heard a small dog yapping. Ed pulled his baseball cap down over his forehead, pulled out sunglasses, and shoved them on his face. His face had been blasted all over the news after the Deavers shooting.

A young woman opened the inner door. She wore a tight T-shirt with red horizontal stripes and faded blue jeans. A roll of fat protruded from the bottom of the shirt, and a belly button ring with a small bell jingled when she moved. The smell of biscuits pushed its way out the door, reminding Ed of summer visits to his relatives in Alabama. Breakfast was always a full spread, and homemade biscuits with real butter were featured prominently.

"I'm here to see—"

"She ain't here," the girl interrupted. "She at General."

Ed knew she was referring to Cleveland Clinic Akron General and hoped he wasn't too late. He muttered his thanks and turned to leave.

"I know who you is," she called, turning to take the dog into the house. The belly button bell announced her departure. "You ain't fooling nobody with that getup."

*If she wants to talk about appearances, we can start with that Michelin roll,* Kevy said.

Ed ignored him.

**Ed had** seen Phyllis Brandt once before from a distance. She had been an imposing woman, though not very tall. The woman reclined on the hospital bed in front of him was not imposing at all. Everything seemed to recede or sag. The corners of her mouth turned down as if gravity had become too strong to resist and pulled her features toward the earth. When Ed saw her the first time, her cheeks were a prominent feature on her face, plump and cherubic. They too sagged, as if a mudslide had occurred

231

under her skin.

"I look different, don't I?" Phyllis said. "I know you saw me outside the courthouse."

"You look fine," Ed lied.

Phyllis's laugh became a cough. A young woman in a denim skirt moved forward and held a cup of water for Phyllis to drink. As she moved past Ed, she glared at him.

"I know Grandma asked for you," the young woman said, "but you're not welcome here, as far as I'm concerned."

"Hush, child," Phyllis said. "Don't pay her no mind. Sit down."

Ed sat on the chair next to the bed. "Is there anything I can do to help?"

The young woman snorted her disapproval.

"You know you can just wait in the hallway if you can't act right," Phyllis snapped.

The girl spun on her heel and walked out.

Phyllis smiled a toothless grin. Ed noticed her dentures were in a jar across the room.

"Why do you think I asked you to come here, Detective Freemen?"

"I don't know," Ed said. "I can't tell you how sorry I am for the way things turned out. You have to know that when I entered that alley, I had no intention to shoot your grandson."

"You're feeling guilty about it, ain't you, son?"

"Yes."

"That's why I wanted you to come. You can't keep carrying this thing with you. I want to tell you about Anthony. There was something wrong with him. We knew it from the time he was six. His mama too. My daughter had the highest aptitude scores in her school, but she turned to pleasures of the flesh, drugs, and men, then prostitution when she couldn't steal anything else from me.

"Anthony was the same way, didn't care about nobody. He'd sooner lie than give you the time of day. And steal, *hmm*... That boy could steal the sweet out of sugar and call it salt, and even if you caught him red-handed, he would look you right in the eye and lie to your face."

Despite the seriousness of the subject, Ed wanted to laugh. His grandfather used to use that phrase.

"We finally took him to the doctor," Phyllis said. "We didn't want him to end up like his mother. They did some tests and said that he had Conduct Disorder, which is what they say when they don't want to call a kid a psychopath."

"I understand," Ed said gently, "but I'm not sure why you're telling me this."

"You shot him because you thought he was pointing a gun at you," Phyllis said. "You had every right to go back to your family."

Ed looked away. He wanted to tell her the truth. There had to be a special punishment for people who lied to the dying. He looked over his shoulder to make sure the girl hadn't slipped back in.

"I'm not sure that's true, Miss Phyllis. At the last minute, I had a sense that the gun was fake. Maybe I could have stopped squeezing the trigger in time, maybe not. I just don't know."

Her old, wise eyes softened even more.

"Then you been carrying around more guilt than I thought. Anthony was a bad boy. It wasn't his fault—he was born that way. But he was a bad boy. He hurt a lot of people, and he wasn't long for this world. Somebody was going to kill him. You can't hurt that many people without coming to a bad end. The only reason he didn't have a real gun that day is because he sold it for drugs. And let me tell you this—if he had a gun that day, he would have shot you and wouldn't have felt bad about it. What I was going to tell you at the funeral is the same thing I'm going to tell you today. I forgive you, son. I couldn't go to my maker without telling you that."

Ed sat there frozen. Miss Phyllis was dying, and her thoughts were not despair about her own condition but concern for the man who shot and killed her grandson. An insatiable flood of emotion rushed to the surface of Ed's consciousness. He turned quickly and thrust his face in the crook of his elbow.

"Ah, ah, don't do that, son!" Miss Phyllis said. "Let it out. Don't go on holding it in like that."

Ed turned away from Miss Phyllis like a child refusing to eat his vegetables at dinner.

"Come on, boy. Let it out!" Miss Phyllis insisted.

The first thing to escape his mouth was a gasp. Then it all came out at once. The pain and guilt he felt for over a year erupted. He cried loud and hard, burying his face on the edge of the hospital bed. He felt Miss Phyllis's hand on the back of his head. The hand was warm. Too warm—the hand of a person whose body was fighting a desperate and losing battle for life.

"I'm so sorry!" Ed cried out. "I'm so sorry!"

The hand continued to caress his head. "That's it, son. Let it out. Let it go."

**Ed felt** emotionally drained when he returned home. He was surprised that Kevy had remained quiet during his trip. It would have been the perfect opportunity to thrust a dagger into Ed's heart. A clever witticism while Ed bawled his eyes out would have broken him.

"You're losing your touch, Kevy," he said.

Ed went into the guest bedroom he used as an office. He sat at the L-shaped desk and powered on his desktop. Ed pulled a flash drive from a small box and plugged it into the USB port. He opened a file marked "Anthony Deavers" and hit play. In preparation for a possible trial on the shooting, Ed had researched all he could about Deavers.

He found and downloaded a video that featured Deavers and a friend talking about which celebrities they would most like to have sex with. It was juvenile and profanity-laced, but at the time, Ed thought that if he could find a video of Deavers brandishing a weapon, it would help his case. Ed was cleared of any wrongdoing, so he never had to use it. When the video began to play, Ed's jaw dropped. The voice that had plagued him the past several weeks was not the voice of the annoying Kevy Chapman from Ed's youth. The voice belonged to Anthony Deavers.

# Chapter 23

"**We were supposed to** meet once a week," Dr. Spicer said. She sat on a straight-backed chair, wearing the same baggy jeans and a different, though still multicolored, blouse. Ed wondered what her closet looked like at home.

"I know. I've been busy, but I found out something," Ed said.

"Hallucinations can be serious, especially in your line of work." Spicer frowned at him.

"That's what I wanted to talk to you about. I was wrong about the voice. It's not Kevy Chapman. It's Anthony Deavers, the boy I shot and killed."

"Oh." Spicer's head cocked. "How are you handling it?"

"I don't know. I don't know what this means."

Spicer pulled her notebook on the table next to her. "It makes more sense though, doesn't it?"

"What do you mean?" Ed looked up.

"You have a hero complex." Spicer folded her arms in her lap.

"Isn't that good in my line of work?"

"Depends. Why did you get into law enforcement?"

"I don't know." Ed frowned. "My mother always taught me to help others. Seemed the best way."

"Tell me about her."

"My mother?"

"Yes, your mother. She seemed to have a great influence on your life."

"Are you Freudian now?"

Spicer gave him a look that made Ed think the last remark was an insult. He continued, talking about his mother and her method for controlling his ADHD and how even the river of marigolds hadn't helped his situation. The entire time Spicer just stared, her jaw set in a deep scowl. She grabbed her notebook and threw it over the back of the chair.

"I feel like I should apologize for something." Ed squinted. "I'm not quite sure what."

Spicer pushed her hands through her dirty blonde curls and slid them down the back of her neck. She looked up and took a deep breath. "How about burying the lead?"

"I'm sorry?" Ed leaned forward.

"This is why we should have met once a week. You just told me that you've been bottling up your emotions for the past thirty years, and you didn't think to mention that?"

Ed looked at the ceiling, his mother's cryptic warning came back to him. *I'm afraid there's going to be a cost.*

Spicer swung her head from side to side. For a moment, Ed thought she was looking for something to throw at him. Finally, she pulled open a small drawer on the table next to her and pulled out another notebook. She looked over her glasses at him. "You probably don't have PTSD."

"I don't?" Ed felt stupid.

"I'm sure your mother was a wonderful woman,

but her coping mechanism forced you to suppress your personality." She cupped her chin. "It's like a pressure cooker. When the pressure gets too high, they have a little valve that pops up and lets the steam out."

"I don't have that valve."

"Everyone needs an outlet," Spicer said. "Keep the valve closed for too long and…"

"Something pops," Ed finished. "So how do I get back to normal?"

"Coming clean was a good first step. Now you make your weekly appointments."

"I didn't intentionally deceive you," Ed said. "Just didn't seem to be relevant to my situation."

"It's all relevant," Spicer said, looking back at him. "I would think that a man of your obvious intelligence would understand that."

"I'm sorry," Ed said.

"You're not going to come weekly, are you?" Spicer said.

"There's something I have to take care of first."

"Something more important than your sanity?"

Ed stood and made his way to the door. "Let's just say if I don't take care of this, these sessions won't be necessary."

**When Ed** returned to work, Nancy and Andy reported that everything remained quiet. If it stayed that way, Ed could get rid of the cameras and return to a normal routine. He would still continue to research Jackie Hudak, if for no other reason than to leave a record for the next poor souls who would encounter him in ten years. Then he could focus on his mental health.

Ed left his office and headed to the bathroom. He

had just passed Andy's desk when a sound made him stop. Ed turned back around and looked at the multiple screens. One was highlighted. He hit it, and the screen filled all forty-two inches of the monitor. The camera overlooked the Hope Furnace area. Ed could see the back of the historical marker. To the left was the outline of the massive Hope Furnace, its stone slabs angling inward like an unfinished pyramid.

What triggered the motion sensor was the figure of a lumbering man carrying an old-style oil lantern. Jackie Hudak moved deliberately, making a beeline for a lone car sitting in the parking lot. The parking lot was not a popular make-out spot. People staying at the park had rooms, cabins, or tents. No high school was close enough to make it a favorite for reckless youth powered by raging hormones. Perhaps the car contained a couple who just thought it was a nice place to sit and watch the stars. In any case, their night was about to get very interesting. Ed grabbed his radio.

*Holy shit*, the voice, now identified as Anthony Deavers, said.

"Holy shit, indeed."

# Chapter 24

**"I wish** it was storming," Robert Feister said. His finger traced the outline of the moon, which now sat above the Hope Furnace.

"What?" Cathy, his wife of three days, punched him in the shoulder.

"No, I mean if it was storming, we might see the ghost."

Cathy smiled, causing her upturned nose to curl upward even more. Robert leaned over and kissed it.

"You mean, the Moonville Ghost?" She feigned an eerie voice.

"No, no," Robert said, shaking his head. "This is another one. This guy was standing at the top of the furnace when a storm came up suddenly. He was struck by lightning and fell into the coals."

"Crispy on the outside and crunchy in the middle," Cathy said, and they both burst into laughter.

"You're terrible." Robert pushed her head back. "Anyway, if you come out here on a stormy night, you can see him standing on the top when the lightning strikes." He leaned over to kiss his bride again, but she palmed his face.

"Wait. You see that?"

"See what?" Robert tried to maneuver his face around her hand, but she turned him to look toward the furnace.

"Looks like we got the other ghost tonight," Cathy said.

"Hey, when's the next train?" Robert said, waving a hand through his open window.

"Robert!" Cathy said. "You don't know. He might be a crazy person."

"Nah. He's just playing a prank."

Robert called to the man as he approached. He was at the picnic tables now, winding through them without looking down. "Dude, seriously. That's a cool costume!"

He was close enough that they could see his facial expression, or lack thereof. He stared straight at them, walking in long strides.

"Robert, start the car." Cathy clawed Robert's arm.

"He's just playing around, trying to scare us."

"Well, it's working. Start the car!" Cathy's body twisted around to look at him.

"Okay, dude, you made your point. It's funny, but you're scaring my wife now." Robert still smiled, but he reached down and turned the ignition. His hands shook as he did so. There was no reason to be scared. He was sure it was a prank. The guy would walk up to the car and utter some spooky phrase.

The man was walking faster, his already long strides lengthening. Robert swallowed, and it felt like ice water sliding down his throat. The moment the engine sprung to life, Cathy stomped on his foot and tugged at his arm.

Robert grabbed the shifting lever, pressed the button, and snatched the car into reverse. Cathy's heel dug even harder into Robert's foot, and the car lurched back just as the man reached for the door. He was holding the lantern up to the driver's window, the red side out, painting the car in a crimson glow. The car shot across the parking lot, hopped the curb, and came to a stop only after Robert pushed Cathy's leg away and moved his foot to the brake.

The man slowly turned to them and began casually walking in their direction. Robert pulled the stick into drive and jammed his foot on the accelerator. He felt the sickening, sliding, sensation of the car slaloming to the left, tires cutting into soft earth. Spinning tires kicked up dirt, pummeling the lamppost behind.

The man had almost reached their front quarter panel when the tires caught dry dirt and peeled forward. The rear of the car fishtailed, nearly hitting the man, who made no attempt to get out of the way. Robert looked into the rearview mirror as they escaped. The man walked slowly toward the woods — his lantern held high.

**"Nancy! We've** got Hudak by the Hope Furnace. Looks like he's after a couple!" Ed's voice over the radio was calm but forceful. Nancy, already driving south on Park Road 1, increased her speed as much as was safe on the winding road. All she would have to do is turn left at 278, and she would be a minute away.

"On my way, chief. I'm close."

"I'm heading out too. Be careful," the chief said.

Nancy reached the intersection of Park Road 1 and Route 278. She had just entered the intersection when she heard tires screech. A white Dodge Charger careened around the corner, the wheels on the left lifting off the pavement. Nancy hit the accelerator and shot across the street.

Most drivers freeze in such situations and slam on the brakes. At that speed, the driver of the other car would have no chance of controlling the vehicle. She drove across the street and onto the shoulder, looking back at the Dodge.

For a second, the Charger looked as if it would make it. Nancy watched the driver frantically turn the wheel as he passed her, but then he made a critical mistake. The driver hit the brakes and skidded sideways like a Tokyo drift gone awry. The car turned backward and slid off the road into the grass. The driver was fortunate not to hit anything, and the car came to a stop, aided by thick bushes.

Nancy made a U-turn and pulled up to the car. The occupants, a man and a woman, appeared to be uninjured and were engaged in animated conversation. Nancy engaged her emergency lights and got out. She approached the passenger side and saw a woman in an agitated state. She pushed the button to roll down the window and clawed at it like a cat in an electrified cage.

"He's after us!" she screamed.

"Who?" Nancy asked.

She instinctively moved past the passenger window and stopped at the edge of the door, so the occupants had to crane their necks to look at her. From this position, she could see their hands if they made any sudden movements. Not that she was worried. She was pretty sure they were victims.

"We don't really know that he's after us," the man said, holding his hands up.

The woman pursed her lips and turned to him. He cocked his head as if to say, "Well?"

Nancy took out her notebook. "Why don't you tell me what happened?"

**Ed drove** down Park Road 1 and stopped at Nancy's cruiser.

"This is the car you saw on the video," she said.

She shot a quick glance over her shoulder to make sure the couple was out of earshot. "Our guy approached them, and they took off. Said he headed west into the woods."

"Crap!" Ed said. "He can cut across to the cabins or skirt around the north side of the lake from there. I'm going to try to follow him. You finish up with the couple and patrol up and down Park Road 1 in case he comes out and cuts across the road."

"That's a lot to cover, chief. I can easily miss him," Nancy said.

"I know, but if he gets to the cabins, Nancy —"

"I got it, chief," she said.

Ed drove to the Hope Furnace Parking area. The three streetlamps were inadequate to illuminate the area, but it wasn't designed for guests to explore at night.

Ed parked next to the space where the car had been and got out. He pulled his flashlight from the pouch in his belt. Crouching, he pointed the beam at the pavement and saw two faint parallel lines where the couple's tires had peeled out. Ed followed the direction of the marks across the parking lot and stopped at the curb. The tires had cut two ruts in the dirt where the car had jumped the curb.

Ed continued straight, reaching the edge of the woods. He played the beam among the trees and shrubbery. A buckeye branch hung loosely where it had been snapped.

Ed ducked his head and entered the woods. He moved slowly, using his light sparingly to remain acclimated to the low light. Hudak was big, and there were signs that he had crashed through the forest, broken branches, and trampled grass.

245

After half a mile, Ed saw a tiny red light bobbing in the distance. He holstered his Mini Maglite, using the moonlight as his only guide. Ed quickened his pace, trying to close the distance. He had to intercept him before he reached the cabins.

For the first time, Ed wondered if his decision had been correct. Perhaps he should have swept the crimes under the rug and blamed Dave Malone for the murder of Meghan Haynes. Maybe Hudak would have stopped after Joshua Morton. Now, Hudak could punish Ed for his hubris.

*Too late now*, Deavers said.

"Too late," Ed agreed.

He moved faster. Branches slashed his face and arms. He thought the light was getting closer but wasn't sure. It bobbed and weaved almost casually as if Hudak was unaware of his pursuit, or worse, he didn't care. Ed looked down to watch his footing. When he looked up again, a rush of cold washed over him. The light was gone. Ed stopped and scanned the darkness for any hint of light. He loathed using his radio in fear of giving away his position, but now he pulled it from the holder.

"Nancy, you on the road yet?"

"Yeah, chief. Nothing so far," Nancy said.

"Had him moving southwest, but now he's gone."

"You need me to come to you?"

Ed could hear the tension in her voice.

"No. Patrol the cabin roads. We can't let him get to one of the guests. I'm going to continue in the same direction. He may be hunkered down."

Ed ran, pushing his way through bushes and going around trees. He thought he was near the road to his left, but the terrain sloped sharply. He realized he was behind the smaller cabins. He was about to come into the clearing when a large dark object swung in his direction. He tried to duck but the object caught him flush on the forehead.

His fall didn't register at first. He only felt the initial whack and his butt hitting the ground. He wasn't knocked out, just lost in a numb fog that started in his forehead and radiated through his body. Ed saw Hudak move in front of him, bend down, and look into his face. There was no anger or aggression, just the detached curiosity of a child looking at a butterfly in a jar.

Ed tried to move his arms and reach for his weapon, but his hands remained collapsed in front of him. Hudak lifted a large boot and kicked Ed in the face. That shook something loose, and he rolled onto his stomach. When he looked back, Hudak was moving quickly behind the cabins.

Ed reached for his radio, but it must have fallen out of its holder. He looked to his left and saw Nancy's cruiser. It was heading back to Park Road 1. He called out, but his voice seemed muted.

Rolling onto his side, he pushed himself up to one knee. Pain ricocheted between the front and back of his head, and a sharp sting at his tailbone where he had plopped to the ground. Ed reached for his holster and was comforted to feel the butt of his Glock 40.

Finding his feet, he pulled out the cell phone in his rear pocket and pushed the side button to bring up the screen. When it lit up, Ed's heart dropped to his stomach. Thick lines radiated from a break in the upper right corner of the screen.

He tapped on it anyway, hoping to bring up the familiar pattern of numbers that would allow him to put in his code. No luck.

*Oops*, Deavers mocked.

In a flash of anger, Ed cocked his arm, preparing to hurl the phone against a tree. He took a deep breath and let it out slowly, dropping the thought into the river and watching it float away. Ed stuffed the phone back into his pocket and continued forward. Nancy would be able to track his phone even if she couldn't talk to him.

Ed continued past the first three cabins, looking into windows as he went. At the fourth cabin, he stopped. The rear door had been ripped off its hinges and hung crookedly like a loose tooth. He drew his weapon and went inside. The door led to a screened-in porch with a picnic table. The table had been moved to the side as if someone had bumped it in a hurry to get out. Red wine dripped onto the floor from an overturned glass.

Ed moved toward the living room, passing the small bathroom and two bedrooms on the way. He cleared the bathroom and the first bedroom, weapon at low ready.

When Ed entered the second bedroom, his mouth dropped open. Savannah's .38 sat unloaded on the small nightstand. Draped across the bed, Ed saw a familiar black dress.

"Oh, no!" Ed backed quickly out of the room and ran into the living room. There was no sign of Savannah Hughes. Ed ran back out of the rear door and to the edge of the woods. Down the steep hill, a light bobbed erratically in the distance.

**Nancy hadn't** heard from the chief in ten minutes. She had been reluctant to use the radio or phone. If the chief was sneaking up on Hudak, the phone could give away his position, but Nancy was sure if he was able, the chief would have contacted her by now. She reached for the mic, pulled her hand back quickly, then reached for it again.

"Chief, you okay?"

Silence.

Again, she hesitated. The chief could have turned off his unit, but she doubted it. He would have texted her to say that he would be on radio silence.

She grabbed her cell phone, opened her contacts, and selected his name. The phone did not immediately go to voicemail, but after the seventh ring, Ed's soothing voice came on saying that he was unavailable to take the call.

Nancy drove up and down Park Road 1, getting out several times to look into the woods. She jumped back into her cruiser and beat the steering wheel with the heels of her hands. Nancy tried to swallow the panic rising in her throat. What would Ed do? She reached over and tapped the "enter" button on her mobile data terminal, bringing it to life. In one of his nerd soliloquies, Andy had said something about a tracking app. Nancy picked up her phone and called Andy.

"Andy, I think the chief's in trouble. He went after Hudak, and I can't get a hold of him."

"What? Why didn't y'all call me?" Andy's voice sounded whiny with frustration.

"Never mind that. I need to track his phone."

"Yeah, just use the app on your MDT," Andy said.

Nancy sighed. "I don't know how to do that."

Now it was Andy's turn to sigh. "I trained y'all on this. You didn't listen, did you?"

"Andy! We don't have time for this. Just walk me through it." Nancy turned back to her terminal.

"All right, just hit 'start' and go to the apps. Fifth one down is the Find Me app. Click on it."

"Okay, got it," Nancy said.

"You should see a map and four triangles on it. The triangles have three digits. The chief is 0-0-1."

"Alright."

"Accuracy depends on reception. The park's coverage is lousy, but it should get you in the same general area. I'm coming in."

Nancy enlarged the display. "The chief's not moving."

"You can't read anything into that. It can take a minute or two to buffer. I'm getting dressed."

"It looks like he's in the woods heading south toward the lake," Nancy said. "You're right, the little thingy moved. Gotta go now."

Hanging up, she drove back toward Park Road 1. The chief was near 278. She assumed Hudak was heading for the Moonville Rail Trail. If she could cut them off before they crossed the road, she had a good chance of intercepting them. At the intersection of Park Road 1 and 278, Nancy stopped and checked the screen. The little triangle that represented the chief had jumped to the east side of the road.

"Goddammit!" Nancy jerked the wheel to the right and jammed her foot on the accelerator.

**Hudak moved** surprisingly fast for a man carrying a woman on his shoulder, but Ed was catching up. He could see the maniac clearly now, heading south on a trail running parallel to 278. Hudak must have known that Ed was getting close, but he didn't even glance over his shoulder.

*He ain't worried about you, hoss,* Anthony Deavers said.

Savannah dangled completely limp, and Ed wondered if she was still alive. Her head bounced as Hudak marched down the trail in hard, regulated strides like a soldier in double time. Ed started to draw his weapon, then decided against it. In the movies, cops always took down suspects with a firearm, but if an unarmed man turned to fight, he would have to re-holster.

*You're just scared you'll punk out again*, Deavers said.

Hudak approached a clearing. This was Ed's chance. He pulled his collapsible baton and sprinted forward. Hudak must have heard him, but still didn't turn to look. The fact the killer didn't consider Ed a threat pissed him off, and he intended to show Jackie the folly in his reasoning.

*Yeah, right*, Deavers said.

When he was about ten feet away, Hudak reacted. Without turning, he shrugged Savannah off his shoulder. She thumped to the ground with a grunt.

*At least she's alive*, Ed thought.

Hudak stood tall but didn't turn around. Ed pulled the baton across his body and swung it hard. He struck the common peroneal nerve. It should have put the big man down, but just made him angry. He turned and swung the lantern. Ed ducked and rolled forward. The lantern whooshed over his head.

"Police! Drop it and get on your knees!" Ed said.

*Are you kidding right now? Shoot him!* Deavers said.

He might've been able to argue that the lantern was a deadly weapon and drop him with his Glock, but he wasn't ready to go there yet.

Hudak came at him. Still clutching the baton, Ed assumed a boxer's stance. He hit Hudak with two quick jabs. Hudak's head popped back like a bobblehead doll in a speeding car. He swung a slow right. Ed dodged it and hit Hudak with a left hook. It twisted the big man's head.

Ed glanced over at Savannah, who still wasn't moving. It was a mistake. Hudak dropped the lantern and smashed a left into Ed's ribs. He covered it with an elbow, but Hudak threw a straight right. Ed tried to weave but caught the fist in his chest. He dropped to a knee. Hudak lifted his right foot. If that connected with Ed's head, it would end the fight. He jammed the end of the baton into Hudak's groin. He groaned and stepped back.

Scrambling to his feet, Ed brought the baton down on Hudak's head. Hudak grabbed his head with both hands. Ed pounced on the opening, thrusting his baton into Hudak's chest. It brought out an *"oof!"*

Hudak staggered, snatched the lantern, and turned the green side toward himself. Ed lunged and swung the baton. The weapon sliced through empty air.

Ed looked around, his mouth forming a big "O." He felt something he couldn't quite identify—a variation in air pressure. He may not have noticed if not for his ADHD. He turned around in time to catch the lantern coming down on top of his head. Ed stumbled back, colliding with a tree. He drew his Glock.

*Shoot him!* Deavers said. *Better to be judged by twelve than carried by six.*

Hudak turned the lantern again and vanished.

*You can do this.*

The sudden words of support surprised Ed. Then he remembered that it wasn't really Anthony Deavers speaking, but his own mind.

The moonlight provided good visibility in the clearing. Taking a deep breath, Ed turned in a slow circle. The air pressure changed again, this time on his left. Ed turned— too late. Hudak slammed him with a right cross. Ed dropped like a marionette.

On his back, he angled the weapon toward Hudak and tried willing his trigger finger to squeeze. Nothing happened. Hudak disappeared again. He stole another look at Savannah and imagined her mangled on the tracks.

*Come on, you crazy son of a bitch, pull the damned trigger!*

The change in air pressure came to his right. He swung the weapon in that direction just as Hudak appeared. Ed's finger convulsed. There was a loud pop and a flash of fiery light. The Glock jumped in his hand, and a forty-caliber missile spat toward Hudak. Hudak spun to his right. Ed squeezed the trigger again, this time with more control. Hudak hunched over, swung the lantern again, and was gone.

Ed was sure he had hit him. He scrambled to a knee, swinging his weapon left and right, but didn't see Hudak. He closed his eyes and tried to sense the change in air pressure. Nothing.

Ed ran over to Savannah and checked for a pulse. Alive.

How far could Hudak teleport? Ed ran to the edge of the path where the hill began to slope down toward the Moonville Rail Trail and saw Hudak stumbling toward the path. Ed aimed. Hudak was about a hundred feet away. No way he could hit him, but he fired anyway and began to run down the hill. Hudak turned and, with another sweep of the lantern, disappeared and reappeared closer to the trail.

Though Ed fired wildly, Hudak made no attempt to dodge. He walked the last few feet to the trail, turned back to Ed, and swung the lantern once more. Hudak was gone in a flash of brilliant light.

"That's very interesting." He re-holstered, dropped to a knee, and stared at the spot where Hudak had disappeared. Warm liquid ran down his forehead. He wiped the blood away before it got into his eyes. Sharp pain thrust daggers into his head and chest.

On the roadway, he saw Nancy's cruiser speeding down 278. Ed went back to the trail and found Savannah sitting up. She rubbed her head.

"You okay?" Ed held out a hand.

"No." Savannah grabbed his arm and pulled herself up. When she reached her full height, she buried her head into his chest and slipped her arms around his waist. Just then, Nancy came into the clearing. She stopped and looked at the two of them.

"What happened?" Ed guided Savannah to the path.

She leaned on him, rubbing her cheek. "I was writing in my journal, having a little wine. I heard a loud bang, and when I turned around, he clobbered me."

"How did you get here?" Nancy asked.

Dazed, Savannah looked around. "Hell, where is here?" She grabbed her head with both hands. "My head is killing me."

"Lack of oxygen. Positional asphyxia from when you were on his shoulder. It should clear up."

"Is he dead?" Savannah said. "I saw you put two in him."

Nancy's head jerked in Ed's direction. "You shot him?"

"Yeah. Two shots, center mass. It slowed him down a little, but it didn't stop him."

Ed watched Nancy's face close down. Her eyes became tiny beads.

"You shot him," Nancy repeated loud enough for them to hear, but low, and then lower, "for her."

Ed looked at Savannah, who appeared to not have heard the last part. As they reached the car, he pressed his mouth closed. This certainly wasn't the place or time to get into it. He frankly thought that Nancy was being unreasonable. He had gotten past his mental block.

That was the important thing. What triggered it was not important.

*That's why you don't —*

Ed smashed his eyelids closed and jerked his head to the right. For the first time, he was successful in cutting Deavers off — the annoying little punk. But it had taken extraordinary effort and probably made him look like a Tourette's patient.

"Ed, you okay?" Savannah asked.

"I'm fine," Ed said.

Nancy didn't turn around as she walked around the car and got in the driver's seat. They wanted to take Savannah to the hospital, but she insisted on going to her cabin right away. When they arrived, Savannah shot to her bedroom, threw a suitcase on the bed, and began to haphazardly throw clothes inside.

"Whoa," Ed said, putting his hand on the suitcase. "What's going on?"

"What does it look like?" Savannah walked quickly past Ed without looking. "I can't stay here!"

"What about getting Hudak?"

"In case you didn't notice, Hudak got *me*." Savannah continued to pack.

Ed stepped in front of her, causing her to stop with a handful of clothes folded across her chest.

"You've been through a lot. Let us take you to the hospital. Take a minute to process."

"I don't need a minute." Savannah stepped around him, shoved the remaining clothes into the suitcase, and, with some effort, smashed it shut.

"You're walking out on the biggest story of your life." Ed probably should have been helping her pack rather than trying to convince her to stay, but she had been helpful after joining their "Scooby" gang, and he hated to lose her. "What about that Pulitzer?"

"Presented posthumously? I don't think so. You put two bullets into his chest, and he walked away like you called him a bad name."

"It hurt him," Ed said lamely.

"You should take Nancy and get the hell out of here." She looked at Nancy. "He's going to kill all of you."

Ed glanced at Nancy who dropped her head.

"What about the equipment?"

"Keep it or send it back. I don't care." Savannah threw up her arms. "He *had* me, Ed. He was going to take me down to the tracks and—"

"Okay." Ed walked over and grabbed Savannah's shoulders. She leaned against him.

"We'll stay with you until you leave."

"No. I'll be okay. I know you've got paperwork or something. I'll stop by the office before I head out."

"Nancy, give her your radio," Ed said. "Anything happens, you push this button and call out. We'll be right here. And your weapon works better if it's loaded."

Savannah accepted the radio. "I'm sorry. I thought I could do this, but—"

Ed touched her shoulder and went out the door.

# Chapter 25

When Ed and Nancy arrived at the office, Andy was sitting at his desk.

"You didn't have to come in early," Nancy said.

Andy ignored her and approached Ed. "What happened?"

"The chief got beat up," Nancy said quickly.

"I didn't get—" Ed closed his eyes. "Nobody got beat up."

"Hudak?" Andy asked.

"Mm-hmm," Nancy went to the breakroom and retrieved an ice pack from the refrigerator. She brought it back and stopped in front of Ed, holding the pack in the palm of her hand.

Ed looked at the pack, then at Nancy. "What?"

"Undo, your shirt. You've got bruised ribs—or broken ribs. You should take your own advice and go to the hospital." Nancy reached out and began to tug on Ed's shirt.

"Somebody gonna tell me what happened?" Andy said.

"I'll do it." Ed pushed Nancy's hand away and

unbuttoned his shirt.

"You fight Hudak, chief?" Andy sounded frustrated.

Ed gingerly lifted his shirt, exposing a dark, circular mark. He touched it with his finger and winced. "How did you know?" he asked Nancy.

"Kandahar. The way you were walking. I've seen that before."

Nancy started to apply the ice pack, but Ed took it from her and pressed it to the wound.

To Andy, he said, "Tracked Hudak through the woods. He had Savannah and was taking her... I guess taking her to the tracks."

"Seriously? Shit," Andy said.

"Yeah, and there's another problem," Ed said.

"Another one? I think we reached our quota."

"His ability to teleport." Ed bared his teeth at another sharp pain that hit him. "He used it to, I don't know, pop around at will. He was able to appear behind me and attack at different angles."

"Wait a minute. He can disappear and reappear at will?" Nancy said. "How?"

"Yeah, short distances, maybe. I don't know. The lantern is the key. He waved it in front of his face before." Ed hesitated. "Before he disappeared, teleported, whatever."

"Chief," Andy said. "That sounds—"

"Crazy?" Ed shifted his position and pressed the ice pack tighter to his ribs.

Andy looked down at his desk.

"What is it, Andy?" Ed asked.

Andy looked up. "Chief, if he has these powers, what chance do we have?"

"We're not talking about that again," Ed said. "He can

be hurt. I clipped him a couple of times. I know I did."

Andy sounded subdued. "Did he go down?"

"He didn't go down, but it hurt him. I could tell."

"He was supposed to have been hurt by Joshua Morton. You see any evidence of that?"

"I know where you're going with this, Andy. We already talked about this. We're not backing off."

"That was before we knew he could pop around like—like the freaking Nightcrawler," Andy said. "When we thought Morton stabbed him. Now it seems like nothing can hurt him."

"It's a moot point now," Ed said.

"What do you mean?"

Ed dropped the ice pack on the table. "He attacked Charlie, and I shot him. There's no going back to our neutral corners."

"And if he kills one of *us*?" Andy asked.

"Andy." Nancy frowned.

Andy waved her off. "I don't mean I'm out. I gave you my word, and I'm going to see it through, but are you going to be able to live with yourself if he takes out Nancy or me?"

"Andy, that's out of line," Nancy said.

"No, it's okay." Ed held a hand up. "He's right. Charlie, Savannah—that's on me. Maybe I should have listened and blamed Malone for a crime he didn't commit. Let Hudak kill with impunity until he got tired and went away."

"Chief, I didn't mean..." Andy said.

Ed buttoned his shirt. "But I didn't, and now I might get everyone killed. Is that it?"

"Boss, that came out way wrong," Andy said.

"Chasing ghosts and demons is not part of your

job. I dragged you into this, and I have to live with that, but there *is* no going back, understand? Either we finish Hudak, or he finishes us. There's no third option. Now, why don't you go get some breakfast? I'll see you tonight."

"Chief."

"We're good. Go get some breakfast."

"Yes, chief," Andy headed for the door, then turned around.

Ed nodded his reassurance.

"Chief, Andy was way out of line." Nancy stepped toward him.

Ed leaned back on the desk. "No, he wasn't."

"You gave us a choice, remember? You didn't order us to do this. Andy is tired and scared. So am I, but we're going to see this thing through."

Ed took a deep breath and let it slip through his teeth. "What if I get one of you killed? What if I get *you* killed?"

"All I know is I'm with you. Whatever happens." Nancy reached for Ed's hand, but he kept it at his side.

The buzzer signaled that someone was at the door. Nancy walked across the room and pulled it open.

Savannah walked in. "I've got something for you."

Ed smiled. "You changed your mind."

"Uh, that's a no. I'm getting the hell out of here. I called Audrey Mason from OU. She's going to let me crash at her place for a bit. I know how that sounds, but I don't care. I'm not willing to die for a story."

"Then what've you got?" Ed asked.

Savannah stared at Ed for a long time before responding. "I've been corresponding with Audrey and a small group of interested individuals."

Ed looked at her incredulously.

"Don't look at me like that." Savannah frowned at him. "These people really want to help."

"That's all we need, Savannah," Ed said, pacing, "a bunch of kooks and wackos running around."

Savannah placed her hands on her hips. "These are serious researchers, and we—*you*—need all the help you can get!"

"Who are they?"

Savannah ran a hand through her hair. She had neglected to color it the last few days, and Ed noticed more streaks of gray.

"They want to remain anonymous. I only have their screen names."

Nancy laughed. "Why don't you put all this on a placard and walk up and down the street advertising what we're doing?"

"Back off!" Savannah said icily.

Nancy stepped forward. "You want to make me back off, princess?"

"Nancy!" Ed said.

Nancy stormed off to the breakroom.

"Look." Savannah moved closer. "No one has come around, right? Now, Athens is not that far away. I'll still be close by."

"Fine." Ed threw up his hands.

"Good." Savannah hugged Ed around the waist, which caused Ed to hiss with pain. Then she kissed him on the cheek and motioned to the breakroom. "That one's a keeper. You take care of her. I mean it."

"We're not—" Ed shook his head and returned the embrace.

Savannah headed for the door with one last wave over her shoulder.

Nancy came in and stared after her. "I shouldn't have given her such a hard time."

"No, you shouldn't have. She took a big risk and almost died for it. You should cut her a break."

# Chapter 26

**"Edward, if you were** anyone else, I'd have you committed," Roland Donegal said after Ed filled him in on Hudak.

They were in the man cave of Donegal's home in Athens. The professor wore a monogrammed robe and slippers. The slippers, shaped like a cow, were a gift from Donegal's daughter.

"Anyone sees you in those slippers, they'll have *you* committed."

Donegal looked down and wiggled his toes, causing one of the cows to bow.

"You say that he was able to teleport short distances during the battle? I can't believe I'm saying this out loud."

"If you can call it that. I got my ass kicked."

"Understandable under the circumstances. But what I don't understand is that if he wanted to get away after you shot him, why not disappear entirely on the spot?"

"I don't know," Ed said.

Donegal picked up the snifter of cognac on the small table next to his oversized chair, swirled it, lifted it to his chin, and inhaled. Ed looked at his glass of Nature

Boost, into which Donegal had dropped ice cubes using metal tongs. There was no drinking out of cans in the professor's home.

"Come on, Edward. You're not even trying. Didn't you say something about a bright light when Hudak disappeared?"

"Yes, and there is no bright light when he teleports."

"Sooo?" Donegal held his hands out wide.

"So his ability to teleport is a different agency than his ability to disappear, and the two times I saw him disappear, he was near the trail."

"Therefore—"

"Therefore, he can only disappear completely when he is near the trail." Ed slapped his forehead. "It holds a special significance, perhaps because he died there."

"It's all right, you got there." Donegal raised the snifter, placed it under his nose one last time and finally sipped, rolling it across his tongue.

"If you had the answer, you could have just told me, Roland," Ed said.

"What fun would that be?" Donegal smiled.

"I just thought of something else. What if his power is directly proportional to his proximity to the trail? He could have dealt with me behind the cabins, but after knocking me down, he ran away."

"Good, Edward."

"Okay, so I know some of his limitations. I just have to find a way to use them against him."

Donegal looked stern.

"What?"

"You can't beat him," Donegal said.

"What do you mean?"

"If you continue down this course, Edward, he will

kill you and maybe your comrades as well."

"I'm finding out more about him every day.."

"What you're finding out is that he has powers beyond your comprehension." Donegal put the snifter down. "Your attacks on him have been completely ineffective."

"So what are you suggesting?"

"Get some help. Government, military, whatever."

"And how would I do that? Who would believe me?"

"You have a couple of witnesses."

"Nancy and Andy were too far away to see anything clearly the first time. Everyone who has seen what he can really do is dead. Except me."

"What about the lovely Miss Hughes?" Donegal said.

"A reporter looking for a story. That's credible."

"You have to try, Edward." Donegal grabbed the snifter again and began to swirl. "I don't want to see you die."

This came as close to affection as Donegal would ever display. Ed smiled. "I appreciate that, but you've known me for thirty years, and until today, you didn't even believe me. How am I going to convince the federal government?"

"All right. Then you're going to have to lure him away from the trail. Get him where he's weakest. Then kill him. No more talk of arrest. Otherwise, he'll kill everyone you care about."

"Not everyone, Roland," Ed said.

**Rubbing his** eyes, Ed tried to focus on Nancy's report. He pushed back from his desk and rolled his neck. It crackled and popped. He looked around his office and wondered if he should do some decorating. On the wall behind him was his police academy photograph. Twenty smiling officers, in uniforms void of badges or patches stood in front of the Harold K. Stubbs Justice Center. They were so young. It seemed like ages ago. Below hung a picture of himself and his partner, Martin Dan, flanking the then-Ohio Attorney General Lee Fisher, who rode along with them. For the first time, he considered that the rule of the four may have been a little extreme.

There were certificates and commendations but nothing personal. No wife or children. Like most men his age, he had been close to marriage. Something always seemed to get in the way, the job mostly. He had always avoided relationships with other law enforcement officers, but perhaps that had been a mistake. Maybe things *could* work out with Nancy, at least after they resolved the Hudak issue and he was no longer her boss.

*You think you're actually going to live through this?* Deavers said.

Ed closed his eyes and rubbed his temples. This had to stop. He conjured the river in his mind.

*Oh, not this shit again,* Deavers said, sounding exasperated.

Ed remained calm. "I thought you were supposed to be gone."

*I thought you were supposed to be gone,* Deavers repeated in Ed's voice.

Ed brought up the image of Anthony Deavers, not the way he was the day he died, but the one from the video. He placed him in the lotus position on one of the marigolds and sent him downriver. Deavers stuck out his tongue before going over the waterfall. Ed waited for another comment but heard none. Ed had no illusions that the imp was gone. Sometimes, he just didn't have anything to say.

Ed unpacked his new cell phone and set it up. After a series of updates, the familiar jingle of his carrier sounded. His phone beeped, whirred, and buzzed after all the messages and notifications he missed flooded in. A name flashed by before it switched to Nancy's name. Ed opened the phone icon and saw a name that brought a deep frown to his face. "Deadbeat." A green dot indicated that a voicemail had been left. He deleted it without listening. The last person on Earth he needed to talk to was his father.

Ed heard the front door buzz. A hint of the morning sun could be seen on the horizon. Nancy had not gone home yet. She walked past his office to the main door. Seconds later, she returned and gestured over her shoulder.

Ed went into the outer office and saw Savannah walk in with Audrey Mason. Savannah's hair, though styled in the same manner, was mildly disheveled. She wore the same outfit she wore on their trip to Athens, blue jeans and a black tank top. A woman like Savannah Hughes would not be seen in the same outfit twice. Audrey Mason, whose appearance was always a bit untidy, looked the same.

Savannah walked straight up to Ed and took his hand. "I owe you an apology. It's just I've never been that scared in my life, and I—well, I panicked."

"You don't owe me anything. You have no obligation to see this through."

To Ed's surprise, Nancy stepped in. "You could have just filed your story, but you came down and got right into the thick of it. That took a hell of a lot of courage in my book."

"I've come bearing gifts." Savannah smiled and

touched Nancy's arm.

"Oh?" Ed looked at Audrey Mason, who stood grinning like a schoolgirl.

"Mr. Freemen, we found her," Audrey said. She pumped her fist as if she had just won money from a scratch-off ticket.

"Who?" Ed looked around.

Savannah moved next to Audrey. They bumped into one another awkwardly as if urging the other to break the news.

"Who did you find?" Ed repeated.

"Jackie Hudak's sister," they both said, then turned to each other and giggled.

"What, did she leave a diary or something?"

"Or something," Savannah said.

"All right, just say it," Nancy said.

"Jackie Hudak's sister Jennifer is still alive," Savannah said.

"That's impossible. She'd have to be—"

"A hundred and three," Audrey said. "And still kicking."

"How did you find her?" Ed motioned for Savannah and Audrey to sit, but they seemed too excited.

"Tell you on the way," Savannah said. She grabbed Audrey's hand, and the two headed for the door.

Ed turned to look at Nancy. "Are they—?"

"Totally," she said.

"And high as kites?"

"Yep," Nancy said. "You want me to go with you, chief?"

Ed looked out the window at the two women. "No, it'll be okay. You go get some sleep." He started to walk.

Nancy grabbed his arm. "Speaking of sleep."

Ed turned to look at himself in the glass of his office door. His eyes were puffy. All the men on his father's side of the family had white hair and looked very distinguished in their later years. Ed's facial hair had remained black, but unshaven he noticed that it too had turned white.

*Damn, you look old*, Deavers said.

"I look bad, huh?"

Nancy reached up and touched his face. "No, you still look good. But you're tired, and it's starting to show."

"Can't be helped. Besides, if Hudak gets his way, I'll be taking a nice long nap under the dirt."

**Jennifer Stewart** lived in, or at least near Blue Creek, West Virginia. The community was little more than an intersection with a U-Haul storage center and a place to rent farm equipment. Down the street was a Baptist church. In fact, all the small towns they passed, and there were many, had a Baptist church.

Ed wondered how they were similar or different from the Baptist church he had grown up attending. Did they sweat profusely while screaming about fire and brimstone until they were hoarse as his pastor? They turned left and crossed the Elk River. Jennifer's granddaughter, Rosemay—not Rosemary—whom they picked up in Parkersburg, drove Savannah's 4Runner. This was a good thing, as Ed suspected that Savannah and Audrey had consumed some mind-altering substance the night before and were just beginning to recover.

After they crossed the Elk River, Ed breathed a sigh of relief. They had to be almost there. He was wrong. They twisted and turned along back roads, some paved, some not, some with names, some without. After a while, it seemed no human being could live so far into the wilderness. Where did they get their services?

Rosemay turned left, and they headed up a slight grade on a dirt road. Every so often, they passed wooden shacks that, at first, appeared to be abandoned. Then, someone would stick his or her head out of a glassless window.

Finally, they arrived at Jennifer Stewart's home. Though it was in better condition than the homes they passed on the way, Ed could tell it was constructed only from material available in the area.

Pillars made from whole trees held up the roof and formed the front porch. The trees had been carefully sanded and smoothed, but you could still see circular marks where branches had once fanned out from the trunks.

The roof was the only prefabricated part of the structure. Made from corrugated tin, it had a layer of red rust that added to the aesthetics of the structure. The walls had once been painted pink, but the paint was so badly chipped only a few flakes clung to the graying wood. Doors of many different types, perhaps a hundred, were piled up, covering the majority of the front porch. Some were entry doors, others flimsy screen doors, but they were all made of wood.

A thought occurred to Ed. Firewood. They were all being used for firewood. It seemed silly at first. A house in a forest would have plenty of available trees, but those trees had to be felled and cut. Wooden doors, especially old ones, could be easily broken apart and tossed into a fireplace.

A tiny woman, not quite five feet tall, emerged from the house. She walked slowly but didn't seem hobbled by age. She started down the three stairs in front of the porch. Ed rushed forward and hooked his right elbow in front of her. She looked up at him with a crinkled smile and grabbed the crook of his arm with her hand. Like Phyllis Brandt, she seemed warmer than most.

Ed guided her to a rocking chair in the dirt. She motioned for her guests to sit on two large logs arranged in a V in front of the chair. Ed introduced himself and his two colleagues.

The old woman greeted them with a wave of her hand. Her silver hair was pulled back into a neat bun. If she had been wearing glasses, she could have passed for Irene Ryan, who played Granny on *The Beverly Hillbillies*. When she spoke, Ed expected the rough timbre of a woman whose vocal cords had been drying for the last seventy years. In fact, the only sign of age was a slight tremulous quality.

"Rosemay said you would be coming, but I knew before that."

"Excuse me, ma'am, but how could you know?" Ed said.

She leaned back and laughed. For a moment, the years were stripped away, and she was a coquettish girl flirting with her young suitor.

"Young man, why do you think the Lord kept me around all these years? And you can ditch that 'ma'am' stuff. You call me Mama Jen. Everybody calls me Mama Jen."

Ed smiled. "Thank you, Mama Jen, and you can call me Ed."

"Excuse me, Mama Jen." Savannah leaned forward. "Why did you think someone would come?"

Mama Jen cocked her head and looked at Savannah,

then Audrey. "Because I know what you're after. You want to know about my brother."

"Jackie Hudak," Ed said.

Her head bobbed. "Yes, Jackie."

"Do you remember what happened?" Ed asked.

Jennifer Stewart turned to the side, and Ed could see the wrinkles fanning out from her eye sockets like rivers snaking out from a lake. He wondered how many stories flowed along those rivers.

"I remember. I remember everything." Jennifer closed her eyes. "Jackie was a good big brother. The other kids — Katie, Merton, Forest, and Grant — never paid attention to me because I was the youngest by a lot, but Jackie always found time for me. Whenever he got home from work, he would come find me, tickle me, and try to make me laugh. He would let me dress him up, and he'd pretend to be a guest at my tea party using little wooden cups and saucers Merton carved."

The old lady paused and looked up. Her eyes glassed over at the memory. "When there wasn't enough to eat, he'd give me some of his. But then he changed. He stopped playing with me and started to get drunk all the time. I didn't understand everything that was going on 'cause I was little, but I heard Father shouting at him, and I heard Mama use the word *haint*."

"What is a haint?" Savannah said, interrupting.

"A ghost or evil spirit," Ed said.

"Belief in haints is thought to have originated with the Gullah Geechee people of the Carolinas but has also appeared in Appalachian myths," Audrey said.

"It ain't no myth," Jennifer said.

"We saw some extra doors on a photo of your old house. Did you guys do that after he changed or after he died?" Ed said.

For the first time, Jennifer seemed confused. "I can't say. I don't remember, but I do remember the bottles. Did you see the bottles?"

"No, ma'am," Ed said.

"You take empty bottles and hang them upside down to keep the evil spirit away. I remember doing that because it was kind of fun." She dropped her head. "I didn't know no better."

"Was this before or after he died?"

"I'm pretty sure it was after 'cause they sent me to live here with my auntie a few weeks after that." She waved a hand to indicate the house, then her voice became a whisper. "I saw him once, you know, after."

Everyone, including Rosemay, leaned in.

"It was only a couple of days after he passed. We didn't have no funeral because, you know, they never found no body. Katie was asleep, but something woke me up. I went to the window, and there was Jackie, circling the house with his railroad lantern. I waved to him, but he didn't pay no mind. I was so happy because I thought he wasn't dead, so I stayed in the window until he came back around.

"This time, he stopped, looked at me, and smiled. I ain't never been that scared before nor since. It was Jackie's smile, but the thing using it wasn't Jackie. He kept a-circling the house like he was waiting for the right time to come in. I told Mama and Daddy, but they didn't believe me. No one did."

Her eyes widened. "They *did* believe me. Now that I think of it, it was the next day that we put out the bottles. They let me think I imagined it. I guess they were trying to protect me, though."

"How did you know it wasn't Jackie?" Savannah asked.

"I don't know." Jennifer swung her head slowly left and right. "It was like when we locked eyes, we knew. I can't explain it. But I knew it wasn't him, and he knew I knew."

A squirrel scampered up a tree and circled to the far side. Ed had to force himself to look away and bring his attention back with some effort. "What happened to your family?"

"I don't know," she said. A wave of sadness washed over her wrinkles. "I never saw them again. My auntie told me they were all gone. We didn't talk about it."

Ed looked around to see if anyone had more questions. He stood and dug his wallet out of his back pocket. He caught Savannah's eye and motioned for her to do the same. Between them, they had about a hundred and seventy dollars. He walked over to Jennifer and handed the money to her.

"Mama Jen, we'd like you to have this as a token of our appreciation."

"We ain't takin' no charity!" Rosemay snapped.

"Mama Jen has given us some valuable information that will help us in an ongoing investigation. We often pay sources for information," Ed said with a smile.

"Hush, child," Mama Jen said, waving an impatient hand at Rosemay. "He don't look down on us. He knows."

Ed did know. He had grown up poor. Sometimes, he and his mother would go a day or two without eating and sang songs to stave off the hunger pangs. She had done the best she could, but Ed's father, a womanizing narcissist, had left his mother broken and penniless.

At least Ed *thought* he was poor. Looking over Jennifer's

property, he understood true poverty was abject and merciless. The broken doors provided the only source of heat in the wintertime. The lack of a meter on the side of the house meant that a pump in the sink probably pulled well water into the home from an underground source. Though Ed's mother had struggled mightily to make ends meet, she had managed to keep a roof over their heads and at least one utility service running. How Jennifer knew that Ed had known poverty was a mystery.

*You just have that look*, Deavers offered.

Mama Jen crooked her finger, and Ed leaned in.

"That thing ain't my brother," she whispered. "Don't you hesitate."

# Chapter 27

**The following evening, Nancy** showered in her small cottage-style home in Nelsonville. She liked her water lukewarm and set her showerhead to its finest setting. The needlelike points of water tingled her skin.

She rubbed soap on her body, a cheap brand called Ocean Breeze or Summer Breeze or something like that. It didn't remind her of the ocean but instead smelled of a dank forest. As the water hit her body, she wondered what Ed would look like in the shower. He was ripped. Nancy knew that much. She imagined him pulling her into his arms, his muscular body pressing against hers. She leaned back, letting the water run down the front of her.

A thump yanked her out of her reverie. Nancy's eyes opened. She turned the water off and listened, then listened again but heard nothing. A sleepy town on the banks of the Hocking River, Nelsonville boasted a crime rate near zero. In normal times, she would have returned to her shower.

Per Ed's instructions, she had placed her weapon on the water closet when she came into the bathroom. She slipped out of the shower, grabbed the gun, and moved naked through the bedroom into the living room, then the kitchen. Her bare feet tapped on the tile like a child who snuck downstairs to peek at Christmas presents.

Nancy searched the kitchen, pantry, and even under the sink. She returned to the bedroom. Her uniform shirt hung on a chair next to the bed, but there was something odd about it. She squinted. Something was missing. A blank space stared at her where a silver name tag with black lettering should have been. This didn't immediately alarm Nancy. She had lost her name tag several times, only to later find it in a laundry basket or on the floor of her closet. To appear at work without her nametag violated procedure, and the chief noticed everything, but he wasn't a stickler for those kinds of rules.

Nancy dropped to the floor, looked under the bed, then in the usual places—the closet and laundry basket. She went through the house, double-checking that all the doors and windows were locked. The entire living area of the small home was on the first floor. Only the storage attic stood above ground level.

Locking doors and windows was something new for Nancy. There had never been a need. When she returned to the bedroom, she saw the window latch wasn't entirely flush against the side. Was it over far enough to engage the lock? Nancy moved to the window and started to push it up. Feeling a chill, she retreated into the room.

She dressed in a white T-shirt and her uniform pants, her usual garb on the nights she worked. Nancy grabbed her Mini Maglite and went outside. She aimed the beam at the grass underneath the window, but the ground was too hard to leave any clues.

"Hey, Nancy."

She turned and saw her next-door neighbor, Mr. Brent, standing on his porch, smoking.

"Everything okay?" Brent said.

"Hey, yeah. Did you see anybody out here a little while ago?"

"Just you," Brent said. The singsong lilt in his voice made Nancy think that he had seen a lot more.

Nancy looked back and forth from her window to where Brent was standing. Her bedroom was partially illuminated by her bathroom light. Her shoulders slumped. Brent could have come out onto his porch for a smoke and been rewarded for his timing with a nice jubbly show. Nancy looked at him. She couldn't tell if he was grinning. She just saw the red glow of the cigarette brighten as he drew the carcinogen into his lungs.

*Suck it in, perv.*

As she started for the house, she heard Brent yell, "You have a nice day now, Nancy."

She started to flip him off, but what would be the point? He had maybe a few seconds to gawk at her breasts. No matter. *Glad to make your day, sir.* Nancy went back inside, pulled her spare name tag off her dress uniform, then walked to the window and slid the latch all the way to the left.

Someone could have climbed through the window and taken her name tag, but why? She decided it couldn't have been Jackie Hudak. He would have come into the shower and beaten her to death or choked her out and taken her to the trail to be flattened by the ghost train. Mr. Brent? She imagined him sneaking into her bedroom, pressing her underwear to his nose, or taking them home to masturbate to, but no. Brent was a harmless ogler who merely enjoyed watching her come and go. Most likely, she had just misplaced the name tag again, but she would be sure to check all her doors and windows from now on. No need to mention it to the chief. Under the circumstances, he wouldn't appreciate her carelessness.

**Ed picked** up his phone and heard the familiar voice of Harry Dean. Dean had been his sergeant when he was a patrol officer and had joined the ranger service, rising to the position of operations supervisor.

"Hey, Harry, what's going on?" Ed said.

"Hey Ed, I just wanted to give you a heads-up. There are some rumblings up here that your predecessor is causing trouble."

"Waddell?"

"Yeah, he's accusing you of unnecessary overtime."

"Unnecessary?" Ed said through clenched teeth.

"He also said you're screwing your hot little ranger."

*You didn't actually put it in her,* Deavers added. *But you wanted to, Ed. You wanted to.*

"Oh my god, if one more person says that!" Ed held the phone away and turned his head.

"It's not true?"

"No, it's not true!" Ed said.

"Ed, I'm speaking as your old sergeant here. If there's anything that can hurt you, you need to let me know."

Ed looked to the sky and groaned. "I'm not banging her, Harry."

"That's good. Make sure you keep it that way. Waddell has a lot of friends up here."

"What does he want?"

"I think he's angling for his old job back."

"That's not good," Ed said. "Can you run interference?"

"Well, not being in your immediate chain of command,

I'm limited in what I can do, but I'll do my best."

"Thanks, sarge."

"Hey, you don't have to thank me, Ed. I owe you my life."

"Will you stop with that 'owe' stuff?"

"No, I won't stop. If you hadn't seen McIntyre hiding in those bushes, he'd have smoked me for sure."

"Whatever," Ed said. "I need to take care of one more thing here. It'd be great if you could keep the jackals off my six while I do it."

"You need any help?"

"No, it's better if you don't know what's going on, believe me."

"All right. Don't hesitate to call if you change your mind. You take care, my friend."

"You too, sarge."

When Ed hung up, Andy was in the outer office talking to Holt Potter. He went to the door, opened it, and waved them into his office.

"Holt, this is a surprise," Ed said.

"I realized that I'd never been here," Holt said. "I wish I had good news."

Ed sat up. "It's not Charlie, is it?"

"No, no. He's fine. But you know when we thought Hudak was lying low?"

"Yeah?"

"He wasn't. He chicken-choked a guy named George Riley in Zaleski. Of course, we can't be sure it's your guy, but a local store owner came out and took a couple of potshots at him. Riley shot at him too. Probably saved his life. They didn't get a good look at him, but the description they gave us fits."

Ed smiled. Holt had finally used the name Hudak.

"That prompted us to contact other surrounding counties," Holt said. "There was another incident in Athens County—big man tried to pull a trucker out of the cab when he stopped at a light. And one just north of here—a woman hiking was being followed by a big man carrying a lantern."

Ed rubbed his chin. "Do Hudak's actions strike you as—"

"Desperate?" Holt finished. "Yes, and careless. It seems like your surveillance forced him to move to the outskirts and take more chances with his targets. A few got away, and he's not happy about it."

"That's why he came after Charlie."

"You boxed him in," Holt said. "You know what happens next."

"Yeah."

"My deputies will be on standby. Call if you need to." Holt walked away.

Ed's cell phone rang. He looked at the display: "Deadbeat." Ed let it go to voicemail.

# Chapter 28

Ed's muscles ached as he arrived at his cabin at around 2:00 a.m. He looked forward to a few hours' sleep. The dim light over his door cast a pitiful glow on his welcome mat. He would have to change it to a higher wattage.

Pulling out his keys, he noticed a rectangular object sticking out from the welcome mat. He drew his weapon and looked around. Situated in an isolated part of the state park, the cabin presented an ideal place for an ambush. Hudak could be hidden on either side, obscured by trees, ready to follow him inside and finish him off. Still looking around, Ed knelt and peeled the end of the mat up. Underneath was a silver nameplate attached to a faded postcard. Ed took it inside and placed it on his dining room table. The name "Sullivan" stenciled in black lettering, stared back at him.

*Uh-oh*, Deavers said.

The postcard had obviously been purchased from the park office. It showed the massive Hope Furnace, used more than a hundred and fifty years ago to smelt iron ore and supply cannon balls to the Union Army during the Civil War. Ed sat and stared at the two objects.

The meaning was clear. Hudak wanted a showdown, and if Ed didn't respond, he would start killing those close to Ed, beginning with Nancy Sullivan. Ed thought of Waddell weeping over his beloved Stella. Ed couldn't understand how Hudak knew about his feelings for Nancy. In the final analysis it didn't matter. He knew.

*You cannot be thinking of going*, Deavers said.

Andy had been right. Ed's actions led them to this point, and if they died, if Nancy died, it would be on his head. Ed got up, went to his bedroom, and dressed in his tactical gear, which included extra magazine pouches and OC spray. He selected four additional magazines instead of the usual two.

*Oh, come on*, Deavers pleaded. *You can't be serious.*

Ed rummaged through his closet and found his old baton from his days as a patrol officer. It was only twelve inches but made of Ebonite, a material used to make bowling balls. It packed more of a punch than his thin metal collapsible baton.

*So you're going to beat him to death?*

Ed's first thought was to empty all five magazines into him.

*That may not work, remember?*

"Then maybe he will reassemble after I've pulverized his bones with this." Ed dropped the baton into the ring on his Sam Browne belt.

*You talking a lot of shit*, Deavers said. *I hope you can back it up.*

"I'd better," Ed said. "I'd better."

**After Ed** left, Nancy settled into her routine. She cruised the rustic cabins near the lodge, then went through the larger housekeeping cabins. The night air felt warm and still. The sounds of every animal native to the Zaleski State Forest made its presence known. Owls, rodents, frogs, cats, and bats all seemed to have something to say, a howling chorus of hunters and the hunted.

Nancy saw flickers of light behind some of the cabins and smelled smoke and barbecued meat. She drove to the Hope Furnace and circled the parking lot where Hudak had scared the bejesus out of that young couple. Next, she drove around the perimeter of the park to the other side of the lake. Parking there for a while, she stared into the darkness. The night shift could be lonely and boring. In the best of circumstances, it was difficult to maintain focus, but lack of focus could get her killed.

Nancy repeated her routine once more. At around three in the morning, her eyes began to get heavy. She decided to go to the office for coffee. On the night shift, all sounds were amplified, and when she opened the door, the buzzer sounded like a naval battle Klaxon. The aroma of freshly brewed coffee met her like an old friend. She had set the pot to brew at three, knowing this was the time she usually became sleepy. Nancy sat at her desk and sipped from a cup that read, "I ain't no lady, so don't f@#k with me."

**When Ed** arrived at Hope Furnace, he found no sign of the hulking maniac. Perhaps he had misread Hudak's intentions. Maybe he was just telling Ed the endgame was near, and they were all destined for death. But he didn't think so. The postcard and nameplate had been an invitation right out of the old West. Instead of a dusty street at high noon, Ed would meet his fate in front of an old furnace in the dead of night.

He sat on one of the large stone blocks that had long

ago fallen away from the furnace. Tiny tree frogs called to prospective mates with a sound that resembled a plucked rubber band. Ed looked at the parking lot where his cruiser stood in the exact spot Hudak had scared the young couple. In the distance, he saw the soft green glow of fireflies winking on and off like tiny stars.

Taking out his flashlight, he played the beam in a wide arc. When he turned to point the beam behind him, it fell on Jackie Hudak. He just stood there, a frighteningly calm expression on his face.

"Shit!" Ed straightened so fast he fell forward onto his knees. He scrambled to his feet and reached for his weapon. Hudak stopped him with a slow shake of his head. Turning, Hudak looked toward the furnace, then back at Ed. When their eyes met, Ed understood that Hudak wanted him to take his gun off and put it there.

They stared at one another for almost a minute. Then Hudak turned slowly, took the lantern to the left side of the furnace and set it down as if it were made of porcelain. Ed understood. Though not in words and not telepathically, they were communicating.

Ed took off his Sam Browne belt and placed it at the other end of the massive furnace. This contest would be fought without magic or firearms. Ed also understood the stakes. Win or lose, his colleagues would be left alone.

*This is really stupid*, Anthony Deavers said. *He's going to kick your ass again.*

A sense of calm washed over Ed. Deep down, he knew he was going to die. Hudak would get the better of him, beat him to within an inch of his life, and finish him off on railroad tracks that weren't there.

Still, he was willing to risk it, to hope against hope he could somehow find the killing blow and end it all here.

Now that he was playing with house money, he could go all out, knowing his colleagues would live. Ed shook his arms out and came forward. He and the big man met in the clearing in front of the furnace.

*Oh boy. Here we go*, Deavers said.

Hudak clenched his fists, causing the fluid between the joints to snap, crackle, and pop. Ed danced on his toes. His strategy—to wear the bigger man down with jabs and straight right hands. If he committed himself to power punches, Hudak would get in a blow. And he may only need one.

Hudak stood waiting. He made no move to close the distance. Ed danced in, popping Hudak with a jab and right cross. Hudak responded with a slow right cross. Ed easily dodged it and punished him for the miss with a straight right to the nose. Hunched over, Hudak tried to tackle Ed. Ed pivoted and kicked him in the side as he went by. Hudak let out a guttural sound of rage, turned, and charged forward. Ed ducked, smashed him with an uppercut, and spun out of the way. Hudak stood, rolled his shoulders, and put up his fists.

**After a** few minutes, Nancy got up from her chair and went into Ed's office. She flicked the light on and sat at his desk. She realized Ed had never really settled in. There were no family pictures, just a few awards and plaques, and a glass block with a 3D image of the Harold K. Stubbs Justice Center and a caption that read "greatest detective ever."

Nancy smiled at Ed's police academy photo. Ed had hair then and was thin—not bony, but thin and wiry. Nancy knew Ed had grown up poor and didn't like to talk about his childhood, but his office was depressing.

Sipping her coffee, Nancy flipped through screens. Occasionally, a camera's motion sensor would interrupt the image and show whatever animal had wandered into the frame. Nancy caught a brief shot of Hope Furnace when the image jumped to a deer nosing its way through the forest on the Peninsula Trail. Nancy kept flipping through the cameras until she realized something strange was going on at Hope Furnace. She quickly jumped back to that camera and shouted when hot coffee hit her thigh. Two men circled one another like 1930s bare-knuckled fighters. One of the men was considerably larger. The other man was Ed Freemen. Grabbing her cell phone, she ran toward the door.

# Chapter 29

**Ed thought he was** doing well. Even in the dark, Ed could see that Hudak's face showed signs of his fast fists. Ed circled, knowing Hudak's right was his most devastating weapon. He shuffled forward, hit Hudak with two lefts, then danced back before the big man could respond. Ed bent his knees and sent a right hook into Hudak's ribs. He grunted in pain but continued to chase Ed around the field.

Ed's breathing grew short and rapid. It was then he realized the folly of his plan. While Ed was scoring points, it wasn't a boxing match, and he was doing no real damage. Hudak could look like he had gone twelve rounds with Tyson Fury and still kill Ed in the end. Ed had to find a way to end it, and that meant taking more chances.

The parking lot lamp provided a dim glow. Ed backed up, drawing Hudak closer to the light. Hudak seemed frustrated at his inability to land a significant blow. Ed's heart pounded. One mistake would be the end.

He dodged to the left and struck with a sidekick to Hudak's leg. The big man dropped to his knees. Ed moved behind him, slipped his right elbow under Hudak's chin, and locked in a chokehold. Hudak tried to get up. Ed kicked his leg and knocked him back down.

Ed leaned back to prevent Hudak from getting leverage, but he managed to get his right hand around Ed's forearm, the meaty paw tightening like a vice. Hudak lifted his right leg to a kneeling position. Ed tried to kick him again, but in doing so, allowed Hudak to straighten his upper body. This gave Hudak just enough leverage. To Ed's horror, he found himself flying over Hudak's shoulder, cracking his back on the edge of the parking lot. Hudak let out a primal scream, clamped both hands around Ed's neck, and lifted him off the ground. Ed's eyes bulged. Hudak tightened his grip. Ed hit, kicked, and scratched but couldn't get loose. He saw spots in front of his eyes and fought to stay conscious.

**When Nancy** arrived at Hope Furnace, Hudak had Ed in the air and was shaking him like a rag doll. Ed's hands were at his sides. *Oh God, is he already dead?* She let out an unintelligible shout, not a command, but a roar of sheer rage. With weapon drawn, she ran forward. Hudak looked at her and dropped Ed's limp body on the asphalt. He ran to the furnace, scooped up his lantern, and ran into the darkness. Though Nancy could no longer clearly see him, she fired wildly into the night, breaking a cardinal rule of law enforcement—never fire at what you can't see. With Hudak out of sight, Nancy dropped to her knees in front of Ed. He was breathing.

"What were you thinking?" Nancy said, shaking and pounding Ed with her fists. "Are you trying to die? Is that what you want?"

Ed groaned.

Nancy realized she was pounding on her boss and stopped. "I'm sorry, chief. Are you okay?"

"From Hudak's beating, or yours?" Ed said, his voice sounding raw. He sucked in a breath and rolled onto his side.

"Uh, I'm sorry I hit you," Nancy said.

"Stop it. You're good."

"Are you really okay?"

Ed stretched his neck. "I wouldn't have been in a few minutes. Let's go to the office."

"No, sir, you're going to the hospital this time." Nancy looked stern.

"Nancy."

"You can fire me for insubordination or for striking a superior officer, take your pick, but you *are* going to the hospital."

"None of us will need a hospital in a little while."

"Sir?"

"I'll explain at the office." Ed clambered to his feet.

**Inside the** office, Nancy reheated the coffee and got Ed a cold compress. He sat in the fluffy chair in the lobby, rubbing his neck with one hand and pressing the cold pack to his forehead with the other. The lack of oxygen gave him a pounding headache. Nancy sat across from him expectantly.

"This was under my doormat when I got home." Ed showed her the postcard and nameplate. He sounded like Redd Foxx.

Nancy's hand shot to the spare nameplate on her uniform and stared at the one in Ed's hand. "You're saying this was some kind of threat?"

"The meaning was clear. Face him down at the Hope

Furnace, or he'd kill everyone close to me."

"And he came to my place first because —" She broke off and looked at Ed, who averted her gaze. He waited for a snarky comment from Anthony Deavers, but none came. "You deduced all that from the postcard and nameplate?"

"Also, there's a — connection."

"A connection?"

"It's hard to explain. I think it's what Charlie was trying to tell us after Hudak attacked him." Ed rolled his neck again. Even on his dark skin, the bruising was visible. "I think it's like empathy, though not the compassionate kind. When you're locked in with him, you can read one another's intentions."

"That's pretty weird, chief,"

"That's the part that sounds weird to you?" Ed switched the ice from his forehead to the back of his neck.

"Good point."

The door buzzed and Ed looked over to see Andy rush into the station.

"Chief, you okay? What happened?"

Nancy shot Ed an icy look before she answered. "The chief went one-on-one with Hudak and almost got himself killed. Hudak had him dangling like a puppet when I got there."

"It sounds pretty bad when you say it like that," Ed said feebly.

"It's not funny, chief." Nancy put her hands on her hips.

"Sorry. And thank you for saving my behind."

"Chief, I've always considered you one of the smartest men I've ever met. But with all due respect, that just wasn't bright," Andy said.

"Never mind that. We've got more pressing things to worry about."

"Worse than you getting attacked by Hudak?"

"Yes." Ed got up. "Like Hudak killing us all."

"What?" Andy said.

Nancy handed him a cup of coffee. "The gloves are off. The chief thinks Hudak's going to take us all out."

"Why is he suddenly going after us?" Andy asked.

Ed rubbed his neck and rolled his shoulders. He thought about the night Nancy came over and the flash of light he thought was a hallucination. "We're dealing with an organized killer. We're an impediment to his mission, so he's removing us from the equation."

"But Hudak is a supernatural being." Andy sat on the edge of his desk. "We can't treat him like any other serial killer."

"Why not?" Ed said. "The clue came from Professor Donegal and Joshua Morton. Roland said it doesn't matter that he's supernatural. He's a killer, and we have to stop him like any other killer. And Morton—you remember, Nancy—Morton described Hudak's demeanor as workmanlike. He compared it to chopping wood. Hudak was able to scare investigators off in the past. But when he couldn't scare me off, he went into *High Noon* mode."

Andy's head dropped. "But, chief, he met you on your turf, away from the trail where his power isn't the greatest."

"I think that was on purpose, Andy. A neutral spot. When I locked in with him, I knew he would leave you alone no matter the outcome. There's no way to lie when that happens."

"That's not what I mean," Andy said. "You faced him at his most vulnerable, and—forgive me—he beat you.

What chance do we have?"

Ed walked to the window and looked out into the darkness. Andy was right. With their current knowledge of Hudak, they had no chance, and they were running out of time.

"We need to buy some time," Ed said, turning around. "Andy, you're going to follow Nancy to her house while she gets her things. Then she's going to follow you to yours. You're going to pack a go-bag and report back here. You're staying here until —"

"Until we get him," Nancy finished.

"Or he gets us," Ed said.

"What about you, chief? You shouldn't be alone either," Nancy said.

"He'll save me for last." Ed took a sip. "He wants me to suffer the pain of seeing you die first."

# Chapter 30

A pale blue light peeked over the horizon as Ed arrived at his cabin that morning. He reached out to grab the doorknob and stopped, noticing a faint scratch on the strike. Snatching his weapon from its holster, Ed crouched, switched the gun to his left hand, and reached for the doorknob. Cracking the door slightly, Ed listened. He didn't quite hear but, instead, sensed rustling coming from the kitchen.

*It's not Hudak*, Deavers offered.

Ed agreed. Hudak wouldn't let him off that easy. He holstered his weapon and went in, noticing a tall man standing in his kitchen eating a sandwich.

"Son!" Gerald Freemen smiled broadly. He was a couple of inches taller than Ed and slender. While Ed had inherited his father's smooth skin and good teeth, Gerald was more classically handsome, with a long, thin face and prominent chin. He wore his hair close-cropped and neat as if he used a ruler to line his sideburns and hairline. Like most of his family, Gerald's hair had gone white, but he colored it. To most women, he passed for a man in his mid-forties and Ed could understand how they believed him. Gerald put the sandwich down on the counter and came forward, arms outstretched.

"I don't want you to call me that, Gerald." Ed maneuvered around his father and began to search the cabin. He opened drawers and pulled boxes from a high shelf in the closet. He took a small strongbox from its hiding place among tennis shoes, shook it, and held his hand out in the direction of his father. "Give it to me."

"What, son?"

"I told you not to call me that. Give it to me." Ed wiggled his fingers while still turned away from his father.

"I don't know what you're talking about."

Ed looked around the cabin. A blue duffle bag sat on the couch. Ed unzipped it and dumped the contents.

"Hey!" Gerald said. "You ever hear of probable cause?"

Ed ignored him, picked up a roll of bills and put them in his safe, along with his watch, wallet, and law enforcement accessories.

"You have a very suspicious nature, s—I mean Edward."

"No, we're not doing this. This is a terrible time, and you have to leave." Ed pointed.

"I contacted you, but you wouldn't take my calls."

Ed scowled. "I wonder why that would be?"

"I came to help," Gerald said.

"Help with what?"

"I know what's going on down here. I'm part of the online group that's doing research." Gerald retrieved a laptop from a case near the door and turned the screen toward Ed.

"Spectral Hunters?"

"I didn't pick the name."

"Wait, is Professor Mason part of this group?" Ed asked.

"Probably." Gerald put the laptop back in its case. "We only know screen names."

"What's your screen name, Deadbeat Dad?"

"ErrolFlynn77, smart-ass," Gerald said.

"Errol Flynn never made it to seventy-seven." Ed put up his hand, not wanting to fight more. "In any case, I can't deal with you right now, or the lying, thieving, womanizing, manipulating, and whatever the hell else you're bringing with you."

"You need me! This is right in my wheelhouse, and you know it!"

"Ah, ah, no. When Mom and I were huddled around an electric heater, shivering and starving—that's when I needed you!"

"I am what I am," Gerald said. "I make no apologies for that."

"Of course not. Never admit, never apologize. That's your mantra." Ed clenched his fists and turned away. "You know what, I'm not doing this."

"This is my area of expertise. No one knows more about the occult than I do. I couldn't help with the other. I'm just not built that way but let me help with this."

"Why?" Ed stepped close to his father. "Why do you want to help now?"

"Because you're my son, and I don't want to see you die."

"No! You don't get to do that. You can't come in here and play the dad card." Ed narrowed his eyes. "So what is it? The truth, or I throw you out on your ass right now."

"I provide a service." Gerald shoved his hands in his

pockets. "Naturally, there would be compensation."

"And there it is."

"That which we are, we are." Gerald quoted Tennyson.

"That's not what he meant," Ed mumbled.

**That evening**, Ed went into the office pulling a shopping cart full of empty bottles. Gerald followed behind him. Andy, Nancy, Savannah, and Audrey were all present. The lounge area looked like a summer camp, with two sleeping bags and an assortment of blankets piled at opposite ends of the room. Wide-eyed with curiosity, they turned to look at the two men when they walked in.

Ed sat on the arm of the couch, which had been pushed away from the middle of the room to accommodate Andy and Nancy's gear. Gerald stood beside him, puffing out his chest.

"Everyone, I want you to meet my...father." Ed hesitated before the word "father" but could think of no other term.

Nancy's mouth dropped open.

Gerald beamed. "Well, you've got quite the little group here, and some really nice—"

"That's enough," Ed said.

He motioned everyone to follow him into the squad area. When they all gathered around, he addressed the group.

"My father, Gerald, has some—we'll call it 'expertise' in these matters and has agreed to help. There are some ground rules, however."

"Ground rules?" Savannah said, smiling. "You sound like a chaperone at a high school dance."

Ed shot her side-eye and continued.

"Ground rules. You are not to shake Gerald's hand

and especially don't allow him to hug you."

Ed heard a loud sigh escape his father's lips. Gerald placed his hand over his chest feigning hurt and surprise.

"Lock all your valuables in your desk drawer, and never go anywhere alone with him."

"Chief, what's this all about?" Andy asked.

"Just do it." Ed was aware that they all looked at him as if he were the worst son in the world, but he had been through this before. Gerald Freemen could sometimes, literally, charm the pants off everyone he met and leave them destitute in the process.

He had done so with Ed's mother, Elizabeth. They had met when she was an undergraduate at the University of Akron. Gerald was pretending to be a Magic, Myth, and Religion professor for some unrelated scheme. By the time she figured out he was lying, she was pregnant with Ed, had dropped out of school, and spent the rest of her short life working minimum-wage jobs.

When Ed was playing football, he would sometimes see Gerald bragging about his son in the crowd. He wondered what they would think if they knew he never visited or provided financial support. Over the years, Ed would hear about Gerald's exploits as a grifter and womanizer. By the time Ed became a cop, Gerald was traveling the world. It was a good thing, as Ed would have no doubt arrested him at some point.

Audrey Mason stepped forward, extending a skinny palm. "ErrolFlynn Seven-Seven?"

Gerald grinned, accepted the hand, and began to pull Audrey into a hug.

"Don't," Ed said, "hug him."

Gerald bowed dramatically and stepped back. "How did you know?"

"You look like your avatar," Audrey said.

"And yours doesn't do you justice."

Ed rolled his eyes. "Let's stay focused."

"Indeed," Gerald said. "Why don't you tell me your plans for dealing with Mr. Hudak?"

"Shooting him in the head is a good plan," Andy said.

"And how effective has that strategy been?"

"He can be hurt. We know that."

Gerald walked around the room. "You can't kill him that way."

"Why not?" Andy pointed at Ed. "The chief put a round or two in him, and he was hurt."

"Perhaps, but if I understand the situation correctly, Hudak only partially lives in this realm. Any physical damage to his body will disappear when he returns to the other side."

"Other side of what?" Nancy asked. Gerald stepped close and looked down into her eyes. She couldn't help but stare back at him.

Ed shifted uncomfortably.

"'Other side' was an awkward use of terms. Think of it as a corridor where the laws governing space and time are merely suggestions. The only way to know it is to die and travel there yourself. The problem is that you won't come back."

"How does Hudak do it?" Savannah asked.

"He died, and he had help."

"This is not making any sense," Andy said. "Help from who?"

"More like help from what," Gerald said.

"A demon?" Audrey suggested.

"Depends on your culture. Demon, evil spirit, it's all the same. Just different names for the same entities. You have to stop thinking of evil in the context of religion. Every culture has some kind of evil entity. Don't you find it strange that they are all similar?"

"Alright, how do we kill him?" Andy asked.

"Kill whom?" Gerald said. "Hudak or the demon?"

Andy scratched his head. "They're not one and the same?"

Gerald Freemen rubbed his knuckles. "Yes and no. I'm not trying to be cryptic, just accurate. Think of Hudak's physical body and soul as a suit that can be worn. The suit has no control over its owner's actions. In fact, it is completely unaware that it is being worn. Like the suit, the demon is wearing Jackie, controlling his actions. And like the suit, Jackie is completely unaware that he is being worn."

"Hudak thinks his actions are his own, but he's actually being controlled by this demon?" Savannah said.

"Exactly."

"Are we calling Hudak a victim?" Savannah caressed her chin.

"In a way. Certainly, at some point, Hudak was offered a Faustian bargain. Now, he took that bargain of his own free will, but these demons prey on the vulnerable. Professor Mason, your online posts indicated that Hudak grew up poor. That is if your screen name was Professor Spooky."

"Guilty on both counts," Audrey said.

"Poverty, disease, despair. These are all things that could make a person susceptible to demonic activity," Gerald said. "Once demons lock onto a person, they can create circumstances that will force the person to make a choice. Give themselves over to the evil spirit or die."

"Are you saying that this demon could have created

the circumstances surrounding Hudak's death—even the train?" Ed asked.

"It's quite possible. I would even say probable," Gerald said. "Think of the startling number of coincidences that would have to happen for Hudak to end up in front of a train. The number of people who die by train is infinitesimal."

"So that brings us back to the question," Andy said. "How do we kill him?"

"That's why I asked whom you want to kill. If it's the demon, you can't kill him because he is technically not alive."

"He exists in that corridor you talked about," Nancy said.

"Head of the class." Gerald flashed a brilliant smile at her. "He can only exist in our world temporarily."

"But by using a host, he can extend that time." Ed pointed at his dad. "That's why they use humans."

Gerald golf clapped.

"If we can't kill the demon, then we have to kill Hudak," Andy said. "And again, I ask, how?"

"Patience, young man," Gerald said. "People who die violent deaths are tied to the place they were killed. In this case, it's the old rail trail where Hudak met his end and encountered an evil spirit who gave him a choice. Die here and now or serve me and live—but it's never the bargain it seems."

"That means his death has to be tied to those areas," Ed said.

"Yep."

"And those areas happen to be where his powers are greatest."

"I didn't say it would be easy," Gerald said.

Andy stood. "Anyone else missing the punch line?"

"What my father is saying is that we have to lure Hudak to the old rail trail and kill him with the same train he used to kill Meghan Haynes," Ed said.

"Excuse me," Nancy said. "We have to conjure up a ghost train to take him out?"

"I imagine he will do the conjuring," Gerald said.

"Oh. Well, I thought it was going to be tough." Andy rolled his eyes.

"Doesn't he call up the train to kill his victims anyway?" Gerald asked.

"That brings up another question," Andy said. "How does he call up the train? Didn't your old professor say time travel was impossible?"

Ed went to the refrigerator and got a can of Nature Boost. He popped the top before saying, "I don't think he actually travels anywhere. I think he can exist in two realms at the same time and his lantern allows him to open a corridor to that time. I'm not sure that's correct but it feels right."

They all turned to Gerald.

"That sounds logical," he said. "There's a lot we don't know about that world. We're still learning."

"Anyway, that plan requires someone to be bait," Nancy said. "Why can't we just wait him out, chief?"

"I'm afraid it's too late for that," Ed said.

"Are you going to join us, Mr. Freemen? We could use the help," Andy asked.

"I'm more of a consultant, not a participant." Gerald looked at Ed.

"Okay. We need to hang these bottles upside down around the station," Ed said, receiving strange looks from the others. "According to Jennifer, it'll keep Hudak

303

at bay."

Audrey Mason stood. "If the myth is true."

With everyone helping, it took only minutes to hang the bottles from trees, light poles, and overhangs. When they finished, the station looked like a hippy trailer park.

"What's Doug going to say when he gets in tomorrow?" Andy said when they were back inside. He leaned against his desk, holding a cup of coffee.

Ed sipped his drink. "One thing at a time."

"He's going to blab to Waddell," Nancy said.

Ed put his hands up in a "who cares" gesture. "Already is. I got a call from Painesville HQ."

"Chief, you going to be all right?" Andy asked.

"Honestly, Andy, I don't know. Apparently, Waddell still has some influence at HQ."

Savannah's eyes flashed with anger. "That bastard knows what you're going through, and he's going to try to use it against you? To what purpose?"

Ed looked away. Their concern touched him, and he nearly smiled. "A friend of mine thinks that he wants his old job back."

"That can't happen," Andy said.

"Here, here." Nancy crossed her fingers.

"In any case, it's all moot if Hudak kills us. Speaking of which, Savannah, I think you and Professor Mason should return to Athens. I have no authority to make you do so, but I would appreciate it."

"I'll go with them," Gerald suggested.

"You most certainly will not," Ed said.

"Well, it was nice meeting you all." Gerald waved with the flourish of a Victorian gentleman.

Savannah walked toward Gerald but stopped near Ed. With puffed out cheeks, she blew a raspberry in Ed's face, then reached up, wrapped her arms around Gerald, and squeezed.

Ed shot Gerald a look, and he quickly put his hands behind his back. Only Ed saw him slide something into his pocket.

Savannah came to Ed and kissed him on the cheek. She whispered, "Remember what I said. That little hottie is a keeper. Take care of yourself."

Savannah and Audrey moved to the door. Gerald Freemen gleefully followed Savannah's every undulation with his eyes.

When they left, Ed turned to his two deputies.

"Okay, I have to get my father settled. Then I'll patrol all the hotspots until Hudak comes out. You guys follow on the monitors. If there's any sign of Hudak, you come running."

"Wait, hold on, chief," Andy said. "Ain't you got that a little backward?"

"Yeah, you can't expect us to sit around here while you take all the risks," Nancy said.

Ed motioned for his father to step outside. "For whatever reason, Hudak can't get past the ring of bottles. I'm not risking anyone else's life."

"Wait. You just brought us here to hide us out?" Nancy's hands went to her hips.

"With all due respect, chief, you tried that strategy twice. It ain't been too successful," Andy said.

"That's the way it is, guys." Ed looked hard at the two rangers. "Stay put. That's an order!"

Ed walked out before there could be any further discussion.

**When they** got to his cabin, Gerald turned to look at him.

"You sticking that little redhead?"

Ed groaned. "Her name is Nancy, and no, I'm not *sticking her*, as you put it."

"Does that mean you want to and haven't gotten there yet?"

"I'm not talking to you about this." Ed went to the kitchen and filled his teapot.

"You mind if I give her a go? You know I like those little spark plugs."

"Is there a type you don't like?"

Gerald smiled broadly. "That which we are, we are."

"Still not what that means." Ed went into the bedroom, opened the safe, and came back with a thick envelope. "You did well tonight. You were right. We needed your expertise. This should get you wherever you're going next and a little extra."

"Could you call me 'Dad,' just once?"

Ed looked at the ceiling. "Why is that so important to you? A dog can produce offspring. A dad is something more. A dad shows up, teaches you how to throw a football, ride a bike, or what to say to a girl you like."

"Suffice it to say that it *is* important, son."

Ed breathed out. "Just take the money."

"All right then, take some advice. Your rangers were right back there. You pose a threat, and Hudak means to stop you. The only way to get him is to draw him out, and, son, time is on his side. You said yourself, he wants to kill them first. You put them in a protective bubble, and he'll hunker down and wait you out. How many others are going to die while he waits?"

"My friend Charlie is in the hospital because of me. I'm not going to get them killed."

"You've always taken responsibility for everything

around you." Gerald placed his hand on Ed's shoulder, something he had never done before, and it made Ed feel awkward. How strange it was that the touch of a blood relative should feel so foreign to him.

Ed cocked his head.

"I know. I wasn't there, but that's my point. You have a team now. It's their job to risk their lives as well. How do you think it makes them feel that you don't trust them?"

"It's not that I don't trust them," Ed said.

"That's not the point. The point is how it makes them feel." Gerald removed his hand. "You know I'm right."

"I have a ride coming for you."

"One more thing, son. Hudak's talisman."

"His lantern."

"Yeah, you have to get it away from him, or none of this will work."

Ed looked up at the taller man. "You mean after I get him to call up the ghost train? No pressure at all."

"Oh, he'll call up the train, all right. He'll want you and your friends to experience maximum terror. He'll want you to see it coming."

"That's comforting." Ed heard a car pull up outside and looked through the curtain. "That's your ride. And one more thing. I'll take the things you stole from Savannah."

"Maybe I'll pay her a visit on the way to the airport. Apologize in person." Gerald grinned.

"You just never quit."

"I know you disapprove of the way I live, but I'm not a person who can work a nine-to-five and maintain a family and house. That's just not me." He placed a small watch and bracelet in Ed's hand and accepted the envelope.

"Whatever else I do, I have certain gifts, and when I can, I use those to help people in situations like this. Maybe it's wrong to ask to be compensated for that, but that's who I am. I hope that at least you can understand that."

"That which we are, we are," Ed said.

"What?"

"You got it right that time. Take care."

"Take care, *Dad*," Gerald said. "Just try it once."

Ed threw his hands up. "Okay, Dad. You happy?"

"I know why you're kicking me out." Gerald walked toward the door. "You don't want Hudak to get me next."

"I'm kicking you out because you're in the way."

"You keep telling yourself that, son." Gerald smiled.

"Your car is waiting." Ed turned away.

After he left, Deavers spoke up. *Aw, you really do love your daddy.*

"Oh my god, if you don't shut the hell up, I swear I'll let Hudak get me just to get rid of you!

# Chapter 31

**A week of camping** in the office had taken a toll on Andy and Nancy. When Ed walked in, they were sitting on the floor playing video games. Their unenthusiastic "Evening, chief" reflected the tedium of their circumstances.

Nancy spoke first. "Chief, I know you mean well, but you really should consider letting us patrol."

Ed stood expressionless. He had already decided to allow them to resume. Though he hated to admit it, his father was right. The only way to draw Hudak out was to put his squad in danger.

"I'm sorry about what I said." Andy put down the game controller. "I don't blame you for anything that happened. I know that's why you faced down Hudak alone. I'm not too good at making speeches, but I just want you to know we got your back. Don't sideline us when you need us the most."

"For someone not good at making speeches, that was pretty good," Ed said. "All right, you're both going out on patrol. And don't look so happy. You're probably going to die tonight."

"One more thing, chief, not related to Hudak," Nancy

said.

"What?"

"Permission to speak freely?"

"Go ahead." Ed gave one quick nod.

"We think you should give your dad a little bit of a break. We understand that he wasn't there for you, and he may be a little frisky, but he *did* come here to help. I know it's none of our business, but maybe you could cut him a little slack."

"You're right. It's none of your business," Ed took out Savannah's bracelet and watch and put it on Nancy's desk. "I forgot to give these back to Savannah."

Nancy said, "Well, now I feel about an inch high."

"Forget it. Let's get Hudak."

Nancy retrieved her Sam Browne belt and hooked it to her waist. "Should we go together for more protection?"

"No, Hudak is more likely to attack if you're alone. Hit all the popular spots. If Hudak shows up, do whatever you have to do to stay alive until we come. I'll be looking at the monitors, and I'll come out to bring you coffee and check on you every hour. We do this every night until it's over."

**The clock** on his computer read 3:33 a.m. Ed scrolled through the cameras for what seemed the four-hundredth time, but he had to stay vigilant. Hudak wouldn't go back to *wherever* until he made them all suffer and die. Ed intended to be ready for whatever came. The thought of losing Nancy before they could explore what they meant to each other frightened him more than anything. On camera six, he saw her cruiser drive down Park Road 9. She was heading for the spot where they'd found poor Meghan Haynes's mangled body weeks ago. There had been no good place to affix a camera at that location, so Ed decided it was a good time to check on her. She probably needed coffee anyway.

Ed went to his cruiser and picked up his radio.

"Andy, how are you doing?"

"Okay, chief. You?" Andy's voice came back.

"Fine. Going to check on Nancy at the rail trail."

"All right. Call if you need anything."

When Ed arrived at the Moonville Rail Trail, Nancy was leaning against her cruiser looking down the hill at where Meghan Haynes had been killed. He parked his car behind hers, walked over, and stood next to her. The moon hung very low on the horizon and cast a soft light on her face. She wasn't wearing her glasses, and as she continued to look ahead. He stared at her surreptitiously.

"I know what you're thinking," Nancy said, still looking ahead.

"You're psychic now?"

"Mm-hmm." She turned toward him, reached up, and released her bun, allowing her ginger hair to fall around her face. "You're thinking that I look beautiful in this light."

"Nancy." Ed held his hand up, but he was thinking something just like that.

"What?" She came toward him. "You're going to quote regulations now? 'We can't. It's against the rules?'"

"Yeah." Ed looked around.

"Seriously? You're still on that?" She got closer.

*Watch out*, Anthony Deavers said.

"We're going to die, Ed." Nancy slipped her arms around Ed's waist and looked into his eyes. "Hudak is going to kill us. Maybe not tonight or tomorrow but soon. You seriously going to stand around quoting rules to me?"

*Watch out.*

"Nancy, we don't know that. We have a plan." Ed knew his words were bullshit the minute they came out of his mouth.

She was right—Hudak had all the cards. Ed had been a fool. He shouldn't have pushed her away that night in his cabin. He had denied himself so many things for so long it became a way of life. His stupid rule of the four. What had following the rules and personal discipline gotten him except beaten up, choked, on the verge of a mental breakdown, and his best friend in the hospital?

"We're going to die without finding out— Don't you want to know where this goes?" Nancy leaned against him and pulled hard. Her body vibrated against him as she sobbed.

"Hey, hey. Come on now." Ed embraced her.

She pulled back a little and tilted her face up to his. He reached up and tenderly brushed a few stray strands of hair out of her face. In the moonlight, he saw her lips part.

*Careful.*

They came together. She tasted sweet, felt good against his body, thick and firm. She sighed into his ear. They kissed tentatively at first, then furiously, like it would be the last one of their lives. Ed lost spatial awareness. Nancy was the only thing that existed, the only thing that mattered. Had he not been so engrossed in her, he might have noticed the subtle change in air pressure behind him and the woosh of a heavy object being swung toward his head. His only warning was Nancy stiffening in his arms. The lantern slammed against his right ear, setting off a deafening gong. As he went down sideways, he heard the voice of Anthony Deavers.

*Told you to watch out.*

Ed's face was pressed against the grass. His neck twisted awkwardly to the right. A dank, earthy smell filled his nostrils.

*Get up*, Deavers said.

Ed put his palms down and tried to push up.

*Get up. He's got Nancy.*

Lifting his head, he saw Nancy battling Hudak. She held her own, using close-quarter combat techniques she probably learned in the army, all elbows and knees, but Hudak was so big, and she was so small.

Ed managed to get up to one knee. Hudak had put his lantern down to fight. He remembered what his father said. With effort, Ed pushed himself to his feet. There would be no hesitation. He reached for his weapon and his hand slapped his side. Empty! Ed's head whipped right and left as he looked for his Sam Browne belt. Hudak must have ripped it off and thrown it while he was out. With the cruiser's lights providing the only illumination, he had no chance of finding it.

Struggling forward, Ed's head throbbed. Hudak punched Nancy in the ribs. Her anguished cry of pain caused his stomach to clench. Ed put his head down and ran forward. The bastard pushed her shoulder back. She slammed into the cruiser. Hudak hit her in the nose. Nancy's head popped back and shattered the driver's window. She went limp and crumpled to the ground.

Rage surged through Ed's body, chasing away the fear he felt for Nancy. Ed yelled, jumped, and brought his elbow down between Hudak's shoulder blades. Hudak roared, arched his back, turned, and swatted with his arm. Ed was too quick. He ducked and hit Hudak with three short punches to the midsection, followed by an uppercut to the chin.

This wasn't the disciplined attack of the battle at Hope Furnace. Wild animal fury took over, and a massive adrenaline dump increased his strength and dulled his pain receptors. Ed grabbed Hudak's collar and rammed the top of his head into his nose. Warm blood spurted into Ed's face. He ignored it, grabbed Hudak behind the head, and thrust his knee into his groin. Hudak doubled over.

Grabbing the collar again, Ed jumped up, put both feet on Hudak's stomach, and leaned back. Hudak fell forward. Ed bent his knees and pushed up with all his might, sending the big man ass-over-end onto his back.

Ed got up and went to Nancy, who still hadn't moved. He reached for her Glock. Too late. Hudak wrenched him from behind, and he tumbled backward down the hill.

Hudak came at him, lantern held high as if he were going to bring it down on him. Ed bounced up, charged and rammed into Hudak's chest then popped his head up into Hudak's chin with a loud bonk. Recovering quickly, Hudak lunged. Ed slipped left and tripped the big man, sending him tumbling toward the Moonville Trail.

*Yeah, now that's what I'm talking about.*

Ed straddled him and got two punches to his face before Hudak swept him off by crashing the lantern into his side. They both got up. Hudak turned the green side of the lantern toward his face and vanished. Ed was ready, he closed his eyes and sensed the change in air pressure to his left. He swung towards thin air, connected with Hudak just as he materialized.

*That's right,* Deavers cheered. *That's a good old fashioned East Akron ass kicking!*

Hudak disappeared again. Ed timed it and kicked him in the stomach. He staggered back, swung the lantern and reappeared behind Ed. Ed bent his knees, teeth bared in a feral snarl. He launched into the air, sending a finishing right hook to Hudak's jaw. The big man leaned just enough to dodge the blow, caught Ed's arm, and spun him around. Hudak tried to hook his free arm around Ed's neck, but Ed wedged his forearm in between, preventing Hudak from choking him out again.

Hudak lifted the lantern high, mumbling in a language unfamiliar to Ed. He elbowed Hudak three times in the ribs. Hudak grunted with each hit but held on and continued his chant.

In front of him, a scene began to unfold that made Ed stop and watch with wonder. An expanding bubble of an alternate reality grew in front of his eyes. It was the same place but different, colder.

In the distance to the right, Ed saw a point of light, and a low rumble reached his ears. Ed twisted, but Hudak tightened his hold.

In desperation, Ed jumped up and came down hard on Hudak's instep with the heel of his boot. Hudak cried out. His grip loosened.

Stepping back, Ed reached behind him and hooked his free arm around Hudak's neck. He dropped to one knee and pulled. Hudak flipped over Ed's shoulder and onto the track that appeared in the bubble. The lantern flew out of Hudak's hand and landed a few feet to his left. He scrambled forward on all fours, but Ed kicked him in the forehead, sending him back onto his butt.

Hudak's look of rage changed to horror at the approaching train. The demon melted from his eyes, and he was just Jackie Hudak, the farm boy who looked after his little sister. He tried to crawl forward again, reaching for Ed as he did so. A look of desperation and genuine terror contorted Hudak's features. Ed raised his foot to kick him again then lowered it to the ground. It was too late anyway.

The train hit Hudak full-on. Blood and gore splashed Ed like wind in a rainstorm. He heard a staccato bumping noise as Hudak's body was dragged across the wooden slats. Ed wondered if they would find Hudak's body in the past, or would things simply reset? A piece of gore, probably Hudak's brain matter, slid off his forehead and onto the corner of his mouth. He spat and swiped at it.

Hudak's lantern blinked rapidly. The scene in front of Ed flickered in time to the light. Its edges became blurry, and it expanded and contracted with each blink. As soon as the light went out, the scene in front of Ed collapsed in a loud *whomp*. The implosion tugged Ed forward.

*Nancy!* Ed turned and sprinted up the hill. Nancy sat on her butt, her legs splayed, and her head flopped over like Pigpen doing his famous dance.

"Nancy—" Ed gently slapped her cheek. When she failed to respond, he went to the trunk of the cruiser and retrieved the first aid kit. Ed took out an ammonia packet and broke it open under her nose.

Nancy's eyes popped open, and she put up her dukes like a punch-drunk fighter. "Whoa, what?"

"It's all right. Hudak's gone," Ed said.

"Ed. He almost—" Nancy hugged his legs.

"I know. It's okay," Ed said.

She tried to rise so he helped her to her feet. She looked bad. The skin around her eyes and nose had turned blue and blood dripped down her mouth, her chin, and onto her uniform.

"What happened to Hudak?" Nancy said.

"In a minute." Ed kissed her forehead. "First, I have something to do."

Ed ran to the trail, picked up the lantern and came back. "This thing has to go."

"It looks new." Nancy touched it.

"Creepy, right?" Ed took the lantern to the road, cocked his arm and stopped.

"Smash it," Nancy said.

"I don't know." Ed set the lantern down again. "What if the demon is trapped inside?"

"Trapped?"

"Yes, and smashing the lantern releases it?"

Nancy rubbed her chin. "We don't know that."

"You want to take a chance on doing this again?"

"No, thank you," Nancy said.

**"Y'all look** like you've been through the washer on spin cycle," Andy said.

They moved from the squad room to the reception area. Ed rolled his neck and felt the lump on the side of his head. Nancy held a cold compress to her nose and mouth.

Ed picked up the lantern and set it on the table between them.

"That looks—" Andy started.

"Brand new?" Ed said. "Maybe it is from Hudak's point of view."

"You think he's gone for good, chief?" Andy said.

Ed tossed his head to one side, then winced from the pain it caused. "I still have his gore on me, and he took a good little ride down the tracks before they disappeared."

"Taste of his own medicine. Good," Andy said.

"I can't be sure of anything," Ed said. "Just before the train hit him, Hudak seemed to change."

"How?" Nancy said.

"His eyes," Ed said. "I had the feeling that it was

just Hudak and not the demon. He looked scared and confused."

"So you think it fled his body," Andy said. "Where did it go?"

Ed nodded toward the lantern.

"You think it's living in that thing?" Andy said.

"If you can call what it does living."

"Well, let's destroy it. Bust it into a thousand pieces." Andy pounded his hand with his fist.

"The chief thinks it might release the demon," Nancy said.

Ed reached over and massaged his sore shoulder. He ached all over. His head, back, and mid-section all showed signs of his battles with Hudak. Ed still had bruising on his neck from being choked to within an inch of his life. "I think it must have a period of dormancy. As long as the light is off, it's not active."

"The ten-year cycle," Nancy offered.

"I'm just guessing," Ed said. "For now, let's throw it in the safe."

Andy grimaced. "I'm going to be creeped out knowing that thing is just feet away from me. Why don't we just take that old demon lamp to the most remote part of the forest and dump it."

"No, it's our responsibility." Ed looked at the lantern and shook his head. "I'm afraid we're stuck with this thing for at least the next ten years."

# Chapter 32

"**Headquarters has initiated a** board of inquiry. I expect all of you to be interviewed," Ed said. He smiled at the group sitting around the conference table. It was two weeks later, just after the end of Doug Weems' shift. Ed had invited all of the principal investigators including Holt, Charlie, Savannah, and Audrey Mason. The afternoon sun illuminated the mahogany table between them, bathing them in a soft glow. The smell of fresh coffee and bagels wafted in from the break room.

"Waddell," Andy said with contempt.

"I suspect so."

"We'll back you, chief. Hundred percent," Andy said. His words were echoed by nods and murmurs around the table.

"No, you won't." Ed turned and winked at Nancy who sat next to him.

"You're not just going to take it?" Savannah said. "If we stick together, they'll have to believe us."

Ed drew a deep breath and let it out slowly. "They'll never believe and even if they do, they won't acknowledge it. They can't."

"You're just going to let them label us as crackpots and kooks?" Savannah said, her face turning red.

"Not you," Ed said. "Nancy and I have decided to resign. You'll have two rangers on temporary duty in the morning."

"We talked about this before, chief," Andy said. "You can't take this all onto yourself. I won't allow it. We won't allow it."

"I appreciate the sentiment," Ed said. Their fierce defense touched him but it would be futile. Headquarters had to have their scapegoat, and he was it. "But there's more at stake here than my job. You have to keep your reputations intact. If you don't, Waddell will take charge and you know what will happen if Hudak returns in ten years and that old coot is still above ground."

"You can't just let Waddell win," Andy said.

"I'm not letting him win, but the fact is that, Hudak or no, I've spent a tremendous amount of the squad's resources to catch a supernatural killer and we have nothing to show for it."

"Chief—" Andy started.

Ed held his hand up. "You're going to say that I made up the Hudak business to cover up an affair with Nancy."

"No!" the group shouted.

"This is the way it has to be, because the alternative is too terrible to contemplate," Ed said.

"We've gotta find another way," Andy said. "We'll show them the video."

"Analyzed by my own computer expert?"

"What about the blood, Ed?" Charlie Cook said. "You can match the DNA to Jennifer Stewart."

They all looked at Ed expectantly. "Sure, she'll come in and say the killer is her brother who was an adult a hundred years ago. Look, I know you all mean well, but I've analyzed this from a hundred different angles. The minute we start talking about ghosts and demons, we lose all credibility. Anything we say after that will be viewed as the ravings of a bunch of lunatics, or worse, liars."

"My last official act will be to make you acting senior ranger." Ed looked at Andy. "I've got one friend at HQ. If you follow this course, he can help make it permanent. If you try to protect me, you'll go down and Waddell waltzes in."

"Ed, I don't think I'm taking a chance when I say that none of us like the course of action you've laid out," Holt Potter said, "but I have to admit that your logic is flawless."

"You going to be okay?" Charlie said.

"Nancy and I have leads on some jobs near Yuma, Arizona. We'll be fine."

"The service is gonna burn you," Andy said. "You'll be unemployable."

"I don't think so, Andy. We're giving them an easy out. We resign and it stays internal. If they make a big deal of it, everything hits the fan, especially in the 'me-too' era. Everyone wins."

"Except you and Nancy," Andy said.

"We've made our peace with it." Ed looked around the room. "I'm afraid I have one more favor to ask of you all. We've been through a unique experience here and I can't think of another group of people I would rather have on my side. We discovered a world that few people know exists. How many incidents labeled as homicide or accidental are actually due to demonic activity? This thing may be over, or in ten years Hudak may come back. Andy, you'll be the gatekeeper. It will be your job to sound the alarm. No matter where I am, or what I'm doing, I'll return if the lantern swings again. I'm asking all of you to take the same pledge."

Ed put his hand flat on the table. One by one they all followed suit.

"Thank you. I guess—I guess that's it," Ed said. He and Nancy got up and headed for the door.

"Chief, you and Nancy—" Andy popped up and stood at attention. Everyone at the table stood as the couple left the office.

**That was** hard," Nancy said after they were outside. "But I think we did the right thing."

"I'm sure we did."

"Did you hear from your friend today?"

"No," Ed said. "I haven't heard from Anthony Deavers since we took care of Hudak."

Nancy looked up at Ed. "In ten years, you'll be in your early sixties. You sure you'll be up for another battle with the supernatural?"

"I guess you'd better keep me in shape."

Nancy nudged Ed with her shoulder. "We can start right now if you want."

"I want," Ed said.

A native of Akron, Ohio, **Allen Grimes** is a retired Special Agent and Supervisor with the Federal Bureau of Investigation and a former Akron Police Officer with over twenty-six years in law enforcement. He graduated from the University of Akron with a Bachelor of Arts in mass media communication. Along with this novel, *When the Lantern Swings*, Grimes is the author of several short stories in the sci-fi/horror genre in magazines such as Potpourri, Nightmares, and Lords of Eternal Darkness. Grimes lives and works in Yuma, Arizona.